GUNS OF THE GODS

A STORY OF YASMINI'S YOUTH

By TALBOT MUNDY

ILLUSTRATED BY
J. CLEMENT COLL

McKINLAY, STONE & MACKENZIE
NEW YORK

At the top of the stairs Yasmini stood waiting

CONTENTS

CONTENTS—Continued

OUT OF THE ASHES

Old Troy reaped rue in the womb of years
For stolen Helen's sake;
Till tenfold retribution rears
Its wreck on embers slaked with tears
That mended no heart-ache.
The wail of the women sold as slaves
Lest Troy breed sons again
Dreed o'er a desert of nameless graves,
The heaps and the hills that are Trojan graves
Deep-runneled by the rain.

But Troy lives on.   Though Helen's rape
And ten-year hold were vain;
Though jealous gods with men conspire
And Furies blast the Grecian fire;
Yet Troy must rise again.
Troy's daughters were a spoil and sport,
Were limbs for a labor gang,
Who crooned by foreign loom and mill
Of Trojan loves they cherished still,
Till Homer heard, and sang.

They told, by the fire when feasters roared
And minstrels waited turns,
Of the might of the men that Troy adored,
Of the valor in vain of the Trojan sword,

With the love that slakeless burns,
That caught and blazed in the minstrel mind
Or ever the age of pen.
So maids and a minstrel rebuilt Troy,
Out of the ashes they rebuilt Troy
To live in the hearts of men.

Guns of the Gods

YASMINI

"Set down my thoughts not yours if the tale is to be worth the pesa."

THE why and wherefore of my privilege to write a true account of the Princess Yasmini's early youth is a story in itself too long to tell here; but it came about through no peculiar wisdom. I fell in a sort of way in love with her, and that led to opportunity.

She never made any secret of the scorn with which she regards those who singe wings at her flame. Rather she boasts of it with limit-overreaching epithets. Her respect is reserved for those rare men and women who can meet her in unfair fight and, if not defeat her, then come close to it. She asks no concessions on account of sex. Men's passions are but weapons forged for her necessity; and as for genuine love-affairs, like Cleopatra, she had but two, and the second ended in disaster to herself. This tale is of the first one that succeeded, although fraught with discontent for certain others.

The second affair came close to whelming thrones, and I wrote of that in another book with an under-

I

standing due, as I have said, to opportunity, and with a measure of respect that pleased her.

She is habitually prompt and generous with her rewards, if far-seeing in bestowal of them. So, during the days of her short political eclipse that followed in a palace that had housed a hundred kings, I saw her almost daily in a room—her holy of holies—where the gods of ancient India were depicted in three primal colors working miracles all over the walls and where, if governments had only known it, she was already again devising plans to set the world on fire.

There, amid an atmosphere of Indian scents and cigarette smoke, she talked and I made endless notes, while now and then, when she was meditative, her maids sang to an accompaniment of rather melancholy wooden flutes. But whenever I showed a tendency to muse she grew indignant.

"Of what mud are you building castles now? Set down my thoughts not yours," she insisted, "if your tale is to be worth the pesa."

By that she referred to the custom of all Eastern story-tellers to stop at the exciting moment and take up a collection of the country's smallest copper coins before finishing the tale. But the reference was double-edged. A penny for my thoughts, a penny for the West's interpretation of the East was what she had in mind.

Nevertheless, as it is to the West that the story must appeal it has seemed wiser to remove it from her lips and so transpose that, though it loses in lore unfortunately, it does gain something of directness and simplicity. Her satire, and most of her metaphor if always set down as she phrased it, would scandalize as well as puzzle Western ears.

This tale is of her youth, but Yasmini's years have not yet done more than ripen her. In a land where most women shrivel into early age she continues, somewhere perhaps a little after thirty, in the bloom of health and loveliness, younger in looks and energy than many a Western girl of twenty-five. For she is of the East and West, very terribly endowed with all the charms of either and the brains of both.

Her quick wit can detect or invent mercurial Asian subterfuge as swiftly as appraise the rather glacial drift of Western thought; and the wisdom of both East and West combines in her to teach a very nearly total incredulity in human virtue. Western morals she regards as humbug, neither more nor less.

In virtue itself she believes, as astronomers for example believe in the precession of the equinox; but that the rank and file of human beings, and especially learned human beings, have attained to the very vaguest understanding of it she scornfully disbelieves. And with a frankness simply Gallic in its freedom from those thought-conventions with which so many people like to deceive themselves she deals with human nature on what she considers are its merits. The result is sometimes very disconcerting to the pompous and all the rest of the host of self-deceived, but usually amusing to herself and often profitable to her friends.

Her ancestry is worth considering, since to that she doubtless owes a good proportion of her beauty and ability. On her father's side she is Rajput, tracing her lineage so far back that it becomes lost at last in fabulous legends of the Moon (who is masculine, by the way, in Indian mythology). All of the great families of Rajputana are her kin, and all the chivalry and derring-do of that royal land of heroines and heroes is part of her conscious heritage.

Her mother was Russian. On that side, too, she can claim blood royal, not devoid of at least a trace of Scandinavian, betrayed by glittering golden hair and eyes that are sometimes the color of sky seen over Himalayan peaks, sometimes of the deep lake water in the valleys. But very often her eyes seem so full of fire and their color is so baffling that a legend has gained currency to the effect that she can change their hue at will.

How a Russian princess came to marry a Rajput king is easier to understand if one recalls the sinister designs of Russian statecraft in the days when India and "warm sea-water" was the great objective. The oldest, and surely the easiest, means of a perplexed diplomacy has been to send a woman to undermine the policy of courts or steal the very consciences of kings. Delilah is a case in point. And in India, where the veil and the rustling curtain and religion hide woman's hand without in the least suppressing her, that was a plan too easy of contrivance to be overlooked.

In those days there was a prince in Moscow whose public conduct so embittered his young wife, and so notoriously, that when he was found one morning murdered in his bed suspicion rested upon her. She was tried in secret, as the custom was, found guilty and condemned to death. Then, on the strength of influence too strong for the czar, the sentence was com-

muted to the far more cruel one of life imprisonment in
the Siberian mines. While she awaited the dreaded
march across Asia in chains a certain proposal was
made to the Princess Sonia Omanoff, and no one who
knew anything about it wondered that she accepted
without much hesitation.

Less than a month after her arrest she was already
in Paris, squandering paper rubles in the fashionable
shops. And at the Russian Embassy in Paris she made
the acquaintance of the very first of the smaller Indian
potentates who made the "grand tour." Traveling
abroad has since become rather fashionable, and is
even encouraged by the British-Indian Government
because there is no longer any plausible means of pre-
venting it; but Maharajah Bubru Singh was a pioneer,
who dared greatly, and had his way even against the
objections of a high commissioner. In addition he
had had to defy the Brahman priests who, all unwilling, are the strong supports of alien overrule; for they
are armed with the iron-fanged laws of caste that forbid crossing the sea, among innumerable other things.

Perhaps there was a hint of moral bravery behind
the warrior eyes that was enough in itself; and she
really fell in love at first sight, as men said. But the
secret police of Russia were at her elbow, too, hinting
that only one course could save her from extradition
and Siberian mines. At any rate she listened to the
Rajah's wooing; and the knowledge that he had a wife
at home already, a little past her prime perhaps and
therefore handicapped in case of rivalry, but nevertheless a prior wife, seems to have given her no pause.

The fact that the first wife was childless doubtless influenced Bubru Singh.

They even say she was so far beside herself with love for him that she would have been satisfied with the Gandharva marriage ceremony sung by so many Rajput poets, that amounts to little more than going off alone together. But the Russian diplomatic scheme included provision for the maharajah of a wife so irrevocably wedded that the British would not be able to refuse her recognition. So they were married in the presence of seven witnesses in the Russian Embassy, as the records testify.

After that, whatever its suspicions, the British Government had to admit her into Rajputana. And what politics she might have played, whether the Russian gray-coat armies might have encroached into those historic hills on the strength of her intriguing, or whether she would have seized the first opportunity to avenge herself by playing Russia false,—are matters known only to the gods of unaccomplished things. For Bubru Singh, her maharajah, died of an accident very shortly after the birth of their child Yasmini.

Now law is law, and Sonia Omanoff, then legally the Princess Sonia Singh, had appealed from the first to Indian law and custom, so that the British might have felt justified in leaving her and her infant daughter to its most untender mercies. Then she would have been utterly under the heel of the succeeding prince, a nephew of her husband, unenamored of foreigners and avowedly determined to enforce on his uncle's widow the Indian custom of seclusion.

But the British took the charitable view, that covering a multitude of sins. It was not bad policy to convert the erstwhile Sonia Omanoff from secret enemy to grateful friend, and the feat was easy.

The new maharajah, Gungadhura Singh, was prevailed on to assign an ancient palace for the Russian widow's use; and there, almost within sight of the royal seraglio from which she had been ousted, Yasmini had her bringing up, regaled by her mother with tales of Western outrage and ambition, and well schooled in all that pertained to her Eastern heritage by the thousand-and-one intriguers whose delight and livelihood it is to fish the troubled waters of the courts of minor kings.

All these things Yasmini told me in that scented chamber of another palace, in which a wrathful government secluded her in later years for its own peace as it thought, but for her own recuperation as it happened. She told me many other things besides that have some little bearing on this story but that, if all related, would crowd the book too full. The real gist of them is that she grew to love India with all her heart and India repaid her for it after its own fashion, which is manyfold and marvelous.

There is no fairer land on earth than that far northern slice of Rajputana, nor a people more endowed with legend and the consciousness of ancestry. They have a saying that every Rajput is a king's son, and every Rajputni worthy to be married to an emperor. It was in that atmosphere that Yasmini learned she must either use her wits or be outwitted, and women begin young to assert their genius in the East. But she outstripped precocity and, being Western too, rode rough-shod on convention when it suited her, reserving her concessions to it solely for occasions when those matched the hand she held. All her life she has had to play in a ruthless game, but the trump that she has learned to lead oftenest is unexpectedness. And now to the story.

ROYAL RAJASTHAN

There is a land where no resounding street
With babel of electric-garish night
And whir of endless wheels has put to flight
The liberty of leisure. Sandaled feet
And naked soles that feel the friendly dust
Go easily along the never measured miles.
A land at which the patron tourist smiles
Because of gods in whom those people trust
(He boasting One and trusting not at all);
A land where lightning is the lover's boon,
And honey oozing from an amber moon
Illumines footing on forbidden wall;
Where, 'stead of pursy jeweler's display,
Parading peacocks brave the passer-by,
And swans like angels in an azure sky
Wing swift and silent on unchallenged way.
No land of fable!   Of the Hills I sing,
Whose royal women tread with conscious grace
The peace-filled gardens of a warrior race,
Each maiden fit for wedlock with a king,
And every Rajput son so royal born
And conscious of his age-long heritage
He looks askance at Burke's becrested page
And wonders at the new-ennobled scorn.
I sing (for this is earth) of hate and guile,
Of tyranny and trick and broken pledge,
Of sudden weapons, and the thrice-keen edge
Of woman's wit, the sting in woman's smile,

But also of the heaven-fathomed glow,
The sweetness and the charm and dear delight
Of loyal woman, humorous and right,
Pure-purposed as the bosom of the snow.

*   *   *

No tale, then, this of motors, but of men
With camels fleeter than the desert wind,
Who come and go.   So leave the West behind,
And, at the magic summons of the pen
Forgetting new contentions if you will,
Take wings, take silent wings of time untied,
And see, with Fellow-friendship for your guide,
A little how the East goes wooing still.

CHAPTER ONE

"Gold is where you find it."

DAWN at the commencement of hot weather in the
hills if not the loveliest of India's wealth of wonders
(for there is the moon by night) is fair preparation
for whatever cares to follow. There is a musical
silence out of which the first voices of the day have
birth; and a half-light holding in its opalescence all the
colors that the day shall use; a freshness and serenity
to hint what might be if the sons of men were wise
enough; and beauty unbelievable. The fortunate sleep
on roofs or on verandas, to be ready for the sweet cool
wind that moves in advance of the rising sun, caused,
as some say, by the wing-beats of departing spirits of
the night.

So that in that respect the mangy jackals, the monkeys, and the chandala (who are the lowest human
caste of all and quite untouchable by the other people
the creator made) are most to be envied; for there is
no stuffy screen, and small convention, between them
and enjoyment of the blessed air.

Next in order of defilement to the sweepers,—or,
as some particularly righteous folk with inside reservations on the road to Heaven firmly insist, even
beneath the sweepers, and possibly beneath the jack-

als—come the English, looking boldly on whatever their eyes desire and tasting out of curiosity the fruit of more than one forbidden tree, but obsessed by an amazing if perverted sense of duty. They rule the land, largely by what they idolize as "luck," which consists of tolerance for things they do not understand. Understanding one another rather well, they are more merciless to their own offenders than is Brahman to chandala, for they will hardly let them live. But they are a people of destiny, and India has prospered under them.

In among the English, something after the fashion of grace notes in the bars of music—enlivening, if sharp at times—come occasional Americans, turning up in unexpected places for unusual reasons, and remaining because it is no man's business to interfere with them. Unlike the English, who approach all quarters through official doors and never trespass without authority, the Americans have an embarrassing way of choosing their own time and step, taking officialdom, so to speak, in flank. It is to the credit of the English that they overlook intrusion that they would punish fiercely if committed by unauthorized folk from home.

So when the Blaines, husband and wife, came to Sialpore in Rajputana without as much as one written introduction, nobody snubbed them. And when, by dint of nothing less than nerve nor more than ability to recognize their opportunity, they acquired the lease of the only vacant covetable house nobody was very jealous, especially when the Blaines proved hospitable.

It was a sweet little nest of a house with a cool

stone roof, set in a rather large garden of its own on the shoulder of the steep hill that overlooks the city. A political dependent of Yasmini's father had built it as a haven for his favorite paramour when jealousy in his seraglio had made peace at home impossible. Being connected with the Treasury in some way, and suitably dishonest, he had been able to make a luxurious pleasaunce of it; and he had taste.

But when Yasmini's father died and his nephew Gungadhura succeeded him as maharajah he made a clean sweep of the old pension and employment list in order to enrich new friends, so the little nest on the hill became deserted. Its owner went into exile in a neighboring state and died there out of reach of the incoming politician who naturally wanted to begin business by exposing the scandalous remissness of his predecessor. The house was acquired on a falling market by a money-lender, who eventually leased it to the Blaines on an eighty per cent. basis—a price that satisfied them entirely until they learned later about local proportion.

The front veranda faced due east, raised above the garden by an eight-foot wall, an ideal place for sleep because of the unfailing morning breeze. The beds were set there side by side each evening, and Mrs. Blaine—a full ten years younger than her husband—formed a habit of rising in the dark and standing in her night-dress, with bare feet on the utmost edge of the top stone step, to watch for the miracle of morning. She was fabulously pretty like that, with her hair blowing and her young figure outlined through the linen; and she was sometimes unobserved.

The garden wall, a hundred feet beyond, was of

rock, two-and-a-half men high, as they measure the
unleapable in that distrustful land; but the Blaines,
hailing from a country where a neighbor's dog and
chickens have the run of twenty lawns, seldom took the
trouble to lock the little, arched, iron-studded door
through which the former owner had come and gone
unobserved. The use of an open door is hardly trespass under the law of any land; and dawn is an excellent time for the impecunious who take thought of the
lily how it grows in order to outdo Solomon.

When a house changes hands in Rajputana there
pass with it, as well as the rats and cobras and the
mongoose, those beggars who were wont to plague the
former owner. That is a custom so based on ancient
logic that the English, who appreciate conservatism,
have not even tried to alter it.

So when a cracked voice broke the early stillness
out of shadow where the garden wall shut off the
nearer view, Theresa Blaine paid small attention to it.

"Memsahib! Protectress of the poor!"

She continued watching the mystery of coming
light. The ancient city's domed and pointed roofs
already glistened with pale gold, and a pearly mist
wreathed the crowded quarter of the merchants.
Beyond that the river, not more than fifty yards wide,
flowed like molten sapphire between unseen banks.
As the pale stars died, thin rays of liquid silver touched
the surface of a lake to westward, seen through a rift
between purple hills. The green of irrigation beyond
the river to eastward shone like square-cut emeralds,
and southward the desert took to itself all imaginable
hues at once.

"Colorado!" she said then. "And Arizona! And Southern California! And something added that I can't just place!"

"Sin's added by the scow-load!" growled her husband from the farther bed. "Come back, Tess, and put some clothes on!"

She turned her head to smile, but did not move away. Hearing the man's voice, the owners of other voices piped up at once from the shadow, all together, croaking out of tune:

"*Bhig mangi shahebi! Bhig mangi shahebi!*" (Alms! Alms!)

"I can see wild swans," said Theresa. "Come and look—five—six—seven of them, flying northward, oh, ever so high up!"

"Put some clothes on, Tess!"

"I'm plenty warm."

"Maybe. But there's some skate looking at you from the garden. What's the matter with your kimono?"

However the dawn wind was delicious, and the night-gown more decent than some of the affairs they label frocks. Besides, the East is used to more or less nakedness and thinks no evil of it, as women learn quicker than men.

"All right—in a minute."

"I'll bet there's a speculator charging 'em admission at the gate," grumbled Dick Blaine, coming to stand beside her in pajamas. "Sure you're right, Tess; those are swans, and that's a dawn worth seeing."

He had the deep voice that the East attributes to manliness, and the muscular mold that never came of armchair criticism. She looked like a child beside him, though he was agile, athletic, wiry, not enormous.

"Sahib!" resumed the voices. "Sahib! Protector of the poor!" They whined out of darkness still, but the shadow was shortening.

"Better feed 'em, Tess. A man's starved down mighty near the knuckle if he'll wake up this early to beg."

"Nonsense. Those are three regular bums who look on us as their preserve. They enjoy the morning as much as we do. Begging's their way of telling people howdy."

"Somebody pays them to come," he grumbled, helping her into a pale blue kimono.

Tess laughed. "Sure! But it pays us too. They keep other bums away. I talk to them sometimes."

"In English?"

"I don't think they know any. I'm learning their language."

It was his turn to laugh. "I knew a man once who learned the gipsy bolo on a bet. Before he'd half got it you couldn't shoo tramps off his door-step with a gun. After a time he grew to like it—flattered him, I suppose, but decent folk forgot to ask him to their corn-roasts. Careful, Tess, or Sialpore'll drop us from its dinner lists."

"Don't you believe it! They're crazy to learn American from me, and to hear your cowpuncher talk. We're social lions. I think they like us as much as we like them. Don't make that face, Dick, one maverick isn't a whole herd, and you can't afford to quarrel with the commissioner."

He chose to change the subject.

"What are your bums' names?" he asked.

"Funny names. Bimbu, Umra and Pinga. Now you can see them, look, the shadow's gone. Bimbu is the one with no front teeth, Umra has only one eye, and Pinga winks automatically. Wait till you see Pinga smile. It's diagonal instead of horizontal. Must have hurt his mouth in an accident."

"Probably he and Bimbu fought and found the biting tough. Speaking of dogs, strikes me we ought to keep a good big fierce one," he added suggestively.

"No, no, Dick; there's no danger. Besides, there's Chamu."

"The bums could make short work of that parasite."

"I'm safe enough. Tom Tripe usually looks in at least once a day when you're gone."

"Tom's a good fellow, but once a day——. A hundred things might happen. I'd better speak to Tom Tripe about those three bums—he'll shift them!"

"Don't, Dick! I tell you they keep others away. Look, here comes Chamu with the *chota hazri.*"

Clad in an enormous turban and clean white linen from head to foot, a stout Hindu appeared, superintending a tall meek underling who carried the customary "little breakfast" of the country—fruit, biscuits and the inevitable tea that haunts all British byways. As soon as the underling had spread a cloth and arranged the cups and plates Chamu nudged him into the background and stood to receive praise undivided. The salaams done with and his own dismissal achieved with proper dignity, Chamu drove the hamal away in front of him, and cuffed him the minute they were out of sight. There was a noise of repeated blows from around the corner.

"A big dog might serve better after all," mused Tess. "Chamu beats the servants, and takes commissions, even from the beggars."

"How do you know?"

"They told me."

"Um, Bing and Ping would better keep away. There's no obligation to camp here."

"Only, if we fired Chamu I suppose the maharajah would be offended. He made such a great point of sending us a faithful servant."

"True. Gungadhura Singh is a suspicious rajah. He suspects me anyway. I screwed better terms out of him than the miller got from Bob White, and now whenever he sees me off the job he suspects me of chicanery. If we fired Chamu he'd think I'd found the gold and was trying to hide it. Say, if I don't find gold in his blamed hills eventually——!"

"You'll find it, Dick. You never failed at anything you really set your heart on. With your experience——"

"Experience doesn't count for much," he answered, blowing at his tea to cool it. "It's not like coal or manganese. Gold is where you find it. There are no rules."

"Finding it's your trade. Go ahead."

"I'm not afraid of that. What eats me," he said, standing up and looking down at her, "is what I've heard about their passion for revenge. Every one has the same story. If you disappoint them, gee whiz, look out! Poisoning your wife's a sample of what they'll do. It's crossed my mind a score of times, little girl, that you ought to go back to the States and wait there till I'm through."

She stood on tiptoe and kissed him.

"Isn't that just like a man!"

"All the same——"

"Go in, Dick, and get dressed, or the sun will be too high before you get the gang started."

She took his arm and they went into the house together. Twenty minutes later he rode away on his pony, looking if possible even more of an athlete than in his pajamas, for there was an added suggestion of accomplishment in the rolled-up sleeves and scarred boots laced to the knee. Their leave-taking was a purely American episode, mixed of comradeship, affection and just plain foolishness, witnessed by more wondering, patient Indian eyes than they suspected. Every move that either of them made was always watched.

As a matter of fact Chamu's attention was almost entirely taken up just then by the crows, iniquitous black humorists that took advantage of turned backs (for Tess walked beside the pony to the gate) to rifle the remains of *chota hazri,* one of them flying off with a spoon since the rest had all the edibles. Chamu threw a cushion at the spoon-thief and called him *"Balibuk,"* which means eater of the temple offerings, and is an insult beyond price.

"That is the habit of crows," he explained indignantly to Tess as she returned, laughing, to the veranda, picking up the cushion on her way. "They are without shame. Garud, who is king of all the birds, should turn them into fish; then they could swim in water and be caught with hooks. But first Blaine sahib should shoot them with a shotgun."

Having offered that wise solution of the problem, Chamu stood with fat hands folded on his stomach.

"The crows steal less than some people," Tess answered pointedly.

He preferred to ignore the remark.

"Or there might be poison added to some food, and the food left for them to see," he suggested, whereat she astonished him, American women being even more incomprehensible than their English cousins.

"If you talk to me about poison I'll send you back to Gungadhura in disgrace. Take away the breakfast things at once."

"That is the hamal's business," he retorted pompously. "The maharajah sahib is knowing me for most excellent butler. He himself has given me already very high recommendation. Will he permit opinions of other people to contradict him?"

The words "opinions of women" had trembled on his lips but intuition saved that day. It flashed across even his obscene mentality that he might suggest once too often contempt for Western folk who worked for Eastern potentates. It was true he regarded the difference between a contract and direct employment as merely a question of degree, and a quibble in any case, and he felt pretty sure that the Blaines would not risk the maharajah's unchancy friendship by dismissing himself; but he suspected there were limits. He could not imagine why, but he had noticed that insolence to Blaine himself was fairly safe, Blaine being super-

humanly indifferent as long as Mrs. Blaine was shown
respect, even exceeding the English in the absurd
length to which he carried it. It was a mad world in
Chamu's opinion. He went and fetched the hamal,
who slunk through his task with the air of a condemned felon. Tess smiled at the man for encourage-
ment, but Chamu's instant jealousy was so obvious
that she regretted the mistake.

"Now call up the beggars and feed them," she
ordered.

"Feed them? They will not eat. It is contrary to
caste."

"Nonsense. They have no caste. Bring bread and
feed them."

"There is no bread of the sort they will eat."

"I know exactly what you mean. If I give them
bread there's no profit for you—they'll eat it all; but
if I give them money you'll exact a commission from
them of one pesa in five. Isn't that so? Go and bring
the bread."

He decided to turn the set-back into at any rate a
minor victory and went in person to the kitchen for
chupatties such as the servants ate. Then, returning
to the top of the steps he intimated that the earth-defil-
ers might draw near and receive largesse, contriving
the impression that it was by his sole favor the concession was obtained. Two of them came promptly and
waited at the foot of the steps, smirking and changing
attitudes to draw attention to their rags. Chamu
tossed the bread to them with expressions of disgust.
If they had cared to pretend they were holy men he
would have been respectful, in degree at least, but

these were professionals so hardened that they dared ignore the religious apology, which implies throughout the length and breadth of India the right to beg from place to place. These were not even true vagabonds, but rogues contented with one victim in one place as long as benevolence should last.

"Where is the third one?" Tess demanded. "Where is Pinga?"

They professed not to know, but she had seen all three squatting together close to the little gate five minutes before. She ordered Chamu to go and find the missing man and he waddled off, grumbling. At the end of five minutes he returned without him.

"One comes on horseback," he announced, "who gave the third beggar money, so that he now waits outside."

"What for?"

"Who knows? Perhaps to keep watch."

"To watch for what?"

"Who knows?"

"Who is it on horseback? A caller? Some one coming for breakfast? You'd better hurry."

The call at breakfast-time is one of the pleasantest informalities of life in India. It might even be the commissioner. Tess ran to make one of those swift changes of costume with which some women have the gift of gracing every opportunity. Chamu waddled down the steps to await with due formality, the individual, in no way resembling a British commissioner, who was leisurely dismounting at the wide gate fifty yards to the southward of that little one the beggars used.

He was a Rajput of Rajputs, thin-wristed, thin-ankled, lean, astonishingly handsome in a high-bred Northern way, and possessed of that air of utter self-assuredness devoid of arrogance which people seem able to learn only by being born to it. His fine features were set off by a turban of rose-pink silk, and the only fault discoverable as he strode up the path between the shrubs was that his riding-boots seemed too tight across the instep. There was not a vestige of hair on his face. He was certainly less than twenty, perhaps seventeen years old, or even younger. Ages are hard to guess in that land.

Tess was back on the veranda in time to receive him, with different shoes and stockings, and another ribbon in her hair; few men would have noticed the change at all, although agreeably conscious of the daintiness. The Rajput seemed unable to look away from her but ignoring Chamu, as he came up the steps, appraised her inch by inch from the white shoes upward until as he reached the top their eyes met. Chamu followed him fussily.

Tess could not remember ever having seen such eyes. They were baffling by their quality of brilliance, unlike the usual slumbrous Eastern orbs that puzzle chiefly by refusal to express emotion. The Rajput bowed and said nothing, so Tess offered him a chair, which Chamu drew up more fussily than ever.

"Have you had breakfast?" she asked, taking the conscious risk. Strangers of alien race are not invariably good guests, however good-looking, especially when one's husband is somewhere out of call. She looked and felt nearly as young as this man, and had already experienced overtures from more than one young prince who supposed he was doing her an honor. Used to closely guarded women's quarters, the East wastes little time on wooing when the barriers are passed or down. But she felt irresistibly curious, and after all there was Chamu.

"Thanks, I took breakfast before dawn."

The Rajput accepted the proffered chair without acknowledging the butler's existence. Tess passed him the big silver cigarette box.

"Then let me offer you a drink."

He declined both drink and cigarette and there was a minute's silence during which she began to grow uncomfortable.

"I was riding after breakfast——up there on the hill where you see that overhanging rock, when I caught sight of you here on the veranda. You, too, were watching the dawn—beautiful! I love the dawn. So I thought I would come and get to know you. People who love the same thing, you know, are not exactly strangers."

Almost, if not quite for the first time Tess grew very grateful for Chamu, who was still hovering at hand.

"If my husband had known, he would have stayed to receive you."

"Oh, no! I took good care for that! I continued my ride until after I knew he had gone for the day."

Things dawn on your understanding in the East one by one, as the stars come out at night, until in the end there is such a bewildering number of points of light that people talk about the "incomprehensible East." Tess saw light suddenly.

"Do you mean that those three beggars are your spies?"

The Rajput nodded. Then his bright eyes detected the instant resolution that Tess formed.

"But you must not be afraid of them. They will be very useful——often."

"How?" ·

The visitor made a gesture that drew attention to Chamu.

"Your butler knows English. Do you know Russian?"

"Not a word."

"French?"

"Very little."

"If we were alone——"

Tess decided to face the situation boldly. She came from a free land, and part of her heritage was to dare meet any man face to face; but intuition combined with curiosity to give her confidence.

"Chamu, you may go."

The butler waddled out of sight, but the Rajput waited until the sound of his retreating footsteps died away somewhere near the kitchen. Then:

"You feel afraid of me?" he asked.

"Not at all. Why should I? Why do you wish to see me alone?"

"I have decided you are to be my friend. Are you not pleased?"

"But I don't know anything about you. Suppose you tell me who you are and tell me why you use beggars to spy on my husband."

"Those who have great plans make powerful enemies, and fight against odds. I make friends where I
can, and instruments even of my enemies. You are to
be my friend."

"You look very young to ——"

Suddenly Tess saw light again, and the discovery
caused her pupils to contract a little and then dilate.
The Rajput noticed it, and laughed. Then, leaning
forward:

"How did you know I am a woman? Tell me. I
must know. I shall study to act better."

Tess leaned back entirely at her ease at last and
looked up at the sky, rather reveling in relief and in
the fun of turning the tables.

"Please tell me! I must know!"

"Oh, one thing and another. It isn't easy to
explain. For one thing, your insteps."

"I will get other boots. What else? I make no
lap. I hold my hands as a man does. Is my voice too
high—too excitable?"

"No. There are men with voices like yours.
There's a long golden hair on your shoulder that
might, of course, belong to some one else, but your
ears are pierced——"

"So are many men's."

"And you have blue eyes——and long fair lashes.
I've seen occasional Rajput men with blue eyes, too,
but your teeth——much too perfect for a man."

"For a young man?"

"Perhaps not. But add one thing to another——"

"There is something else. Tell me!"

"You remember when you called attention to the butler before I dismissed him? No man could do that. You're a woman and you can dance."

"So it is my shoulders? I will study again before the mirror. Yes, I can dance. Soon you shall see me. You shall see all the most wonderful things in Rajputana!"

"But tell me about yourself," Tess insisted, offering the cigarettes again. And this time her guest accepted one.

"My mother was the Russian wife of Bubru Singh, who had no son. I am the rightful maharanee of Sialpore, only those fools of English put my father's nephew on the throne, saying a woman can not reign. They are no wiser than apes! They have given Sialpore to Gungadhura who is a pig and loathes them instead of to a woman who would only laugh at them, and the brute is raising a litter of little pigs, so that even if he and his progeny were poisoned one by one, there would always be a brat left——he has so many!"

"And you?"

"First you must promise silence."

"Very well."

"Woman to woman!"

"Yes."

"Womb to womb—heart to heart——?"

"On my word of honor. But I promise nothing else, remember!"

"So speaks one whose promises are given truly! We are already friends. I will tell you all that is in my heart now."

"Tell me your name first."

She was about to answer when interruption came
from the direction of the gate. There was a restless
horse there, and a rider using resonant strong
language.

"Tom Tripe!" said Tess. "He's earlier than
usual."

The Rajputni smiled. Chamu appeared through
the door behind them with suspicious suddenness and
waddled to the gate, watched by a pair of blue eyes
that should have burned holes in his back and would
certainly have robbed him of all comfort had he been
aware of them.

THAW ON OLYMPUS

Bright spurs that add their roweled row
To clanking saber's pride;
Fierce eyes beneath a beetling brow;
More license than the rules allow;
A military stride;
Years' use of arbitrary will
And right to make or break;
Obedience of men who drill
And willy nilly foot the bill
For authorized mistake;
The comfort of the self-esteem
Deputed power brings———
Are fickler than the shadows seem,
Less fruitful than the lotus-dream,
And all of them have wings
When blue eyes, laughing in your own,
Make mockery of rules!

      *   *   *

And when those fustian shams have flown
The wise their new allegiance own,
Leaving dead form to fools!

CHAPTER TWO

"Friendship's friendship and respect's respect, but duty's what I'm paid to do!"

THE man at the gate dallied to look at his horse's fetlocks. Tess's strange guest seemed in no hurry either, but her movements were as swift as knitting-needles. She produced a fountain pen, and of all unexpected things, a Bank of India note for one thousand rupees—a new one, crisp and clean. Tess did not see the signature she scrawled across its back in Persian characters, and the pen was returned to an inner pocket and the note, folded four times, was palmed in the subtle hand long before Tom Tripe came striding up the path with jingling spurs.

"Morning, ma'am,——morning! Don't let me intrude. I'd a little accident, and took a liberty. My horse cut his fetlock—nothing serious—and I set your two *saises* (grooms) to work on it with a sponge and water. Twenty minutes will see it right as a trivet. Then I'm off again——I've a job of work."

He stood with back to the sun and hands on his hips, looking up at Tess—a man of fifty—a soldier of another generation, in a white uniform something like a British sergeant-major's of the days before the Mutiny. His mutton-chop whiskers, dyed dark-brown,

30

were military mid-Victorian, as were the huge brass spurs that jingled on black riding-boots. A great-chested, heavy-weight athletic man, a few years past his prime.

"Come up, Tom. You're always welcome."

"Ah!" His spurs rang on the stone steps, and, since Tess was standing close to the veranda rail, he turned to face her at the top. Saluting with martinet precision before removing his helmet, he did not get a clear view of the Rajputni. "As I've said many times, ma'am, the one house in the world where Tom Tripe may sit down with princes and commissioners."

"Have you had breakfast?"

He made a wry face.

"The old story, Tom?"

"The old story, ma'am. A hair of the dog that bit me is all the breakfast I could swallow."

"I suppose if I don't give you one now you'll have two later?"

He nodded. "I must. One now would put me just to rights and I'd eat at noon. Times when I'm savage with myself, and wait, I have to have two or three before I can stomach lunch."

She offered him a basket chair and beckoned Chamu.

"Brandy and soda for the sahib."

"Thank you, ma'am!" said the soldier piously.

"Where's your dog, Tom?"

"Behaving himself, I hope, ma'am, out there in the sun by the gate."

"Call him. He shall have a bone on the veranda. I want him to feel as friendly here as you do."

Tom whistled shrilly and an ash-hued creature, part Great Dane and certainly part Rampore, came up the path like a catapulted phantom, making hardly any sound. He stopped at the foot of the steps and gazed inquiringly at his master's face.

"You may come up."

He was an extraordinary animal, enormous, big-jowled, scarred, ungainly and apparently aware of it. He paused again on the top step.

"Show your manners."

The beast walked toward Tess, sniffed at her, wagged his stern exactly once and retired to the other end of the veranda, where Chamu, hurrying with brandy, gave him the widest possible berth. Tess looked the other way while Tom Tripe helped himself to a lot of brandy and a little soda.

"Now get a big bone for the dog," she ordered.

"There is none," the butler answered.

"Bring the leg-of-mutton bone of yesterday."

"That is for soup to-day."

"Bring it!"

Chamu was standing between Tom Tripe and the Rajputni, with his back to the latter; so nobody saw the hand that slipped something into the ample folds of his sash. He departed muttering by way of the steps and the garden, and the dog growled acknowledgment of the compliment.

Tess's Rajput guest continued to say nothing; but made no move to go. Introduction was inevitable, for it was the first rule of that house that all ranks met there on equal terms, whatever their relations else-where. Tom Tripe had finished wiping his mustache, and Tess was still wondering just how to manage without betraying the sex of the other or the fact that she herself did not yet know her visitor's name, when Chamu returned with the bone. He threw it to the dog from a safe distance, and was sniffed at scornfully for his pains.

"Won't he take it?" asked Tess.

"Not from a black man. Bring it here, you!"

The great brute, with a sidewise growl and glare at the butler that made him sweat with fright, picked up the bone and, at a sign from his master, laid it at the feet of Tess.

"Show your manners!"

Once more he waved his stern exactly once.

"Give it to him, ma'am."

Tess touched the bone with her foot, and the dog took it away, scaring Chamu along the veranda in front of him.

"Why don't you ever call him by name, Tom?"

"Bad for him, ma'am. When I say, 'Here, you!' or whistle, he obeys quick as lightning. But if I say, 'Trotters!' which his name is, he knows he's got to do his own thinking, and keeps his distance till he's sure what's wanted. A dog's like an enlisted man, ma'am; ought to be taught to jump at the word of command and never think for himself until you call him out of the ranks by name. Trotters understands me perfectly."

"Speaking of names," said Tess, "I'd like to introduce you to my guest, Tom, but I'm afraid——"

"You may call me Gunga Singh," said a quiet voice full of amusement, and Tom Tripe started. He turned about in his chair and for the first time looked the third member of the party in the face.

"Hoity-toity! Well, I'm jiggered! Dash my drink and dinner, it's the princess!"

He rose and saluted cavalierly, jocularly, yet with a deference one could not doubt, showing tobacco-darkened teeth in a smile of almost paternal indulgence.

"So the Princess Yasmini is Gunga Singh this morning, eh? And here's Tom Tripe riding up-hill and down-dale, laming his horse and sweating through a clean tunic—with a threat in his ear and a reward promised that he'll never see a smell of—while the princess is smoking cigarettes——"

"In very good company!"

"In good company, aye; but not out of mischief, I'll be bound! Naughty, naughty!" he said, wagging a finger at her. "Your ladyship'll get caught one of these days, and where will Tom Tripe be then? I've got my job to keep, you know. Friendship's friendship and respect's respect, but duty's what I'm paid to do. Here's me, drill-master of the maharajah's troops and a pension coming to me consequent on good behavior, with orders to set a guard over you, miss, and prevent your going and coming without his highness' leave. And here's you giving the guard the slip! Somebody tipped his highness off, and I wish you'd heard what's going to happen to me unless I find you!"

"You can't find me, Tom Tripe! I'm not Yasmini to-day; I'm Gunga Singh!"

"Tut-tut, Your Ladyship; that won't do! I swore on my Bible oath to the maharajah that I left you day

before yesterday closely guarded in the palace across
the river. He felt easy for the first time for a week.
Now, because they're afraid for their skins, the guard
all swear by Krishna you were never in there, and that
I've been bribed! How did you get out of the grounds,
miss?"

"Climbed the wall."

"I might have remembered you're as active as a
cat! Next time I'll mount a double guard *on* the wall,
so they'll tumble off and break their necks if they fall
asleep. But there are no boats, for I saw to it, and
the bridge is watched. How did you cross the river?"

"Swam."

"At night?"

The blue eyes smiled assent.

"Missy——Your Ladyship, you mustn't do that.
Little ladies that act that way might lose the number
of their mess. There's crockadowndillies in that river
—aggilators—what d'ye call the dam' things?——
mugger. They snap their jaws on a leg and pull you
under! The sweeter and prettier you are the more
they like you! Besides, missy, princesses aren't supposed to swim; it's vulgar."

He contrived to look the very incarnation of offended prudery, and she laughed at him with a voice like
a golden bell.

He faced Tess again with a gesture of apology.

"You'll pardon me, ma'am, but duty's duty."

Tess was enjoying the play immensely, shrewdly
suspecting Tom Tripe of more complaisance than he
chose to admit to his prisoner.

"You must treat my house as a sanctuary, Tom. Outside the garden wall orders I suppose are orders. Inside it I insist all guests are free and equal."

The Princess Yasmini slapped her boot with a little riding-switch and laughed delightedly.

"There, Tom Tripe! Now what will you do?"

"I'll have to use persuasion, miss! Tell me how you got into your own palace unseen and out again with a horse without a soul knowing?"

" 'Come into my net and get caught,' said the hunter; but the leopard is still at large. 'Teach me your tracks,' begged the hunter; but the leopard answered, 'Learn them!' "

"Hell's bells!"

Tom Tripe scratched his head and wiped sweat from his collar. The princess was gazing away into the distance, not apparently inclined to take the soldier seriously. Tess, wondering what her guest found interesting on the horizon all of a sudden, herself picked out the third beggar's shabby outline on the same high rock from which Yasmini had confessed to watching before dawn.

"Will your ladyship ride home with me?" asked Tom Tripe.

"No."

"But why not?"

"Because the commissioner is coming and there is only one road and he would see me and ask questions. He is stupid enough not to recognize me, but you are too stupid to tell wise lies, and this memsahib is so afraid of an imaginary place called hell that I must stay and do my own——"

"I left off believing in hell when I was ten years old," Tess answered.

"I hope to God you're right, ma'am!" put in Tom Tripe piously, and both women laughed.

"Then I shall trust you and we shall always understand each other," decided Yasmini. "But why will you not tell lies, if there is no hell?"

"I'm afraid I'm guilty now and then."

"But you are ashamed afterward? Why? Lies are necessary, since people are such fools!"

Tom Tripe interrupted, wiping the inside of his tunic collar again with a big bandanna handkerchief.

"How do you know the commissioner is coming, Your Ladyship? Phew! You'd better hide! I'll have to answer too many questions as it is. *He'd* turn you outside in!"

"There is no hurry," said Yasmini. "He will not be here for five minutes and he is a fool in any case. He is walking his horse up-hill."

Tess too had seen the beggar on the rock remove his ragged turban, rewind it, and then leisurely remove himself from sight. The system of signals was pretty obviously simple. The whole intriguing East is simple, if one only has simplicity enough to understand it.

"Can your horse be seen from the road?" Yasmini asked.

"No, miss. The *saises* are attending to him under the neem-trees at the rear."

"Then ask the memsahib's permission to pass through the house and leave by the back way."

Tess, more amused than ever, nodded consent and

clapped her hands for Chamu to come and do the honors.

"I'll wait here," she said, "and welcome the commissioner."

"But you, Your Ladyship?" Tom Tripe scratched his head in evident confusion. "I've got to account for you, you know."

"You haven't seen me. You have only seen a man named Gunga Singh."

"That's all very fine, missy, but the butler—that man Chamu—he knows you well enough. He'll get the story to the maharajah's ears."

"Leave that to me."

"You dassen't trust him, miss!"

Again came the golden laugh, expressive of the worldly wisdom of a thousand women, and sheer delight in it.

"I shall stay here, if the memsahib permits."

Tess nodded again. "The commissioner shall sit with me on the veranda," Tess said. "Chamu will show you into the parlor."

(The Blaines had never made the least attempt to leave behind their home-grown names for things. Whoever wanted to in Sialpore might have a drawing-room, but whoever came to that house must sit in a parlor or do the other thing.)

"Is it possible the burra-sahib will suppose my horse is yours?" Yasmini asked, and again Tess smiled and nodded. She would know what to say to any one who asked impertinent questions.

Yasmini and Tom Tripe followed Chamu into the house just as the commissioner's horse's nose appeared past the gate-post; and once behind the curtains in the long hall that divided room from room, Tom Tripe called a halt to make a final effort at persuasion.

"Now, missy, Your Ladyship, please!"

But she had no patience to spare for him.

"Quick! Send your dog to guard that door!"

Tom Tripe snapped his fingers and made a motion with his right hand. The dog took up position full in the middle of the passage blocking the way to the kitchen and alert for anything at all, but violence preferred. Chamu, all sly smiles and effusiveness until that instant, as one who would like to be thought a confidential co-conspirator, now suddenly realized that his retreat was cut off. No explanation had been offered, but the fact was obvious and conscience made the usual coward of him. He would rather have bearded Tom Tripe than the dog.

Yasmini opened on him in his own language, because there was just a chance that otherwise Tess might overhear through the open window and put two and two together.

"Scullion! Dish-breaker! Conveyor of uncleanness! You have a son?"

"Truly, heavenborn. One son, who grows into a man—the treasure of my old heart."

"A gambler!"

"A young man, heavenborn, who feels his manhood—now and then gay—now and then foolish——"

"A *budmash!*" (Bad rascal.)

"Nay, an honest one!"

"Who borrowed from Mukhum Dass the moneylender, making untrue promises?"

"Nay, the money was to pay a debt."

"A gambling debt, and he lied about it."

"Nay, truly, heavenborn, he but promised Mukhum Dass he would repay the sum with interest."

"Swearing he would buy with the money, two horses which Mukhum Dass might seize as forfeit after the appointed time!"

"Otherwise, heavenborn, Mukhum Dass would not have lent the money!"

"And now Mukhum Dass threatens prison?"

"Truly, heavenborn. The money-lender is without shame—without mercy—without conscience."

"And that is why you—dog of a spying butler set to betray the sahib's salt you eat—man of smiles and welcome words!——stole money from me? Was it to pay the debt of thy gambling brat-born-in-a-stable?"

"I, heavenborn? I steal from thee? I would rather be beaten!"

"Thou shalt be beaten, and worse, thou and thy son! Feel in his *cummerbund,* Tom Tripe! I saw where the money went!"

Promptly into the butler's sash behind went fingers used to delving into more unmilitary improprieties than any ten civilians could think of. Tripe produced the thousand-rupee note in less than half a minute and, whether or not he believed it stolen, saw through the plan and laughed.

"Is my name on the back of it?" Yasmini asked.

Tom Tripe displayed the signature, and Chamu's clammy face turned ashen-gray.

"And," said Yasmini, fixing Chamu with angry blue eyes, "the commissioner sahib is on the veranda!

For the reputation of the English he would cause an example to be made of servants who steal from guests in the house of foreigners."

Chamu capitulated utterly, and wept.

"What shall I do? What shall I do?" he demanded.

"In the jail," Yasmini said slowly, "you could not spy on my doings, nor report my sayings."

"Heavenborn, I am dumb! Only take back the money and I am dumb forever, never seeing or having seen or heard either you or this sahib here! Take back the money!"

But Yasmini was not so easily balked of her intention.

"Put his thumb-print on it, Tom Tripe, and see that he writes his name."

The trembling Chamu was led into a room where an ink-pot stood open on a desk, and watched narrowly while he made a thumb-mark and scratched a signature. Then:

"Take the money and pay thy puppy's debt with it. Afterward beat the boy. And see to it," Yasmini advised, "that Mukhum Dass gives a receipt, lest he claim the debt a second time!"

Speechless between relief, doubt and resentment Chamu hid the bank-note in his sash and tried to feign gratitude—a quality omitted from his list of elements when a patient, caste-less mother brought him yelling into the world.

"Go!"

Tom Tripe made a sign to Trotters, who went and lay down, obviously bored, and Chamu departed backward, bowing repeatedly with both hands raised to his forehead.

"And now, Your Ladyship?"

"Take that eater-of-all-that-is-unnamable," (she meant the dog), "and return to the palace."

"Your Ladyship, it's all my life's worth!"

"Tell the maharajah that you have spoken with a certain Gunga Singh, who said that the Princess Yasmini is at the house of the commissioner sahib."

"But it's not true; they'll——"

"Let the commissioner sahib deny it then! Go!"

"But, missy——"

"Do as I say, Tom Tripe, and when I am maharanee of Sialpore you shall have double pay—and a troupe of dancing girls—and a dozen horses—and the title of bahadur—and all the brandy you can drink. The sepoys shall furthermore have modern uniforms, and you shall drill them until they fall down dead. I have promised. Go!"

With a wag of his head that admitted impotence in the face of woman's wiles Tom strode out by the back way, followed at a properly respectful distance by his "eater-of-all-that-is-unnamable."

Then the princess walked through the parlor to the deeply cushioned window-seat, outside which the commissioner sat quite alone with Mrs. Blaine, trying to pull strings whose existence is not hinted at in blue books. Yasmini from earliest infancy possessed an uncanny gift of silence, sometimes even when she laughed.

NO TRESPASS!

There's comfort in the purple creed
Of rosary and hood;
There's promise in the temple gong,
And hope (deferred) when evensong
Foretells a morrow's good;
There's rapture in the royal right
To lay the daily dole
In cash or kind at temple-door,
Since sacrifice must go before,
The saving of a soul.
The priests who plot for power now,
Though future glory preach,
Themselves alike the victims fall
Of law that mesmerizes all——
Each subject unto each——
Though all is well if all obey
And all have humble heart,
Nor dare to hold in cursèd doubt
Those gems of truth the church lets out;
But where's the apple-cart,
And where's the sacred fiction gone,
And who's to have the blame
When any upstart takes a hand
And, scorning what the priests have planned,
Plays Harry with the game?

CHAPTER THREE

*"Give a woman the last word always; but be sure it is
a question, which you leave unanswered."*

HE WAS a beau ideal commissioner. The native
newspaper said so when he first came, having pain-
fully selected the phrase from a "Dictionary of Polite
English for Public Purposes" edited by a college grad-
uate at present in the Andamans. True, later it had
called him an "overbearing and insane procrastinator"
—"an apostle of absolutism"—and, plum of all literary
gleanings, since it left so much to the imagination of
the native reader,—*"laudator temporis acti."* But that
was because he had withdrawn his private subscrip-
tion prior to suspending the paper *sine die* under Para-
graph so-and-so of the Act for Dealing with Sedition;
it could not be held to cancel the correct first judgment, any more than the unmeasured early praise had
offset later indiscretion. Beau ideal must stand.

It was not his first call at the Blaines' house,
although somehow or other he never contrived to find
Dick Blaine at home. As a bachelor he had no domestic difficulties to pin him down when office work was
over for the morning, and, being a man of hardly more
than forty, of fine physique, with an astonishing capacity for swift work, he could usually finish in an hour

44

before breakfast what would have kept the routine rank and file of orthodox officials perspiring through the day. That was one reason why he had been sent to Sialpore—men in the higher ranks, with a pension due them after certain years of service, dislike being hurried.

He was a handsome man—too handsome, some said—with a profile like a medallion of Mark Antony that lost a little of its strength and poise when he looked straight at you. A commissionership was an apparent rise in the world; but Sialpore has the name of being a departmental cul-de-sac, and they had laughed in the clubs about "Irish promotion" without exactly naming Judge O'Mally. (Mrs. O'Mally came from a cathedral city, where distaste for the conventions is forced at high pressure from early infancy.)

But there are no such things as political blind alleys to a man who is a judge of indiscretion, provided he has certain other unusual gifts as well. Sir Roland Samson, K. C. S. I., was not at all a disappointed man, nor even a discouraged one.

Most people were at a disadvantage coming up the path through the Blaines' front garden. There was a feeling all the way of being looked down on from the veranda that took ten minutes to recover from in the subsequent warmth of Western hospitality. But Samson had learned long ago that appearance was all in his favor, and he reenforced it with beautiful buff riding-boots that drew attention to firm feet and manly bearing. It did him good to be looked at, and he felt, as a painstaking gentleman should, that the sight did spectators no harm.

"All alone?" he asked, feeling sure that Mrs. Blaine was pleased to see him, and shifting the chair beside her as he sat down in order to see her face better. "Husband in the hills as usual? I must choose a Sunday next time and find him in."

Tess smiled. She was used to the remark. He always made it, but always kept away on Sundays.

"There was a party at my house last night, and every one agreed what an acquisition you and your husband are to Sialpore. You're so refreshing—quite different to what we're all used to."

"We're enjoying the novelty too—at least, Dick doesn't have much time for enjoyment, but——"

"I suppose he has had vast experience of mining?"

"Oh, he knows his profession, and works hard. He'll find gold where there is any," said Tess.

"You never told me how he came to choose Sialpore as prospecting ground."

Tess recognized the prevarication instantly. Almost the first thing Dick had done after they arrived was to make a full statement of all the circumstances in the commissioner's office. However, she was not her husband. There was no harm in repetition.

"The maharajah's secretary wrote to a mining college in the States for the name of some one qualified to explore the old workings in these hills. They gave my husband's name among others, and he got in correspondence. Finally, being free at the time, we came out here for the trip, and the maharajah offered terms on the spot that we accepted. That is all."

Samson laughed.

"I'm afraid not all. A contract with the British

Government would be kept. I won't say a written agreement with Gungadhura is worthless, but——"

"Oh, he has to pay week by week in advance to cover expenses."

"Very wise. But how about if you find gold?"

"We get a percentage."

Every word of that, as Tess knew, the commissioner could have ascertained in a minute from his office files. So she was quite as much on guard as he—quite as alert to discover hidden drifts.

"I'm afraid there'll be complications," he went on with an air of friendly frankness. "Perhaps I'd better wait until I can see your husband?"

"If you like, of course. But he and I speak the same language. What you tell me will reach him—— anything you say, just as you say it."

"I'd better be careful then!" he answered, smiling. "Wise wives don't always tell their husbands everything."

"I've no secrets from mine."

"Unusual!" he smiled. "I might say obsolete! But you Americans with your reputation for divorce and originality are very old-fashioned in some things, aren't you?"

"What did you want me to tell my husband?" countered Tess.

"I wonder if he understands how complicated conditions are here. For instance, does your contract stipulate where the gold is to be found?"

"On the maharajah's territory."

"Anywhere within those limits?"

"So I understand."

"Is the kind of gold mentioned?"

"How many kinds are there?"

He gained thirty seconds for reflection by lighting a cigar, and decided to change his ground.

"I know nothing of geology, I'm afraid. I wonder if your husband knows about the so-called islands? There are patches of British territory, administered directly by us, within the maharajah's boundaries; and little islands of native territory administered by the maharajah's government within the British sphere."

"Something like our Indian reservations, I suppose?"

"Not exactly, but the analogy will do. If your husband were to find gold—of any kind—on one of our 'islands' within the maharajah's territory, his contract with the maharajah would be useless."

"Are the boundaries of the islands clearly marked?"

"Not very. They're known, of course, and recorded. There's an old fort on one of them, garrisoned by a handful of British troops—a constant source of heart-burn, I believe, to Gungadhura. He can see the top of the flag-staff from his palace roof; a predecessor of mine had the pole lengthened, I'm told. On the other hand, there's a very pretty little palace over on our side of the river with about a half square mile surrounding it that pertains to the native State. Your husband could dig there, of course. There's no knowing that it might not pay—if he's looking for more kinds of gold than one."

Tess contrived not to seem aware that she was being pumped.

"D'you mean that there might be alluvial gold down by the river?" she asked.

"Now, now, Mrs. Blaine!" he laughed. "You Americans are not so ingenuous as you like to seem! Do you really expect us to believe that your husband's purpose isn't in fact to discover the Sialpore Treasure?"

"I never heard of it."

"I suspect he hasn't told you."

"I'll bet with you, if you like," she answered. "Our contract against your job that I know every single detail of his terms with Gungadhura!"

"Well, well,——of course I believe you, Mrs. Blaine. We're not overheard, are we?"

Not forgetful of the Princess Yasmini hidden somewhere in the house behind her, but unsuspicious yet of that young woman's gift for garnering facts, Tess stood up to look through the parlor window. She could see all of the room except the rear part of the window-seat, a little more than a foot of which was shut out of her view by the depth of the wall. A cat, for instance, could have lain there tucked among the cushions perfectly invisible.

"None of the servants is in there," she said, and sat down again, nodding in the direction of a gardener. "There's the nearest possible eavesdropper."

Samson had made up his mind. This was not an occasion to be actually indiscreet, but a good chance to pretend to be. He was a judge of those matters.

"There have been eighteen rajahs of Sialpore in direct succession father to son," he said, swinging a beautiful buff-leather boot into view by crossing his knee, and looking at her narrowly with the air of a man who unfolds confidences. "The first man began accumulating treasure. Every single rajah since has added to it. Each man has confided the secret to his successor and to none else—father to son, you understand. When Bubru Singh, the last man, died he had no son. The secret died with him."

"How does anybody know that there's a secret then?" demanded Tess.

"Everybody knows it! The money was raised by taxes. Minister after minister in turn has had to hand over minted gold to the reigning rajah——"

"And look the other way, I suppose, while the rajah hid the stuff!" suggested Tess.

Samson screwed up his face like a man who has taken medicine.

"There are dozens of ways in a native state of getting rid of men who know too much."

"Even under British overrule?"

He nodded. "Poison—snakes—assassination—jail on trumped-up charges, and disease in jail—apparent accidents of all sorts. It doesn't pay to know too much."

"Then we're suspected of hunting for this treasure? Is that the idea?"

"Not at all, since you've denied it. I believe you implicitly. But I hope your husband doesn't stumble on it."

"Why?"

"Or if he does, that he'll see his way clear to notify me first."

"Would that be honest?"

He changed his mind. That was a point on which Samson prided himself. He was not hidebound to one plan as some men are, but could keep two or three possibilities in mind and follow up whichever suited him. This was a case for indiscretion after all.

"Seeing we're alone, and that you're a most exceptional woman, I think I'll let you into a diplomatic secret, Mrs. Blaine. Only you mustn't repeat it. The present maharajah, Gungadhura, isn't the saving kind; he's a spender. He'd give his eyes to get hold of that treasure. And if he had it, we'd need an army to suppress him. We made a mistake when Bubru Singh died; there were two nephews with about equal claims, and we picked the wrong one—a born intriguer. I'd call him a rascal if he weren't a reigning prince. It's too late now to unseat him—unless, of course, we should happen to catch him in *flagrante delicto.*"

"What does that mean? With the goods? With the treasure?"

"No, no. In the act of doing something grossly *ultra vires*—illegal, that's to say. But you've put your finger on the point. If the treasure should be found—as it might be—somewhere hidden on that little plot of ground with a palace on it on our side of the river, our problem would be fairly easy. There'd be some way of—ah—making sure the fund would be properly administered. But if Gungadhura found it in the hills, and kept quiet about it as he doubtless would, he'd have every sedition-monger in India in his pay within a year, and the consequences might be very serious."

"Who is the other man—the one the British didn't choose?" asked Tess.

"A very decent chap named Utirupa—quite a sportsman. He was thought too young at the time the selection was made; but he knew enough to get out of the reach of the new maharajah immediately. They have a phrase here, you know, 'to hate like cousins.' They're rather remote cousins, but they hate all the more for that."

"So you'd rather that the treasure stayed buried?"

"Not exactly. But"——he tossed ash from the end of his cigar to illustrate offhandedness—— "I think I could promise ten per cent. of it to whoever brought us exact information of its whereabouts before the maharajah could lay his hands on it."

"I'll tell that to my husband."

"Do."

"Of course, being in a way in partnership with Gungadhura, he might——"

"Let me give you one word of caution, if I may without offense. We—our government—wouldn't recognize the right of—of any one to take that treasure out of the country. Ten per cent. would be the maximum, and that only in case of accurate information brought in time to us."

"Aren't findings keepings? Isn't possession nine points of the law?" laughed Tess.

"In certain cases, yes. But not where government knows of the existence somewhere of a hoard of public funds—an enormous hoard—it must run into millions."

"Then, if the maharajah should find it would you take it from him?"

"No. We would put the screws on, and force him

to administer the fund properly if we knew about it. But he'd never tell."

"Then how d'you know he hasn't found the stuff already?"

"Because many of his personal bills aren't paid, and the political stormy petrels are not yet heading his way. He's handicapped by not being able to hunt for it openly. Some ill-chosen confidant might betray the find to us. I doubt if he trusts more than one or two people at a time."

"It must be hell to be a maharajah!" Tess burst out after a minute's silence.

"It's sometimes hell to be commissioner, Mrs. Blaine."

"If I were Gungadhura I'd find that money or bu'st! And when I'd found it——"

"You'd endow an orphan asylum, eh?"

"I'd make such trouble for you English that you'd be glad to leave me in peace for a generation!"

Samson laughed good-naturedly and twisted up the end of his mustache.

"'Pon my soul, you're a surprising woman! So your sympathies are all with Gungadhura?"

"Not at all. I think he's a criminal! He buys women, and tortures animals in an arena, and keeps a troupe of what he is pleased to call dancing-girls. I've seen his eyes in the morning, and I suspect him of most of the vices in the calendar. He's despicable. But if I were in his shoes I'd find that money and make it hot for you English!"

"Are you of Irish extraction, Mrs. Blaine?"

"No, indeed I'm not. I'm Connecticut Yankee, and my husband's from the West. I don't have to be Irish to think for myself, do I?"

Samson did not know whether or not to take her seriously, but recognized that his chance had gone that morning for the flirtation he had had in view—very mild, of course, for a beginning; it was his experience that most things ought to start quite mildly, if you hoped to keep the other man from stampeding the game. Nevertheless, as a judge of situations, he preferred not to take his leave at that moment. Give a woman the last word always, but be sure it is a question, which you leave unanswered.

"You've a beautiful garden," he said; and for a minute or two they talked of flowers, of which he knew more than a little; then of music, of which he understood a very great deal.

"Have you a proper lease on this house?" he asked at last.

"I believe so. Why?"

"I've been told there's some question about the title. Some one's bringing suit against your landlord for possession on some ground or another."

"What of it? Suppose the other should win—could he put us out?"

"I don't know. That might depend on your present landlord's power to make the lease at the time when he made it."

"But we signed the agreement in good faith. Surely, as long as we pay the rent——?"

"I don't know, I'm sure. Well——if there's any

trouble, come to me about it and we'll see what can be done."

"But who is this who is bringing suit against the landlord?"

"I haven't heard his name—don't even know the details. I hope you'll come out of it all right. Certainly I'll help in any way I can. Sometimes a little influence, you know, exerted in the right way—well— Please give my regards to your husband— Good morning, Mrs. Blaine."

It was a pet theory of his that few men pay enough attention to their backs,—not that he preached it; preaching is tantamount to spilling beans, supposing that the other fellow listens; and if he doesn't listen it is waste of breath. But he bore in mind that people behind him had eyes as well as those in front. Accordingly he made a very dignified exit down the long path, tipped Mrs. Blaine's *sais* all the man had any right to expect, and rode away feeling that he had made the right impression. He looked particularly well on horseback.

Theresa Blaine smiled after him, wondering what impression she herself had made; but she did not have much time to think about it. From the open window behind her she was seized suddenly, drawn backward and embraced.

"You are perfect!" Yasmini purred in her ear between kisses. "You are surely one of the fairies sent to live among mortals for a sin! I shall love you forever! Now that *burra-wallah* Samson sahib will ride into the town, and perhaps also to the law-court, and to other places, to ask about your landlord, of

whom he knows nothing, having only heard a servant's tale. But Tom Tripe will have told already
that I am at the burra commissioner's house, and
Gungadhura will send there to ask questions. And
whoever goes will have to wait long. And when the
commissioner returns at last he will deny that I have
been there, and the messenger will return to Gungadhura, who will not believe a word of it, especially as
he will know that the commissioner has been riding
about the town on an unknown errand. So, after he
has learned that I am back in my own palace, Gungadhura will try to poison me again. All of which is as it
should be. Come closer and let me——"

"Child!" Tess protested. "Do you realize that
you're dressed up like an extremely handsome man,
and are kissing me through a window in the sight of
all Sialpore? How much reputation do you suppose I
shall have left within the hour?"

"There is only one kind of reputation worth the
having," laughed Yasmini; "that of knowing how to
win!"

"But what's this about poison?" Tess asked her.

"He always tries to poison me. Now he will try
more carefully."

"You must take care! How will you prevent
him?"

By quite unconscious stages Tess found herself
growing concerned about this young truant princess.
One minute she was interested and amused. The next
she was conscious of affection. Now she was posi-
tively anxious about her, to use no stronger word.

Nor had she time to wonder why, for Yasmini's methods were breathless.

"I shall eat very often at your house. And then you shall take a journey with me. And after that the great pig Gungadhura shall be very sorry he was born, and still more sorry that he tried to poison me!"

"Tell me, child, haven't you a mother?"

"She died a year ago. If there is such a place as hell she has gone there, of course, because nobody is good enough for Heaven. But I am not Christian and not Hindu, so hell is not my business."

"What are you, then?"

"I am Yasmini. There is nobody like me. I am all alone, believing only what I know and laughing at the priests. I know all the laws of caste, because that is necessary if you are to understand men. And I have let the priests teach me their religion because it is by religion that they govern people. And the priests," she laughed, "are much more foolish than the fools they entice and frighten. But the priests have power. Gungadhura is fearfully afraid of them. The high priest of the temple of Jinendra pretends to him that he can discover where the treasure is hidden, so Gungadhura makes daily offerings and the priest grows very fat."

"Who taught you such good English?" Tess asked her; for there was hardly even a trace of foreign accent, nor the least hesitation for a word.

"Father Bernard, a Jesuit. My mother sent for him, and he came every day, year after year. He had a little chapel in Sialpore where a few of the very low-caste people used to go to pray and make confessions to him. That should have given him great power; but the people of this land never confess completely, as he told me the Europeans do, preferring to tell lies about one another rather than the truth about themselves. I refused to be baptized because I was tired of him, and after my mother died and she was burned with the Hindu ritual, he received orders to go elsewhere. Now there is another Jesuit, but he only has a little following among the English, and can not get to see me because I hide behind the *purdah*. The *purdah* is good—if you know how to make use of it and not be ruled by it."

They were still in the window, Yasmini kneeling on the cushions with her face in shadow and Tess with her back to the light.

"Ah! Hasamurti comes!" said Yasmini suddenly. "She is my *cheti*." (Hand-maiden.)

Tess turned swiftly, but all she saw was one of the three beggars down by the little gate twisting himself a garland out of stolen flowers.

"Now there will be a carriage waiting, and I must leave my horse in your stable." .

The beggar held the twisted flowers up to the sunlight to admire his work.

"I must go at once. I shall go to the temple of Jinendra, where the priest, who is no man's friend, imagines I am a friend of his. He will promise me anything if I will tell him what to say to Gungadhura; and I shall tell him, without believing the promises. One of these days perhaps he will plot with Gungadhura to have me poisoned, being in agreement with the commissioner sahib who said to you just now that it is not good to know too much! But neither is it good to be too late! Lend me a covering, my sister——see, this is the very thing. I shall leave by the little gate. Send the gardener on an errand. Are the other servants at the back of the house? Of course yes, they will be spying to see me leave by the way I came."

Tess sent the gardener running for a basket to put flowers in, and when she turned her head again Yasmini had stepped out through the window shrouded from head to heels in a camel-hair robe such as the Bikanir Desert men wear at night. The lower part of her face was hooded in it.

Provided you wear a turban you can wear anything else you like in India without looking incongruous. It is the turban that turns the trick. Even the spurs on the heels of riding-boots did not look out of place.

"You'll sweat," laughed Tess. "That camel-hair is hot stuff."

"Does the panther sweat under his pelt? I am stronger than a panther. Now swiftly! I must go, but I will come soon. You are my friend."

She was gone like a shadow without another word, with long swift strides, not noticing the beggars and not noticed by them as far as any one could tell. Tess sat down to smoke a cigarette and think the experience over.

She had not done thinking when Dick Blaine returned unexpectedly for early lunch and showed her a bag-full of coarsely powdered quartz.

"There's color there," he said jubilantly. "Rather more than merely color! It's not time to talk yet, but

I think I've found a vein that may lead somewhere.
Then won't Gungadhura gloat?"

She told him at great length about Yasmini's visit,
dwelling on every detail of it, he listening like a man at
a play, for Tess had the gift of clear description.

"Go a journey with her, if you feel like it, Tess,"
he advised. "You have a rotten time here alone all
day, and I can't do much to 'liven it. Take sensible
precautions but have a good time anyway you can."

Because Yasmini had monopolized imagination she
told him last of all, at lunch, about the commissioner's
call, rehearsing that, too, detail by detail, word for
word.

"Wants me to find the treasure, does he, and call
the game on Gungadhura? What does he take me
for? One of his stool-pigeons? If it's a question
of percentage, I'd prefer one from the maharajah than
from him. If I ever stumble on it, Gungadhura shall
know first go off the bat, and I'll see the British Government in hell before I'll answer questions!"

"They'd never believe Gungadhura hadn't
rewarded you," said Tess.

"What of it?" he demanded. "What do we care
what they believe? And supposing it were true, what
then? Just at present I'm in partnership with
Gungadhura."

JINENDRA'S SMILE

Deep broods the calm where the cooing doves are
    mating
And shadows quiver noiseless 'neath the courtyard
    trees,
Cool keeps the gloom where the suppliants are waiting
Begging little favors of Jinendra on their knees.
Peace over all, and the consciousness of nearness,
Charity removing the remoteness of the gods;
Spirit of compassion breathing with new clearness
"There's a limit set to khama; there's a surcease from
    the rods."
"Blessed were the few, who trim the lights of kindness,
Toiling in the temple for the love of one and all,
If it were not for hypocrisy and gluttony and
    blindness,"
Smiles the image of Jinendra on the courtyard wall.

CHAPTER FOUR

"The law....is like a python after monkeys in the tree-tops."

YASMINI, hooded like a bandit in the camel-hair cloak, resumed an air of leisurely dignity in keeping with the unhurried habit of Sialpore the moment she was through the gate. It was just as well she did, for Mukhum Dass, the money-lender, followed by a sweating lean parasite on foot, was riding a smart mule on his customary morning round to collect interest from victims and oversee securities.

He was a fat, squat, shiny-looking person in a black alpaca coat, with a black umbrella for protection from the sun, and an air of sour dissatisfaction for general business purposes—an air that was given the lie direct by a small, acquisitive nose and bright brown eyes that surely never made bad bargains. Yasmini's hooded figure brought him to a halt just at the corner, where the little road below the Blaines' wall joined the wider road that led down-hill. Business is business, and time a serious matter only for those who sign promissory notes; he drew rein without compunction.

"This house is yours?" she asked, and he nodded, his sharp eyes shining like an animal's, determined to recognize his questioner.

62

"There is a miscalculating son of lies who brings a lawsuit to get the title?"

He nodded again—a man of few words except when words exacted interest.

"Dhulap Singh, is it not? He is a secret agent of Gungadhura."

"How do you know? Why should the maharajah want my property?"

"He hunts high and low for the Sialpore treasure. Jengal Singh, who built this house, was in the confidence of Gungadhura's uncle, and a priest says there will be a clue found to the treasure beneath the floor of this house."

"A likely tale indeed!"

"Very well, then——lose thine house!"

Yasmini turned on a disdainful heel and started down-hill. Mukhum Dass called after her, but she took no notice. He sent the sweating parasite to bring her back, but she shook him off with execrations. Mukhum Dass turned his mule and rode down-hill after her.

"True information has its price," he said. "Tell me your name."

"That also has its price."

He cackled dryly. "Names cost money only to their owners—on a *hundi*." (Promissory note.)

"Nevertheless there is a price."

"In advance? I will give a half-rupee!"

Once more Yasmini resumed her way down-hill. Again Mukhum Dass rode after her.

"At any rate name the price."

"It is silence firstly; second, a security for silence."

"The first part is easy."

"Nay, difficult. A woman can keep silence, but men chatter like the apes, in every coffee shop."

His bargain-driver's eyes watched hers intently, unable to detect the slightest clue that should start him guessing. He was trying to identify a man, not a woman.

"How shall I give security for silence?" he asked.

"I already hold it."

"How? What? Where?"

The money-lender betrayed a glimpse of sheer pugnacity that seemed to amuse his tormentor.

"Send thy jackal out of ear-shot, tiger."

He snapped at his parasite angrily, and the man went away to sit down. Then:

"Where are the title-deeds of the house you say you own?" she asked him suddenly.

Mukhum Dass kept silence, and tried to smother the raging anger in his eyes.

"Was it Mukhum Dass or another, who went to the priest in the temple of Jinendra on a certain afternoon and requested intercession to the god in order that a title-deed might be recovered, that fell down the *nullah* when the snakes frightened a man's mule and he himself fell into the road? Or was it another accident that split that car of thine in two pieces?"

"Priests cackle like old women," growled the money-lender.

"Nay, but this one cackled to the god. Perhaps Jinendra felt compassionate toward a poor *shroff* (money-lender) who can not defend his suit successfully without that title-deed. Jengal Singh died and his son, who ought to know, claims that the house was really sold to Dhulap Singh, who dallies with his suit because he suspects, but does not know, that Mukhum Dass has lost the paper;——eh?"

"How do you know these things?"

"Maybe the god Jinendra told! Which would be better, Mukhum Dass—to keep great silence, and be certain to receive the paper in time to defend the law-suit,——or to talk freely, and so set others talking? Who knows that it might not reach the ears of Jengal Singh that the title-deed is truly lost?"

"He who tells secrets to a priest," swore the money-lender, "would better have screamed them from the housetop!"

"Nay—the god heard. The priest told the god, and the god told a certain one to whom the finder brought the paper, asking a reward. That person holds the paper now as security for silence!"

"It is against the law to keep my paper!"

"The law catches whom it can, Mukhum Dass, let-ting all others go, like a python after monkeys in the tree-tops!"

"From whom am I to get my paper for the law-suit at the proper time?"

"From Jinendra's priest perhaps."

"He has it now? The dog's stray offspring! I will——"

"Nay, he has it not! Be kind and courteous to Jinendra's priest, or perhaps the god will send the paper after all to Dhulap Singh!"

"As to what shall I keep silence?"

"Two matters. Firstly, Chamu the butler will presently pay his son's debt. Give Chamu a receipt with the number of the bank-note written on it, saying nothing."

"Second?"

"Preserve the bank-note carefully for thirty days and keep silence."

"I will do that. Now tell me thy name?"

Yasmini laughed. "Do thy victims repay in advance the rupees not yet lent? Nay, the price is silence! First, pay the price; then learn my name. Go——get thy money from Chamu the butler. Breathe as much as a hint to any one, and thy title-deed shall go to Dhulap Singh!"

Eying her like a hawk, but with more mixed emotions than that bird can likely compass, the money-lender sat his mule and watched her stride round the corner out of sight. Then, glancing over her shoulder to make sure the man's parasite was not watching her at his master's orders, she ran along the shoulder of the hill to where, in the shelter of a clump of trees, a carriage waited.

It was one of those lumbering, four-wheeled affairs with four horses, and a platform for two standing attendants behind and wooden lattice-work over the windows, in which the women-folk of princes take the air. But there were no attendants—only a coachman, and a woman who came running out to meet her; for Yasmini, like her cousin the maharajah, did not trust too many people all at once.

"Quick, Hasamurti!"

Fussing and giggling over her (the very name means Laughter), the maid bustled her into the carriage, and without a word of instruction the coachman tooled his team down-hill at a leisurely gait, as if told in advance to take his time about it; the team was capable of speed.

Inside the carriage, with a lot more chuckling and giggling a change was taking place almost as complete as that from chrysalis to butterfly. The toilet of a lady of Yasmini's nice discrimination takes time in the easiest circumstances; in a lumbering coach, not built for leg-room, and with a looking-glass the size of a saucer, it was a mixture of horse-play and miracle. Between them they upset the perfume bottle, as was natural, and a shrill scream at one stage of the journey (that started a rumor all over Sialpore to the effect that Gungadhura was up to the same old game again) announced, as a matter of plain fact that Yasmini had sat on the spurs. There was long, spun-gold hair to be combed out—penciling to do to eyebrows—lac to be applied to pretty feet to make them exquisitely pretty—and layer on layer of gossamer silk to be smothered and hung exactly right. Then over it all had to go one of those bright-hued silken veils that look so casually worn but whose proper adjustment is an art.

But when they reached the bottom of the long hill and began twisting in and out among the narrow streets, it was finished. By the time they reached the temple of Jinendra, set back in an old stone courtyard with images of the placid god carved all about in the shade of the wide projecting cornice, all was quiet

and orderly inside the carriage and there stepped out
of it, followed by the same dark-hooded maid, a swift
vision of female loveliness that flitted like a flash of
light into the temple gloom.

It was not so squalid as the usual Hindu temple,
although so ancient that the carving of the pillars in
some places was almost worn away, and the broad
stone flags on the floor were hollowed deep by ages of
devotion. The gloom was pierced here and there by
dim light from brass lamps, that showed carvings
blackened by centuries of smoke, but there was an
unlooked-for suggestion of care, and a little cleanli-
ness that the fresh blossoms scattered here and there
accentuated.

There were very few worshipers at that hour——
only a woman, who desired a child and was praying to
Jinendra as a last recourse after trying all the other
gods in vain, and a half-dozen men—all eyes—who
gossiped in low tones in a corner. Yasmini gave them
small chance to recognize her. Quicker than their gaze
could follow, a low door at the rear, close beside the
enormous, jeweled image of the god, closed behind her
and the maid, and all that was left of the vision was
the ringing echo of an iron lock dying away in dark
corners and suggesting nothing except secrecy.

The good square room she had entered so abruptly
unannounced was swept and washed. Sunlight poured
into it at one end through a window that opened on an
inner courtyard, and there were flowers everywhere—
arranged in an enormous brass bowl on a little table—
scattered at random on the floor——hung in plaited

garlands from the hooks intended to support lamps. Of furniture there was little, only a long cushioned bench down the length of the wall beneath the window, and a thing like a throne on which Jinendra's high priest sat in solitary grandeur.

He did not rise at first to greet her, for Jinendra's priest was fat; there was no gainsaying it. After about a minute a sort of earthquake taking place in him began to reach the surface; he rocked on his center in increasing waves that finally brought him with a spasm of convulsion to the floor. There he stood in full sunlight with his bare toes turned inward, holding his stomach with both hands, while Yasmini settled herself in graceful youthful curves on the cushioned bench, with her face in shadow, and the smirking maid at her feet. Then before climbing ponderously back to his perch on the throne the priest touched his forehead once with both hands and came close to a semblance of bowing, the arrogance of sanctity combining with his paunch to cut that ceremony short.

"Send the girl away," he suggested as soon as he was settled into place again. But Yasmini laughed at him with that golden note of hers that suggests illimitable understanding and unfathomable mirth.

"I know the ways of priests," she answered. "The girl stays!"

The priest's fat chops darkened a shade.

"There are things she should not know."

"She knows already more in her small head than there is in all thy big belly, priest of an idol!"

"Beware, woman, lest the gods hear sacrilege!"

"If they are real gods they love me," she answered.
"If they have any sense they will be pleased whenever
I laugh at your idolatry. Hasamurti stays."

"But at the first imaginary insult she will run with
information to wherever it will do most harm. If she
can be made properly afraid, perhaps——"

Yasmini's golden laugh cut him off short.

"If she is made afraid now she will hate me later.
As long as she loves me she will keep my secrets, and
she will love me because of the secrets—being a woman
and not a belly-with-a-big-tongue, who would sell me
to the highest bidder, if he dared. I know a Brahman.
Thou and I are co-conspirators because my woman's
wit is sharper than thy greed. We are confidants
because I know too much of thy misdeeds. We are
going to succeed because I laugh at thy fat fears, and
am never deceived for a moment by pretense of sanctity or promises however vehement."

She said all that in a low sweet voice, and with a
smile that would have made a much less passionate
man lose something of his self-command. Jinendra's
priest began to move uneasily.

"Peace, woman!"

"There is no peace where priests are," she retorted
in the same sweet-humored voice. "I am engaged in
war, not honey-gathering. I have lied sufficient times
to-day to Mukhum Dass to need ten priests, if I
believed in them or were afraid to lie! The *shroff*
will come to ask about his title-deed. Tell him you are
told a certain person has it, but that if he dares
breathe a word the paper will go straight to Dhulap

Singh, who will destroy it and so safely bring his lawsuit. Then let Dhulap Singh be told also that the title-deed is in certain hands, so he will put off the lawsuit week after week, and one who is my friend will suffer no annoyance."

"Who is this friend?"

"Another one who builds no bridges on thy sanctity."

"Not one of the English? Beware of them, I say; beware of them!"

"No, not one of the English. Next, let Gungadhura be told that Tom Tripe has ever an open-handed welcome at Blaine sahib's——"

"Ah!" he objected, shaking his fat face until the cheeks wabbled. "Women are all fools sooner or later. Why let a drunken English soldier be included in the long list of people to be reckoned with?"

"Because Gungadhura will then show much favor to Tom Tripe, who is my friend, and it amuses me to see my friends prosper. Also I have a plan."

"Plans—plans—plans! And whither does the tangle lead us?"

"To the treasure, fool!"

"But if you know so surely where the treasure is, woman, why not tell me and——"

Again the single note of mocking golden laughter cut him off short.

"I would trust thee with the secret, Brahman, just as far as the herdsman trusts a tiger with his sheep."

"But I could insure that Gungadhura should divide it into three parts, and——"

"When the time comes," she answered, "the priest of Jinendra shall come to me for his proportion, not I to the priest. Nor will there be three portions, but one—with a little percentage taken from it for the sake of thy fat belly. Gungadhura shall get nothing!"

"I wash my hands of it all!" the priest retorted indignantly. "The half for me, or I wash my hands of it and tell Gungadhura that you know the secret! I will trust him to find a way to draw thy cobra from its hole!"

"Maybe he might," she nodded, smiling, "after the English had finished hanging thee for that matter of the strangling of Rum Dass. Thy fat belly would look laughable indeed hanging by a stretched neck from a noose. They would need a thick rope. They might even make the knot slippery with cow-grease for thy special benefit."

The priest winced.

"None can prove that matter," he said, recovering his composure with an effort.

"Except I," she retorted, "who have the very letter that was written to Rum Dass that brought him into thy clutches—and five other proofs beside! Two long years I waited to have a hold on thee, priest, before I came to blossom in the odor of thy sanctity; now I am willing to take the small chance of thy temper getting the better of discretion!"

"You are a devil," he said simply, profoundly convinced of the truth of his remark; and she laughed like a mischievous child, clapping her hands together.

"So now," she said, "there is little else to discuss.

If Gungadhura should be superstitious fool enough to come to thee again for auguries and godly counsel—"

"He comes always. He shows proper devotion to Jinendra."

"Repeat the former story that a clue to the treasure must be found in Blaine sahib's house——"

"In what form? He will ask me again in what form the clue will be, that he may recognize it?"

"Tell him there is a map. And be sure to tell him that Tom Tripe is welcome at the house. Have you understood? Then one other matter: when it is known that I am back in my palace Gungadhura will set extra spies on me, and will double the guard at all the doors to keep me from getting out again. He will not trust Tom Tripe this time, but will give the charge to one of the Rajput officers. But he will have been told that I was at the commissioner sahib's house this morning, and therefore he will not dare to have me strangled, because the commissioner sahib might make inquiries. I have also made other precautions——and a friend. But tell Gungadhura, lest he make altogether too much trouble for me, that I applied to the commissioner sahib for assistance to go to Europe, saying I am weary of India. And add that the commissioner sahib counseled me not to go, but promised to send English memsahibs to see me." (She very nearly used the word American, but thought better of it on the instant.)

"He will ask me how I know this," said the Brahman, turning it all over slowly in his mind and trying to make head or tail of it.

"Tell him I came here like himself for priestly counsel and made a clean breast of everything to thee! He will suspect thee of lying to him; but what is one lie more or less?"

With that final shaft she gathered up her skirts, covered her face, nudged the giggling maid and left him, turning the key in the lock herself and flitting out through gloom into the sunlight as fast as she had come. The carriage was still waiting at the edge of the outer court, and once again the driver started off without instructions, but tooling his team this time at a faster pace, with a great deal of whip-cracking and shouts to pedestrians to clear the way. And this time the carriage had an escort of indubitable maharajah's men, who closed in on it from all sides, their numbers increasing, mounted and unmounted, until by the time Yasmini's own palace gate was reached there was as good as a state procession, made up for the most part of men who tried to look as if they had made a capture by sheer derring-do and skill.

And down the street, helter-skelter on a sweating thoroughbred, came Maharajah Gungadhura Singh just in time to see the back of the carriage as it rumbled in through the gateway and the iron doors clanged behind it. Scowling—altogether too round-shouldered for the martial stock he sprang from—puffy-eyed, and not so regal as overbearing in appearance, he sat for a few minutes stroking his scented beard upward and muttering to himself.

Then some one ventured to tell him where the carriage had been seen waiting, and with what abundant skill it had been watched and tracked from Jinendra's

temple to that gate.   At that he gave an order about
the posting of the guard, and, beckoning only one
mounted attendant to follow him, clattered away down-
street, taking a turn or two to throw the curious off
the scent, and then headed straight for the temple on
his own account.

AN AUDIT BY THE GODS

(I)

Thus spake the gods from their place above the
    firmament
Turning from the feasting and the music and the
    mirth:
"There is time and tide to burn;
Let us stack the plates a turn
And study at our leisure what the trouble is with
    earth."

Down, down they looked through the azure of the
    Infinite
Scanning each the meadows where he went with men
    of yore,
Each his elbows on a cloud,
Making reckoning aloud——
Till the murmur of God wonder was a titan thunder-
    roar.

"War rocks the world! Look, the arquebus and
    culverin
Vanish in new sciences that presage T. N. T!
Lo, a dark, discolored swath
Where they drive new tools of wrath!
Do they justify invention? Will they scrap the Laws
    that Be?

"Look! Mark ye well: where we left a people
    flourishing
Singing in the sunshine for the fun of being free,
Now they burden man and maid
With a law the priests have laid,
And the bourgeois blow their noses by a communal
    decree!

"Where, where away are the liberties we left to them—
Gift of being merry and the privilege of fun?
Is delight no longer praise?
Will they famish all their days
For a future built on fury in a present scarce begun?"

CHAPTER FIVE

"Most precious friend......please visit me!"

THE one thing in India that never happens is the expected. If the actual thing itself does occur, then the manner of it sets up so many unforeseen contingencies that only the subtlest mind, and the sanest and the least hidebound by opinion, can hope to read the signs fast enough to understand them as they happen. Naturally, there are always plenty of people who can read backward after the event; and the few of those who keep the lesson to themselves, digesting rather than discussing it, are to be found eventually filling the senior secretaryships, albeit bitterly criticized by the other men, who unraveled everything afterward very cleverly and are always unanimous on just one point—that the fellow who said nothing certainly knew nothing, and is therefore of no account and should wield no influence, Q. E. D.

And as we belong to the majority, in that we are uncovering the course of these events very cleverly long after they took place, we must at this point, to be logical, denounce Theresa Blaine. She was just as much puzzled as anybody. But she said much less than anybody, wasted no time at all on guesswork, pon-

dered in her heart persistently whatever she had actually seen and heard, and in the end was almost the
only non-Indian actor on the stage of Sialpore to reap
advantage. If that does not prove unfitness for one of
the leading parts, what does? A star should scintil-
late—should focus all eyes on herself and interrupt
the progress of the play to let us know how wise and
beautiful and wonderful she is. But Tess apparently
agreed with Hamlet that "the play's the thing," and
was much too interested in the plot to interfere with it.

She attended the usual round of dinners, teas and
tennis parties, that are part of the system by which
the English keep alive their courage, and growing
after a while a little tired of triviality, she tried to scandalize Sialpore by inviting Tom Tripe to her own garden party, successfully overruling Tripe's objections.

"Between you and I and the gate-post, lady, they
don't hanker for my society. If somebody—especially
colonels, or a judge maybe,—wanted to borrow a horse
from the maharajah's stable,—or perhaps they'd like
a file o' men to escort a picnic in the hills,—then it's
'Oh, hello, good morning, Mr. Tripe. How's the dog
this morning? And oh, by the way——' Then I
know what's coming an' what I can do for 'em I do,
for I confess, lady, that I hanker for a little bit o' flattery and a few words o' praise I'm not entitled to. I
don't covet any man's money—or at least not enough
to damn me into hell on that account. Finding's keeping, and a bet's a bet, but I don't covet money more
than that dog o' mine covets fleas. He likes to scratch
'em when he has 'em. Me the same; I can use money
with the next man, his or mine. But I wouldn't go to

hell for money any more than Trotters would for
fleas, although, mind you, I'm not saying Trotters
hasn't got fleas. He has 'em, same as hell's most folks'
destiny. But when it comes to praise that ain't due me,
lady, I'm like Trotters with another dog's bone—I've
simply got to have it, reason or no reason. A common ordinary bone with meat on it is just a meal.
Praise I've earned is nothing wonderful. But praise I
don't deserve is stolen fruit, and that's the sweetest.
Now, if I was to come to your party I'd get no praise,
ma'am. I'd be doing right by you, but they'd say I
didn't know my place, and by and by they'd prove it to
me sharp and sneery. I'll be a coward to stop away,
but—— 'Sensible man,' they'll say. 'Knows when he
isn't wanted.' You see, ma'am, yours is the only house
in Sialpore where I can walk in and know I'm welcome whether you're at home or not."

"All the more reason for coming to the party,
Tom."

"Ah-h-h! If only you understood!"

He wagged his head and one finger at her in his
half-amused paternal manner that would often win for
him when all else failed. But this time it did not work.

"I don't care for half-friends, Tom. If you expect
to be welcome at my house you must come to my parties when I ask you."

"Lady, lady!"

"I mean it."

"Oh, very well. I'll come. I've protested. That
absolves me. And my hide's thick. It takes more than
just a snub or two—or three to knock my number
down! Am I to bring Trotters?"

"Certainly. Trotters is my friend too. I count on him to do his tricks and help entertain."

"They'll say of you, ma'am, afterward that you don't know better than ask Tripe and his vulgar dog to meet nice people."

"They'll be right, Tom. I don't know better. I hope they'll say it to me, that's all."

But Tess discovered when the day came that no American can scandalize the English. They simply don't expect an American to know how to behave, and Tom Tripe and his marvelous performing dog were accepted and approved of as sincerely as the real American ice-cream soda—and forgotten as swiftly the morning following.

The commissioner was actually glad to meet Tripe in the circumstances. If the man should suppose that because Sir Roland Samson and a judge of appeal engaged in a three-cornered conversation with him at a garden party, therefore either of them would speak to the maharajah's drill-master when next they should meet in public, he might guess again, that was all.

One of the things the commissioner asked Tripe was whether he was responsible for the mounting of palace guards—of course not improperly inquisitive about the maharajah's personal affairs but anxious to seem interested in the fellow's daily round, since just then one couldn't avoid him.

"In a manner, and after a fashion, yes, sir. I'm responsible that routine goes on regularly and that the men on duty know their business."

"Ah. Nothing like responsibility. Good for a man. Some try to avoid it, but it's good. So you look

after the guard on all the palaces? The Princess Yasmini's too, eh? Well, well; I can imagine that might
be nervous work. They say that young lady is——!
Eh, Tripe?"

"I couldn't say, sir. My duties don't take me inside
the palace."

"Now, now, Tripe! No use trying to look inno-
cent! They tell me she's a handful and you encourage
her!"

"Some folks don't care *what* they say, sir."

"If she should be in trouble I dare say, now, you'd
be the man she'd apply to for help."

"I'd like to think that, sir."

"Might ask you to take a letter for instance, to
me or his honor the judge here?"

The judge walked away. He did not care to be
mixed up in intrigue, even hypothetically, and especially with a member of the lower orders.

"I'd do for her what I'd do for a daughter of my
own, sir, neither more nor less."

"Quite so, Tripe. If she gave you a letter to bring
to me, you'd bring it, eh?"

"Excepting barratry, the ten commandments, earthquake and the act of God, sir, yes."

"Without the maharajah knowing?"

"Without his highness knowing."

"You'd do that with a clear conscience, eh?"

Tom Tripe screwed his face up, puffed his cheeks,
and struck a very military attitude.

"A soldier's got no business with a conscience, sir.
Conscience makes a man squeamish o' doing right for
fear his wife's second cousin might tell the neighbors."

"Ha-ha! Very profoundly philosophic! I dare wager you've carried her letters at least a dozen times —now come."

Again Tom Tripe puffed out his cheeks and struck an attitude.

"Men don't get hanged for murder, sir."

"For what, then?"

"Talking before and afterward!"

"Excellent! If only every one remembered that! Did it ever occur to you how the problem might be reversed?"

"Sir?"

"There might one day be a letter for the Princess Yasmini that, as her friend, you ought to make sure should reach her."

"I'd take a letter from you to her, sir, if that's your meaning."

Sir Roland Samson, K. C. S. I., looked properly shocked.

There are few things so appalling as the abruptness with which members of the lower orders divest diplomacy's kernel of its decorative outer shell. "What I meant is—ah——" He set his monocle, and stared as if Tripe were an insect on a pin-point. "Since you admit you're in the business of intriguing for the princess, no doubt you carry letters to, as well as from her, and hold your tongue about that too?"

"If I should deliver letters they'd be secret or they'd have gone through the mail. I'd risk my job each time I did it. Would I risk it worse by talking? Once the maharajah heard a whisper——"

"Well—I'll be careful not to drop a hint to his

highness. As you say, it might imperil your job. And, ah——" (again the monocle,) "—— the initials r. s.——in small letters, not capitals, in the bottom left-hand corner of a small white envelope would—ah—you understand?—you'd see that she received it, eh?"

Tom Tripe bridled visibly. Neither the implied threat nor the proposal to make use of him without acknowledging the service afterward, escaped him. Samson, who believed among other things in keeping all inferiors thoroughly in their place decided on the instant to rub home the lesson while it smarted.

"You'd find it profitable. You'd be paid whatever the situation called for. You needn't doubt that."

Tess, talking with a group of guests some little distance off, observed a look of battle in Tom Tripe's eye, and smiled two seconds later as the commissioner let fall his monocle. Two things she was certain of at once: Tom Tripe would tell her at the first opportunity exactly what had happened, and Samson would lie about it glibly if provoked. She promised herself she would provoke him. As a matter of fact Tom gave her two or three versions afterward of what his words had been, their grandeur increasing as imagination flourished in the comfortable warmth of confidence. But the first account came from a fresh memory:

"No money *you'll* ever touch would buy my dog's silence, let alone mine, sir! If you've a letter for the princess, send it along and I'll see she gets it. If she cares to answer it, I'll see the answer reaches you. As for dropping hints to the maharajah about my doing little services for the princess,——a gentleman's a gentleman, and don't need instruction—nor advice from me. If I was out of a job to-morrow I'd still be a man on two feet, to be met as such."

A man of indiscretion, and a diplomat, must have fireproof feelings. As Tess had observed, Samson blenched distinctly, but he recovered in a second and put in practise some of that opportunism that was his secret pride, reflecting how a less finished diplomatist would have betrayed resentment at the snub from an inferior instead of affecting not to notice it at all. As a student of human nature he decided that Tom Tripe's pride was the point to take advantage of.

"You're the very man I can trust," he said. "I'm glad we have had this talk. If ever you receive a small white envelope marked r. s. in the left-hand bottom corner, see that the princess gets it, and say nothing."

"Trust me, eh?" Tripe muttered as Samson walked away. "You never trusted your own mother without you had a secret hold over her. I wouldn't trust you that far!" He spat among the flowers, for Tom could not pretend to real garden-party manners. "And if she trusts you, letters or no letters, I'll eat my spurs and saber cold for breakfast."

Then, as it to console himself with proof that some one in the world did trust him thoroughly, Tom swaggered with a riding-master stride to where Tess stood talking with a Rajput prince, who had come late and threatened to leave early. The prince had puzzled her by referring two or three times to his hurry, once even going so far as to say good-by, and then not going. It was as if he expected her to know something that she did not know, and to give him a cue that he waited for in vain. She felt he must think her stupid, and the

thought made her every minute less at ease; but Tom's
approach, eyed narrowly by Samson for some reason,
seemed to raise the Rajput's spirits.

"If only my husband were here," she said aloud,
"but at the last minute—there was blasting, you know,
and——"

The prince—he was quite a young one—twenty-one
perhaps—murmured something polite and with eyes
that smoldered watched Tom take a letter from his
tunic pocket. He handed it to Tess with quite a
flourish.

"Some one must have dropped this, ma'am."

The envelope was scented, and addressed in Persian characters. She saw the prince's eyes devour the
thing—saw him exchange glances with Tom Tripe—
and realized that Tom had rather deftly introduced her
to another actor in the unseen drama that was going
on. Clearly the next move was hers.

"Is it yours, perhaps?" she asked.

Prince Utirupa Singh bowed and took the letter.
Samson with a look of baffled fury behind the monocle, but a smile for appearance's sake, joined them at
that minute and Utirupa seemed to take delight in so
manipulating the sealed envelope that the commissioner could only see the back of it.

The prince was an extremely handsome young
man, as striking in one way as Samson in another.
Polo and pig-sticking had kept him lean, and associa-
tion with British officers had given him an air of being
frankly at his ease even when really very far from
feeling it. He had the natural Oriental gift of smoth-
ering excitement, added to a trick learned from the

West of aggressive self-restraint that is not satisfied
with seeming the opposite of what one is, but insists on
extracting humor from the situation and on calling
attention to the humor.

"I shall always be grateful to you," he said, smiling
into Tess's eyes with his own wonderful brown ones
but talking at the commissioner. "If I had lost this letter I should have been at a loss indeed. If some one
else had found it, that might have been disastrous."

"But I did not find it for you," Tess objected.

Utirupa turned his back to the commissioner and
answered in a low voice.

"Nevertheless, when I lose letters I shall come here
first!"

He bowed to take his leave and showed the back of
the envelope again to Samson, with a quiet malice
worthy of Torquemada. The commissioner looked
almost capable of snatching it.

"Mrs. Blaine," he said with a laugh after the prince
had gone, "skill and experience, I am afraid, are not
much good without luck. Luck seems to be a thing I
lack. Now, if I had picked up that letter I've a notion
that the information in it would have saved me a year's
work."

Tess was quite sure that Tom had not picked the
letter up, but there was no need to betray her
knowledge.

"Do you mean you'd have opened a letter you
picked up in my garden?" she demanded.

His eyes accepted her challenge.

"Why not?"

"But why? Surely————"

"Necessity, dear lady, knows no law. That's one of the first axioms of diplomacy. Consider your husband as a case in point. Custom, which is the basis of nearly all law, says he ought to be here entertaining your guests. Necessity, ignoring custom, obliges him to stay in the hills and supervise the blasting, disappointing every one but me. I'm going to take advantage of his necessity."

If he had seen the swift glance she gave him he might have changed the course of one small part of history. Tess knew nothing of the intrigue he was engaged in, and did not propose to be keeper of his secrets; if he had glimpsed that swift betrayal of her feelings he would certainly not have volunteered further confidences. But the poison of ambition blinds all those who drink it, so that the "safest" men unburden themselves to the wrong unwilling ears.

"Walk with me up and down the path where every one can see us, won't you?"

"Why?" she laughed. "Do you flatter yourself I'd be afraid to be caught alone with you?"

"I hope you'd like to be alone with me! I would like nothing better. But if we walk up and down together on the path in full view, we arouse no suspicion and we can't be overheard. I propose to tell some secrets."

Not many women would resist the temptation of inside political information. Recognizing that by some means beyond her comprehension she was being drawn into a maze of secrets all interrelated and any of them likely to involve herself at any minute, Tess had no compunction whatever.

"I'll be frank with you," she said. "I'm curious."

Once they walked up the path and down again, talking of dogs, because it happened that Tom Tripe's enormous beast was sprawling in the shadow of a rose-bush at the farther end. The commissioner did not like dogs. "Something loathsome about them—degrading—especially the big ones." She disagreed. She liked them, cold wet noses and all, even in the dark. Tom Tripe, stepping behind a bush with the obvious purpose of smoking in secret the clay pipe that he hardly troubled to conceal, whistled the dog, who leapt into life as if stung and joined his master.

The second time up and down they talked of professional beggars and what a problem they are to India, because they both happened as they turned to catch sight of Umra with the one eye, entering through the little gate in the wall and shuffling without modesty or a moment's hesitation to his favorite seat among the shrubs, whence to view proceedings undisturbed.

"Those three beggars that haunt this house seem to claim all our privileges," she said. "They wouldn't think of letting us give a garden party without them."

"Say the word," he said, "and I'll have them put in prison."

But she did not say the word.

The third time up the path he chose to waste on very obvious flattery.

"You're such an unusual woman, you know, Mrs. Blaine. You understand whatever's said to you, and don't ask idiotic questions. And then, of course, you're American, and I feel I can say things to you that my own countrywoman wouldn't understand. As an American, in other words, you're privileged."

As they turned at the top of the path she felt a cold wet something thrust into her hand from behind. She had never in her life refused a caress to a dog that asked for one, and her fingers closed almost unconsciously on Trotters' muzzle, touching as they did so the square unmistakable hard edges of an envelope. There was no mistaking the intent; the dog forced it on her and, the instant her fingers closed on it, slunk out of sight.

"Wasn't that Tripe's infernal dog again?"

"Was it? I didn't see." She was wiping slobber on to her skirt from an envelope whose strong perfume had excited the dog's salivary glands. But it was true that she did not see.

"May I call you Theresa?"

"Why?"

"It would encourage confidences. There isn't another woman in Sialpore whom I could tell what I'm going to say to you. The others would repeat it to their husbands, or——"

"I tell mine everything. Every word!"

"Or they'd try to work me on the strength of it for little favors——"

"Wait until you know me! Little favors don't appeal to me. I like them big—very big!"

"Honestly, Theresa——"

"Better call me Mrs. Blaine."

"Honestly, there's nothing under heaven that——"

"That you really know about me. I know there isn't. You were going to tell secrets. I'm listening."

"You're a hard-hearted woman!"

She had contrived by that time to extract a letter from the envelope behind her back, but how to read it without informing Samson was another matter. As she turned up the path for the sixth time, the sight of Tom Tripe making semi-surreptitious signals to attract her attention convinced her that the message was urgent and that she should not wait to read it until after her last guests were gone. It was only one sheet of paper, written probably on only one side—she hoped in English. But how————

Suddenly she screamed, and Samson was all instant concern.

"Was that a snake? Tell me, was that a snake I saw. Oh, do look, please! I loathe them."

"Probably a lizard."

"No, no, I know a lizard. Do please look!"

Unbelieving, he took a stick and poked about among the flowers to oblige her; so she read the message at her leisure behind the broad of his back, and had folded it out of sight before he looked up.

"No snakes. Nothing but a lizard."

"Oh, I'm so glad! Please forgive me, but I dread snakes. Now tell me the secrets while I listen properly."

He noticed a change in her voice—symptoms of new interest, and passed it to the credit of himself.

"There's an intrigue going on, and you can help me. Sp —— people whose business it is to keep me informed have reported that Tom Tripe is constantly carrying letters from the Princess Yasmini of Sialpore to that young Prince Utirupa who was here this after-

noon. Now, it's no secret that if Gungadhura Singh
were to get found out committing treason (and I'm
pretty sure he's guilty of it five days out of six!) we'd
depose him————"

"You mean the British would depose him?"

"Depose him root and branch.   Then Utirupa
would be next in line. He's a decent fellow. He'd be
sure of the nomination, and he'd make a good ruler."

"Well?"

"I want to know what the Princess Yasmini has to
do with it."

"It seems to me you're not telling secrets, but asking favors for nothing."

"Not for nothing—not for nothing! There's pos-
itively nothing that I won't do!"

"In return for ————?"

"Sure information as to what is going on."

"Which you think I can get for you?"

"I'm positive!   You're such an extraordinary
woman. I'm pretty sure it all hinges on the treasure
I told you about the other day. Whoever gets first
hold of that holds all the trumps. I'd like to get it
myself. That would be the making of me, politically
speaking. If Gungadhura should get it he'd ruin himself with intrigue in less than a year, but he might
cause my ruin in the process. If the local priests
should get it—and that's likeliest, all things considered
—there'd be red ruin for miles around; money and
the church don't mix without blood-letting, and you
can't unscramble that omelet forever afterward. I confess I don't know how to checkmate the priests.

Gungadhura I think I can manage, especially with your aid. But I must have information."

"Is there any one else who'd be dangerous if he possessed the secret?"

"Anybody would be, except myself. Anybody else would begin playing for political control with it, and there'd be no more peace on this side of India for years. And now, this is what I want to say: The most dangerous individual who could possibly get that treasure would be the Princess Yasmini. The difficulty of dealing with her is that she's not above hiding behind *purdah* (the veil), where no male man can reach her. There are several women here whom I might interest in keeping an eye on her—Tatum's wife, and Miss Bent, and Miss O'Hara, and the Goole sisters—lots of 'em. But they'd all talk. And they'd all try to get influence for their male connections on the strength of being in the know. But somehow, Theresa, you're different."

"Mrs. Blaine, please."

"I know Tom Tripe thinks the world of you. I want you to find out for me from him everything he knows about this treasure intrigue and whatever's behind it."

"You think he'd tell me?"

"Yes. And I want you to make the acquaintance of the Princess Yasmini, and find out from her if you can what the letters are that she writes to Utirupa. You'll find the acquaintance interesting."

Tess crumpled a folded letter in her left hand.

"If you could give me an introduction to the princess—they say she's difficult to see—some sort of letter that would get me past the maharajah's guards," she answered.

"I can. I will. The girl's a minor. I've the right to appoint some one to visit her and make all proper inquiries. I appoint you."

"Give me a letter now and I'll go to-night."

He stopped as they turned at the end of the path, and wrote on a leaf of his pocket-book. Behind his back Tess waved her secret letter to attract Tom Tripe's notice, and nodded.

"There." said Samson. "That's preliminary. I'll confirm it later by letter on official paper. But nobody will dare question that. If any one does, let me know immediately."

"Thank you."

"And now, Theresa———"

"You forget."

"I forget nothing. I never forget! You'll be wondering what you are to get out of all this———"

"I wonder if you're capable of believing that nothing was further from my thoughts!"

"Don't think I want all for nothing! Don't imagine my happiness—my success could be complete without———"

"Without a whisky and soda. Come and have one. I see my husband coming at last."

"Damn!" muttered Samson under his breath.

She had expected her husband by the big gate, but he came through the little one, and she caught sight of him at once because through the corner of her eye she was watching some one else—Umra the beggar.

Umra departed through the little gate thirty seconds before her husband entered it.

Blaine was so jubilant over a sample of crushed quartz he had brought home with him that there was no concealing his high spirits. He was even cordial to Samson, whom he detested, and so full of the milk of human kindness toward everybody else that they all wanted to stay and be amused by him. But Tess got rid of them at last by begging Samson to go first ostentatiously and set them an example, which he did after extracting a promise from her to see him tête-à-tête again at the earliest opportunity.

Then Tess showed her husband the letter that Tom's dog had thrust into her hand.

"You dine alone to-night, Dick, unless you prefer the club. I'm going at once. Read this."

It was written in a fine Italic hand on expensive paper, with corrections here and there as if the writer had obeyed inspiration first and consulted a dictionary afterward—a neat letter, even neat in its mistakes.

"Most precious friend," it ran, "please visit me. It is necessary that you find some way of avoi—elu—tricking the guards, because there are orders not to admit any one and not to let me out. Please bring with you food from your house, because I am hungry. A cat and two birds and a monkey have died from the food cooked for me. I am also thirsty. My mother taught me to drink wine, but the wine is finished, and I like water the best. Tom Tripe will try to help you past the guards, but he has no brains, so you must give him orders. He is very faithful. Please come soon, and bring a very large quantity of water. Yours with love, YASMINI."

He read the letter and passed it back.

"D'you think it's on the level, Tess?"

"I know it is! Imagine that poor child, Dick, cooped up in a palace, starving and parching herself for fear of poison!"

"But how are you going to get to her? You can't bowl over Gungadhura's guards with a sunshade."

"Samson wrote this for me."

Dick Blaine scowled.

"I imagine Samson's favors are paid for sooner or later."

"So are mine, Dick! The beast has called me Theresa three times this afternoon, and has had the impudence to suggest that his preferment and my future happiness may bear some relation to each other."

"See here, Tess, maybe I'd better beat him and have done with it."

"No. He can't corrupt me, but he might easily do you an injury. Let him alone, Dick, and be as civil as you can. You did splendidly this evening———"

"Before I knew what he'd said to you!"

"Now you've all the more reason to be civil. I must keep in touch with that young girl in the palace, and Samson is the only influence I can count on. Do as I say, Dick, and be civil to him. Pretend you're not even suspicious."

"But say, that guy's suggestions aggregate an ounce or two! First, I'm to draw Gungadhura's money while I hunt for buried treasure; but I'm to tip off Samson first. Second, I'm to look on while he makes his political fortune with my wife's help. And third—what's the third thing, Tess?"

She kissed him. "The third is that you're going to seem to be fooled by him, for the present at all events. Let's know what's at the bottom of all this, and help the princess and Tom Tripe if it's possible. Are you tired?"

"Yes. Why?"

"If you weren't tired I was going to ask you to put a turban on as soon as it's dark, and dress up like a *sais* and drive me to Yasmini's palace, with a revolver in each pocket in case of accidents, and eyes and ears skinned until I come out again."

"Oh, I'm not too tired for that."

"Come along then. I'll put up a hamper with my own hands. You get wine from the cellar, and make sure the corks have not been pulled and replaced. Then get the dog-cart to the door. I'll keep it waiting there while you run up-stairs and change. Hurry, Dick, hurry——it's growing dark! I'll put some sandwiches under the seat for you to eat while you're waiting in the dark for me."

AN AUDIT BY THE GODS

(2)

Loud laughed the gods (and their irony was pestilence;
Pain was in their mockery, affliction in their scorn.
The ryotwari cried
On a stricken countryside,
For the scab fell on the sheepfold and the mildew on
*   the corn).*

"Write, Chitragupta!*   Enter up your reckoning!
Yum**awaits in anger the assessment of the dead!
We left a law of kindness,
But they bowed themselves in blindness
To a cruelty consummate and a mystery instead!

"Write, Chitragupta!   Once we sang and danced with
*   them.*
Now in gloomy temples they lay foreheads in the dust!
To us they looked for pleasure
And we never spared the measure
Till they set their priests between us and we left them
*   in disgust.*

"Fun and mirth we made for them (write it,
*   Chitragupta!*
Set it down in symbols for the awful eye of Yum!)

*In Hindu mythology Yum is the judge of the dead
and Chitragupta writes the record for him.

But they traded fun for fashion
And their innocence for passion,
Till they murmur in their wallow now the consequences
    come!

"Look!   Look and wonder how the simple folk are out
    of it!
Empirics are the teachers and the liars leading men!
We were generous and free——
Aye, a social lot were we,
But they took to priests instead of us, and trouble
    started then!"

CHAPTER SIX

"Peace, Maharajah sahib!   Out of anger came no wise counsel yet!"

TOM TRIPE had done exactly what Yasmini ordered
him. Like his dog Trotters, whom he had schooled to
perfection, and as he would have liked to have the
maharajah's guards behave, he always fell back on
sheer obedience whenever facts bewildered him or circumstances seemed too strong.

Yasmini had ordered him to report to the maharajah a chance encounter with an individual named
Gunga Singh. Accordingly he did. Asked who
Gunga Singh was, he replied he did not know. She
had told him to say that Gunga Singh said the Princess
Yasmini was at the commissioner's house; so he told
the maharajah that and nothing further. Gungadhura
sent two men immediately to make inquiries. One
drew the commissioner's house blank, bribing a servant
to let him search the place in Samson's absence; the
other met the commissioner himself, and demanded of
him point-blank what he had been doing with the princess. The question was so bluntly put and the man's
attitude so impudent that Samson lost his temper and
couched his denial in blunt bellicose bad language.
The vehemence convinced the questioner that he was

lying, as the maharajah was shortly informed. So the fact became established beyond the possibility of refutation that Yasmini had been closeted with Samson for several hours that morning.

Remained, of course, to consider why she had gone to him and what might result from her visit; and up to a certain point, and in certain cases accurate guessing is easier than might be expected for either side to a political conundrum in India, ample provision having been made for it by all concerned.

The English are fond of assuring strangers and one another that spying is "un-English"; that it "isn't done, you know, old top"; and the surest way of heaping public scorn and indignation on the enemies of England is to convict them, correctly or otherwise, of spying on England secretly. So it would be manifestly libelous, ungentlemanly and proof conclusive of crass ignorance to assert that Samson in his capacity of commissioner employed spies to watch Gungadhura Singh. He had no public fund from which to pay spies. If you don't believe that, then ponder over a copy of the Indian Estimates. Every rupee is accounted for.

The members of the maharajah's household who came to see Samson at more or less frequent intervals were individuals of the native community whom he encouraged to intimacy for ethnological and social reasons. When they gave him information about Gungadhura's doings, that was merely because they were incurably addicted to gossip; as a gentleman, and in some sense a representative of His Majesty the King, he would not dream, of course, of paying attention to any such stuff; but one could not, of course, be so rude and high-handed as to stop their talking even if it did tend toward an accurate foreknowledge of the maharajah's doings that was hardly "cricket."

As for money, certainly none changed hands. The indisputable fact that certain friends and relatives of certain members of the maharajah's household enjoyed rather profitable contracts on British administered territory was coincidence. Everybody knows how long is the arm of coincidence. Well, then, so are its ears, and its tongue.

As for the maharajah, the rascal went the length of paying spies in British government offices. There was never any knowing who was a spy of his and who wasn't. People were everlastingly crossing the river from the native state to seek employment in some government department or other, and one could not investigate them really thoroughly. It was so easy to forge testimonials and references and what not. One of Samson's grooms had once been caught red-handed eavesdropping in the dark. Samson, of course, took the law into his own hands on that occasion and thrashed the blackguard within an inch of his treacherous life; and in proof that the thrashing was richly deserved, some one reported to Samson the very next day how the groom had gone straight to the maharajah and had been solaced with silver money.

It was even said, although never proved, that the fat, short-sighted young babu Sita Ram who typed the commissioner's official correspondence was one of Gungadhura's spies. There was a mystery about where he spent his evenings. But his mother's uncle

was a first-class magistrate, so one could not very well
dismiss him without clear proof. Besides, he was un-
commonly painstaking and efficient.

One way and another it is easy to see that Gungadhura had a deal of dovetailed information from which
to draw conclusions as to the probable reason of Yasmini's alleged visit to the commissioner. One false
conclusion invariably leads to another, and so Samson
got the blame for the secret bargain with the Rangar
stable-owner, with whose connivance Yasmini had contrived to keep a carriage available outside her palace
gates. Her palace gates having closed on the carriage now, the guards would pay attention that it
stayed inside, but there was no knowing how many
riding horses she might have at her beck and call in
various khans and places. Doubtless Samson had
arranged for that. Gungadhura sent men immediately
to search Sialpore for horses that might be held in
waiting for her, with orders to hire or buy the animals
over her head, or in the alternative to lame them.

As for her motive in visiting the commissioner, that
was not far to seek. There was only one motive in
Sialpore for anything—the treasure. No doubt Samson lusted for it as sinfully and lustily and craftily as
any one. If, thought Gungadhura, Yasmini had a clue
to its whereabouts, as she might have, then whoever
believed she was not trafficking with the commissioner
must be a simpleton. The commissioner was known to
have written more than one very secret report to Simla
on the subject of the treasure, and on the political consequences that might follow on its discovery by natives
of the country. The reports had been so secret and

important that Gungadhura had thought it worth while
to have the blotting paper from Samson's desk photo-
graphed in Paris by a special process. Adding two
and two together now by the ancient elastic process,
Gungadhura soon reached the stage of absolute conviction that Yasmini was in league with Samson to
forestall him in getting control of the treasure of his
ancestors; and Gungadhura was a dark, hot-blooded,
volcanic-tempered man, who stayed not on the order
of his anger but blew up at once habitually.

We have seen how he came careering down-street
just in time to behold Yasmini's carriage rumble into
her stone-paved palace courtyard. After ordering the
guards not to let her escape again on pain of unnamed,
but no less likely because illegal punishment, he rode
full pelt to the temple of Jinendra, whence they assured
him Yasmini had just come, and his spurs rang presently on the temple floor like the footfalls of avenging
deity.

Jinendra's priest welcomed him with that mixture
of deference and patronage that priests have always
known so well how to extend to royalty, showing him
respect because priestly recognition of his royalty
entitled him in logic to the outward form of it——
patronage because, as the "wisest fool in Christendom"
remarked, "No bishop no king!" The combination of
sarcastic respect and contemptuous politeness produced
an insolence that none except kings would tolerate for
a moment; but Jinendra's fat high priest could guess
how far he dared go, as shrewdly as a marksman
guesses windage.

"She has betrayed us! That foreign she-bastard

has betrayed us!" shouted Gungadhura, slamming the priest's private door behind him and ramming home the bolt as if it fitted into the breach of a rifle.

"Peace! Peace, Maharajah sahib! Out of anger came no wise counsel yet!"

"She has been to the commissioner's house!"

"I know it."

"You know it? Then she told you?"

The priest was about to lie, but Gungadhura saved him.

"I know she was here," he burst out. "My men followed her home."

"Yes, she was here. She told."

"How did you make her tell? The she-devil is more cunning than a cobra!"

Jinendra's high priest smiled complacently.

"A servant of the gods, such as I am, is not altogether without power. I found a way. She told."

"I, too, will find a way!" muttered Gungadhura to himself. Then to the priest: "What did she say? Why did she go to the commissioner?"

"To ask a favor."

"Of course! What favor?"

"That she may go to Europe."

"Then there is no longer any doubt whatever! By Saraswati (the goddess of wisdom) I know that she has discovered where the treasure is!"

"My son," said the priest, "it is not manners to call on other gods by name in this place."

"By Jinendra, then! Thou fat sedentary appetite, what a great god thine must be, that he can choose no cleverer servant than thee to muddle his affairs!

While you were lulling me to sleep with dreams about a clue to be found in a cellar, she has already sucked the secret out from some cobra's hole and has sold it to the commissioner! As soon as he has paid her a proportion of it she will escape to Europe to avoid me—will she?"

"But the commissioner refused the desired permission," said the priest, puffing his lips and stroking his stomach, as much as to add, "It's no use getting impatient in Jinendra's temple. We have all the inside information here."

"What do you make of that?" demanded Gungadhura.

The priest smiled. One does not explain everything to a mere maharajah. But the mere maharajah was in no mood to be put off with smiles just then. As Yasmini got the story afterward from the bald old mendicant, whose piety had recently won him permission to bask on the comfortable carved stones just outside the window, Gungadhura burst forth into such explosive profanity that the high priest ran out of the room. The mendicant vowed that he heard the door slam—and so he did; but it was really Gungadhura, done with argument, on his way to put threat into action.

The mildest epithet he called Yasmini was "Widyadhara," which meant in his interpretation of the word that she was an evil spirit condemned to roam the earth because her sins were so awful that the other evil spirits simply could not tolerate her.

"It is plain that the commissioner fears to let her go to Europe!" swore Gungadhura. "Therefore it is plain that she and he have a plan between them to loot the treasure and say nothing. Neither trusts the other, as is the way of such people! He will not let her out of sight until he can leave India himself!"

"He has promised to send European memsahibs to call on her," said the priest, and the maharajah gnashed his teeth and swore like a man stung by a hornet.

"That is to prevent me from using violence on her! He will have frequent reports as to her health! After a time, when he has his fingers in the treasure, he will not be so anxious about her welfare!"

"There was another matter that she told me," said the priest.

"Repeat it then, Belly-of-Jinendra! Thy paunch retains a tale too long!"

"Tripe, the drill-master, is a welcome guest at the house built by Jengal Singh."

"What of it?"

"He may enter even when the sahibs are away from home. The servants have orders to admit him."

"Well?"

The priest smiled again.

"If it should chance to be true that the princess knows the secret of the treasure, and that she is selling it to the commissioner, Tripe could enter that house and discover the clue. Who could rob you of the treasure once you knew the secret of its hiding-place?"

It was at that point that the maharajah grew so exasperated at the thought of another's knowledge of a secret that he considered rightly his own by heritage, that his language exceeded not only the bounds of decorum but the limits of commonplace blasphemy as well. Turning his back on the priest he rushed from

the room, slamming the door behind him. And, being
a ruminant fat mortal, the priest sat so still considering on which side of the equation his own bread might
be buttered as to cause the impression that the room
was empty; whereas only the maharajah had left it.
And a little later the babu Sita Ram came in.

Gungadhura was in no mood to be trifled with.
He knew pretty well where to find Tom Tripe during
any of the hours of duty, so he cornered him without
delay and, glaring at him with eyes like an animal's at
bay, ordered him to search the Blaines' house at the
first opportunity.

"Search for what?" demanded Tripe.

"For anything! For everything! Search the cellar; search the garden; search the roof! Are you a
fool? Are you fit for my employment? Then search
the house, and report to me anything unusual that you
find in it! Go!"

After several stiff brandies and soda Gungadhura
then conceived a plan that might have been dangerous supposing Yasmini to have been less alert,
and supposing that she really knew the secret. He
spent an evening coaching Patali, his favorite dancing
girl, and then sent her to Yasmini with almost full
powers to drive a bargain. She might offer as much
as half of the treasure to Yasmini, provided Gungadhura should receive the other half and the British
should know nothing. That was the one point on
which Patali's orders permitted no discretion. The
whole transaction must be secret from the British.

Reporting the encounter afterward to her employer
Patali hardly seemed proud of her share in it. All the

information she brought back was to the effect that Yasmini denied all knowledge of the treasure, and all desire to possess it.

"I think she knows nothing. She said very little to me. She laughed at the idea of bargaining with Englishmen. She said you are welcome to the treasure, maharajah sahib, and that if she should ever find its hiding-place she will certainly tell you. She plays the part of a woman whose spirit is already broken and who is weary of India."

Having a very extensive knowledge of dancing girls and their ways, Gungadhura did not believe much more than two per cent. of Patali's account of what had taken place, and he was right, except that he grossly overestimated her truthfulness. And even with his experienced cynicism it never entered his head to suppose that Patali was the individual who warned Yasmini in advance of the preparations being made to poison her by Gungadhura's orders. Yet, as it was Patali's own sister who made the sweetmeats, and tampered with the charcoal for the filter, and put the powdered diamonds in the chutney, it was likely enough that Patali would know the facts; and as for motives, dancing girls don't have them. They fear, they love, they desire, they seek to please. If Yasmini could pluck heart-strings more cleverly than Gungadhura could break and bruise them, so much the worse for Gungadhura's plans, that was all, as far as Patali was concerned.

For several days after that, as Yasmini more than hinted in her letter to Tess, repeated efforts were made to administer poison in the careful undiscoverable

ways that India has made her own since time immemo-
rial. But you can not easily poison any one who does
not eat, and who drinks wine that was bottled in
Europe; or at any rate, to do it you must call in experts
who are expensive in the first place as well as adepts
at blackmail in the second. Yasmini enjoyed a
charmed life and an increasing appetite, Gungadhura's
guards attending to it however, that she took no more
forbidden walks and rides and swims by moonlight to
make the hunger really unendurable. Supplies were
allowed to pass through the palace gate, after they had
been tampered with.

Finally Gungadhura, biting his nails and drinking
whisky in the intervals between consultation with a
dozen different sets of priests, made up his mind to
drastic action. It dawned on his exasperated mind
that every single priest, including Jinendra's obese
incumbent, was trying to take advantage of his pre-
dicament in order to feather a priestly nest or forward
plans diametrically opposed to his own. (Not that
recognition of priestly deception made him less superstitious, or any less dependent on the priest; if that
were the way discovery worked, all priests would have
vanished long ago. It simply made him furious, like a
tiger in a net, and spurred him to wreak damage in
which the priests might have no hand.)

Whisky, drugs, reflection and the hints of twenty
dancing girls convinced him that Jinendra's priest
especially was playing a double game; for what was
there in the fat man's mental ingredients that should
anchor his loyalty to an ill-tempered prince, in case a
princess of wit and youth and brilliant beauty should

stake her cunning in the game? Why was not Yasmini
already ten times dead of poison? Nothing but the
cunning inspired by partnership with priests, and alert-
ness born of secret knowledge, could have given her
the intelligence to order her maids to boil a present of
twenty pairs of French silk stockings—nor the malice
to hang them afterward with her own hands on a line
across her palace roof in full view of Gungadhura's
window!

Hatred of Yasmini was an obsession of his in any
case. He had loathed her mother, who dared try to
wear down the rule that women must be veiled. Even
his own dancing girls were heavily veiled in public,
and all his relations with women of any sort took place
behind impenetrable screens. He was a stickler for
that sort of thing and, like others of his kidney, rather
proud of the rumors that no curtains could confine.
So he loathed and despised Yasmini even more than
he had detested her mother, because she coupled to her
mother's Western notions about freedom a wholly
Eastern ability to take advantage of restraint. In
other words she was too clever for him.

On top of all that she had dared outrage his royal
feelings by refusing to be given in marriage to the
husband he selected for her—a fine, black-bristling,
stout cavalier of sixty with a wife or two already and
impoverished estates that would have swallowed Yasmini's fortune nicely at a gulp. Incidentally, the husband would have eagerly canceled a gambling debt in
exchange for a young wife with an income.

There was no point at which Yasmini and himself
could meet on less than rapier terms. Her exploits in

disguise were notorious—so notorious that men sang songs about them in the drinking places and the khans. And as if that were not bad enough there was a rumor lately that she had turned Abhisharika. The word is Sanskrit and poetic. To the ordinary folk, who like to listen to love-stories by moonlight on the roofs or under trees, that meant that she had chosen her own lover and would go to him, when the time should come, of her own free will. To Gungadhura, naturally, such a word bore other meanings. As we have said, he was a stickler for propriety.

Last, and most uncomfortable crime of all, it seemed that she had now arranged with Samson to have English ladies call on her at intervals. Not a prophet on earth could guess where that might lead to, and to what extremes of Western fashion; for though one does not see the high-caste women of Rajputana, they themselves see everything and know all that is going on. But it needed no prophet to explain that a woman visited at intervals by the wives of English officers could not be murdered easily or safely.

All arguments pointed one way. He must have it out with Yasmini in one battle royal. If she should be willing to surrender, well and good. He would make her pay for the past, but no doubt there were certain concessions that he could yield without loss of dignity. If she knew the secret of the hiding-place of the treasure he would worm it out of her. There are ways, he reflected, of worming secrets from a woman—ways and means. If she knew the secret and refused to tell, then he knew how to provide that she should never tell any one else. If she had told some one else already,

—Samson, for instance, or Jinendra's priest—then he would see to it that priest or commissioner, as the case might be, must carry on without the cleverest member of the firm.

But he must hurry. Poison apparently would not work and he did not dare murder her outright, much as he would have liked to. It was maddening to think how one not very violent blow with a club or a knife would put an end to her wilfulness forever, and yet that the risk to himself in that case would be almost as deadly as the certainty for her. But accidents might happen. In a land of elephants, tigers, snakes, wild boars and desperate men there is a wide range for circumstance, and the sooner the accident the less the risk of interference by some inquisitive English woman with a ticket-of-admission signed by Samson.

An "accident" in Yasmini's palace, he decided would be nearly as risky as murder. But he had a country-place fifty miles away in the mountains, to which she could be forcibly removed, thus throwing inquisitive Englishwomen off the scent for a while at any rate. That secluded little hunting box stood by a purple lake that had already drowned its dozens, not always without setting up suspicion; and between the city of Sialpore and the "Nesting-place of Seven Swans" lay leagues of wild road on which anything at all might happen and be afterward explained away.

As for the forcible abduction, that could best be got around by obliging her to write a letter to himself requesting permission to visit the mountains for a change of air and scenery. There were ways and means of obliging women to write letters.

Best of all, of course, would be Yasmini's unconditional surrender, because then he would be able to make use of her wits and her information, instead of having to explain away her "accident" and cope alone with any one whom she might already have entrusted with her secret. There should be a strenuous effort first to bring her to her senses. Physical pain, he had noticed, had more effect on people's senses than any amount of argument. There had been a very amusing instance recently. One of his dancing girls named Malati had refused recently to sing and dance her best before a man to whom Gungadhura had designed to make a present of her; but the mere preliminaries of removing a toe-nail behind the scenes had changed her mind within three minutes.

Then there were other little humorous contrivances. There is a way of tying an intended convert to your views in such ingenious fashion that the lightest touch of a finger on taut catgut stretched from limb to limb, causes exquisite agony. And a cigarette end, of course, applied in such circumstances to the tenderer parts has great power to persuade.

As to accomplices, those must be few and carefully chosen. Alone against Yasmini he knew he would have no chance whatever, for she was physically stronger than a panther, and as swift and graceful. But there are creatures, not nearly yet extinct from Eastern courts, known as eunuchs, whose strongest quality is seldom said to be mercy, and whose chief business in life is to be amenable to orders and to guard with their lives their master's secrets. Three were really too many to be let into such a secret; but it had needed two to hold Malati properly while the third experimented on the toe-nail, and Yasmini was much stronger than Malati; so he must chance it and take three.

The only remaining problem did not trouble him much. The palace guards were his own men, and were therefore not likely to question his right to ignore the first law of *purdah* that forbids the crossing of a woman's threshold, especially after dark, unless she is your property. Besides, they all knew already what sort of prowl-by-night their master was, and laws, especially such laws, were made for other people, not for maharajahs.

A bloody enlisted man—that's me,
A peg in the officer's plan—maybe.
Drunk on occasion,
Disgrace to a nation
And proper societee.
Yet I've a notion the sky—pure blue
Ain't more essential than I—clear through.
I'm a man.   I can think.
In the chain of eternal
Affairs I'm a link,
And the chain ain't no stronger than me—or you.

CHAPTER SEVEN

"That will be the end of Gungadhura!"

It took longer to get the hamper ready than Tess expected, partly because it did not seem expedient to have the butler Chamu in the secret. By the time she and her husband were up side by side in the dog-cart there was already a nearly full moon silvering the sky, and the jackals were yelping miserably on the hillside. Before they reached the stifling town a slow breeze had moved the river-mist, until a curtain shut off the whole of the bazaar and merchants' quarters from the better residential section where the palaces stood. It was an ideal night for adventure; an almost perfect night for crime; one could step from street to street and leave no clue, because of the drifting vapor.

Here and there a solitary policeman coughed after they had passed, or slunk into a shadow lest they recognize and report him for sleeping at his post. All sahibs have unreasonable habits, and not even a constable can guess which one will not make trouble for him. An occasional stray dog yapped at the wheels, and more than once heads peered over roof-tops to try and glimpse them, because gossip—especially about sahibs who are out after dark—is a coinage of its own that buys welcome and refreshment almost anywhere. But nothing in particular happened until the horse struck sparks from the granite flagstones outside Yasmini's gate, and a sleepy Rajput sentry brought his rifle to the challenge.

Then it was not exactly obvious what to do next. Tess felt perfectly confident on the high seat, with the pistol in her husband's pocket pressing against her and his reassuring bulk between her and the sentry; but everywhere else was insecurity and doubt. One does not as a rule descend from dog-carts after dark and present half-sheets of paper by way of passports for admission to Rajput palaces. The sentry looked mildly interested, no more. He had been so thoroughly warned and threatened in case of efforts to escape from within, that it did not enter his head that any one might want to enter. However, since the dog-cart continued to stand still in front of the gate, he turned the guard out as a matter of routine; one never knew when sahibs will not complain about discourtesy.

The guard lined up at attention—eight men and a risaldar (officer)—double the regular number by Gungadhura's orders. The risaldar stepped up close to the dog-cart and spoke to the man he imagined was the *sais,* using, as was natural, the Rajput tongue. But Dick Blaine only knew enough of the language for fetch and carry purposes—not enough to deceive a native as to his nationality after the first two words.

"Now I feel foolish!" said Tess, and the risaldar of the guard thrust his bearded face closer, supposing she spoke to him. Dick answered her.

"Shall I drive you home again, little woman? Say the word and we're off."

"Not yet. I haven't tried my ammunition."

She pulled out Samson's scribbled permit and was about to offer it to the guard. But there was a risk that whatever she did would only arouse and increase his suspicions, and she offered it nervously.

"What if he won't give it back to you?" asked her husband.

"Oh, Dick, you're a regular prophet of evil to-night!"

However, she withdrew the paper before the guard's fingers closed on it. The next moment a figure like a phantom, making no noise, almost made her scream. Dick produced a repeating pistol with that sudden swiftness that proves old acquaintance with the things, and the corporal of the guard sprang back with a shout of warning to his men, imagining the pistol was intended for himself. Tess recovered presence of mind first.

"It's all right, Dick. Put the gun out of sight."

She stretched out her hand and a cold nose touched her finger-ends, sniffing them. A dog's forefeet were on the shaft, and his eyes gleamed balefully in the carriage lamp light.

"Good Trotters! Good boy, Trotters!"

She remembered Tom Tripe's lecture about calling dogs by name, wondering whether the rule applied to owners only, or whether she, too, could make the creature "do this own thinking." Before she could decide what she would like the dog to think about he was gone again as silently as he had come. The guard was thoroughly on the *qui vive* by that time, if not suspicious, then officious. How should one protect the pri-

vacy of a palace gate if unknown memsahibs in dog-
carts, with *saises* who knew English but did not answer
when spoken to in the native tongue, were to be allowed to draw up in front of the gate at unseemly
hours and remain there indefinitely.   The risaldar
ordered Tess away without further ceremony, making
his meaning plain by taking the horse's head and
starting him.

Dick Blaine drew the horse back on his haunches
and cursed the man for that piece of impudence, in
language and with mannerisms that banished forever
any delusions as to his nationality; and it occurred to
the officer that his extra complement of men, standing
in a row like dummies at attention, were not there after
all for nothing. He despatched two of them at a run to
Gungadhura's palace, the one to tell the story of what
had happened and the other to add to it whatever the
first might omit. Between them they were likely to
produce results of some sort.

"Now we're done for!" sighed Tess. "No chance
to-night, I'm afraid. If only I'd done what she told me
to and consulted with Tom Tripe first. Better drive
home now, Dick, before we make the case worse."

The unreasonableness of the attempt convinced and
discouraged her. It was like a nightmare. But as
Dick reined the horse about there came out of the mist
the sound of another horse at a walk, and two men
marching in step. Then a man's voice broke the stillness. Dick reined in, and a second later Trotters' huge
paws rested on the shaft again. Tess could see his
long, unenthusiastic tail wagging to and fro.

"Tom!" she called. "Tom Tripe!"

"Coming, lady!"

Three figures emerged out of the gloom, one of them mounted and loquacious.

"I'd like to know what these rascally guards are doing off their post! Give these sons of camp-follow-ers an inch and they'll take three leagues, every moth-er's son of them! Halt, there, you! Now then, where's your officer? Give an account of yourselves!"

There followed an interlude in Rajasthani.* Tom Tripe becoming more blasphemously vehement as it grew clearer that the risaldar had done entirely right.

"Lady," he said presently, riding round to Tess's side of the dog-cart. "I'm going to have hard work to convince this man. I'd orders from Gungadhura to search your house, Krishna knows what for, and I rode up to ask your leave to do it, hoping you'd be alone after the party. Chamu told me you and your husband had gone out, and one of the three beggars gave me a message intended for you that tallied pretty close with one I knew you'd received already, so I guessed where to head for, and sent the dog in advance. He came back with his hair on end reporting trouble, and then as luck would have it I rode into these two men on their way to Gungadhura. If they'd reached him, we'd all have had to make new plans to-morrow morning! You want to see the princess, of course? But what have you got that can get by the guard?"

Tess produced Samson's scribbled note, and he studied it in the carriage lamplight. Then she recalled Yasmini's warning that Tom Tripe had no brains and

*The native language of Rajputana.

must be told what to do. Her own wits began to work desperately.

"I'm the lady doctor, Tom. That is my written order from the *burra* sahib." (Commissioner).

Tom scratched his head and swore in a low voice fervently.

"The difficulty's this, lady: since the escape from the palace across the river, the maharajah has taken the posting of palace guards out of my hands entirely. I've still the duty to inspect and make sure they're on the job—— Oh, I see! I have it!"

He turned on the corporal with all the savagery that the white man generates in contact with Eastern subordinates.

"What do you mean," he demanded in the man's own language, "by standing in the way of the maharajah sahib's orders? Here's his highness sending a lady doctor to the princess for an excuse to confine her elsewhere and have all this trouble off our hands, and you, like a blockhead, stand in the way to prevent it! See——there's the letter!"

The Rajput looked perplexed. All the world knows what privileges the rare American women doctors enjoy in that land of sealed seraglios.

"But it is written in English," he objected. "The maharajah sahib does not write English."

"Idiot! Of what use would a letter in Persian be to an American lady doctor?"

"But to me? It is I who command the guard and must read the letter. How can I read the letter?"

"I'll read it to you. What's more, I'll explain it.

The princess has been appealing to the commissioner
sahib——"

The Rajput nodded. It was all over town that Yasmini had been closeted with the commissioner on the
morning of her recent escape. She herself had deliberately sown the seeds of that untruth.

"So the commissioner sahib and the maharajah
sahib had a conference——"

The Rajput nodded again. It was common knowledge, too that the commissioner and Gungadhura had
had a rather stormy interview the day before; and it
was none of the corporal's privilege to know that all
they had argued about was the ill-treatment of prison-
ers in the Sialpore jail.

"—It was agreed at the conference that if the
princess can be proved mad, then the maharajah sahib
may do as he's minded about sending her away into
the hills. If she's not mad, then he's to give her her
liberty. Do you understand, you dunderhead?"

"Hah! I understand. But why at night? Why
not the maharajah sahib's signature in his own
writing?"

"Son of incomprehension! Does the maharajah
sahib wish still more scandal than already has been by
permitting such a visit in the daytime? Strike me
everlasting dumb if he hasn't had more than enough
already! Does he want the responsibility? Does he
wish the British to say afterward that it was all the
maharajah's doing? No, you ass! At the conference
he agreed solely on condition that the commissioner
sahib should sign the letter and relieve his highness of
all blame in case of a verdict of madness. And it was

decided to send an American, lest there be too much talk among the British themselves. Now, do you understand?"

"Hah! I understand. If all this is true the matter is easy. I will send one of the guard with that letter to the maharajah sahib. He will write his name on it and send it back, and all is well."

"Suit yourself!" sneered Tom Tripe. "The maharajah sahib is with his dancing girls this minute. What happened to the last man who interrupted his amusements?"

The Rajput hesitated. The answer to that question could be seen any day near the place they call the Old Gate, where beggars sit in rags.

"Shall I offer him money?" whispered Tess.

"For God's sake, no, lady! The man's a decent soldier. He'd refuse it and we'd all be in the apple-cart! Leave him to me."

He turned again on the Rajput.

"You know who I am, don't you? You know it's my duty to see that the palace guards attend to business, eh? That's why I'm here to-night. His highness particularly warned me to see that if anything unusual wanted doing it should get done. If you want to question my authority you'll have it out with me before his highness in the morning first thing."

The Rajput obviously wavered. Everybody knew that the first thing in the morning was no good time to appear on charges before a man who spent his nights as Gungadhura did.

"Who is to enter? A man and a woman?"

"No, you idiot! A lady doctor only. And nobody's

to know. You'd better warn your men that if there's
any talk about this night's business the palace guard
will catch the first blast of the typhoon. Gungadhura's
anger isn't mild in these days!"

"Show me the letter again," said the Rajput. "Let
me keep it in case I am brought to book."

Tom translated that to Tess and her husband.

"It's this way, ma'am. If you let him keep the letter I suspect he'll let you go in. But he may show it to
the maharajah in the morning, and then there'll be hot
fat in the fire. If you don't let him keep it, perhaps
he'll admit you and perhaps he won't; but if you keep
the letter, and trouble comes of it, he and I'll both be in
the soup! Never mind about me. Maybe I'm too valuable to be sent packing. I'll take the chance. But
this man's a decent soldier, and he'd be helpless."

"Let him keep it," said Tess.

Tom turned on the Rajput again.

"Here's the letter. Take it. But mark this! What
his highness wants to-night is discretion. There might
be promotion for a man who'd say nothing about this
night's work. If, on top of that, he was soldier enough
to keep his men from talking he'd be reported favor-
ably to his highness by Tom Tripe. Who got you
made risaldar, eh? Who stood up for you, when you
were charged with striking Gullam Singh? Was Tom
Tripe's friendship worth having then? Now suit
yourself! I've said all I'm going to say."

The Rajput muttered something in his beard, stared
again at the letter as if that of itself would justify him,
looked sharply at Tess, whose hamper might or might

not be corroborative evidence, folded the letter away in his tunic pocket, and made a gesture of assent.

"Now, lady, hurry!" said Tom. "And here's hoping you're right about there being no hell! I've told lies enough to-night to damn my soul forever! Once you're safely through the gate I'll have a word or two more with the guard, and then your husband and I will go to a place close by that I know of and wait for you."

But Tess objected to that. "Please don't leave me waiting for you in the dark outside the gate when I return! Why not keep the carriage here; my husband won't mind."

"Might make talk, ma'am. I'll leave Trotters here to watch for you. He'll bring word in less than a minute."

Tom Tripe dismounted to help her out of the dog-cart. The Rajput struck the iron gate as if he expected to have to wake the dead and take an hour about it. But it opened suspiciously quickly and a bearded Afridi, of all unlikely people, thrust an expectant face outward, rather like a tortoise emerging from its shell, blinking as he tried to recognize the shadowy forms that moved in the confusing lamplight. He seemed to know whom to expect and admit, for he beckoned Tess with a long crooked forefinger the moment she approached the gate, and in another ten seconds the iron clanged behind her, shutting her off from husband and all present hope of succor. The chance of any rescuer entering the palace that night, whether by force or sublety, was infinitesimal.

The strange gateman—he had a little kennel of a place to sleep in just inside the entrance—snatched the hamper from Tess and led her almost at a run across an ancient courtyard whose outlines were nearly invisible except where the yellow light of one ancient oil lantern on an iron bracket showed a part of the palace wall and a steep flight of stone steps, worn down the middle by centuries of sandals. Everything else was in gloom and shadow, and only one chink of light betrayed the whereabouts of a curtained window. The Afridi led her up the stone steps, and paused at the top to hammer on a carved door with his clenched fist; but the door moved while his fist was in mid-air, and the merry-eyed maid who opened it mocked him for a lunatic. Dumb, apparently, in the presence of woman, he slunk down the steps again, leaving Tess wondering whether it were not good manners to remove her shoes before entering. Natives of the country always removed their shoes before entering her house, and she supposed it would be only decent to reciprocate.

However, the maid took her by the hand and pulled her inside without further ceremony, not letting go of the hand even to close the door, but patting it and making much of her, smiling the welcome that they had no words in common to express. The little outer hall in which they stood was shut off by curtains six yards high, all smothered in a needlework of peacocks that generations of patient fingers must have toiled at. Pulling these apart the maid led her into an inner hall fifty or sixty feet long, the first sight of which banished all diffidence about her shoes; for never had she seen such medley of East and West, such toning down of Oriental mysticism with the sheer utility of European importations; and that without incongruity.

The lamps, of which there were dozens, were mostly Russian. Some of the furniture was Buhl, some French. There were hangings that looked like loot from the Pekin Summer Palace, and tapestry from Gobelin. In a place of honor on a side wall was an *ikon,* framed in gold, and facing that an image of the Buddha done in greenish bronze, flanked by a Dutch picture of the Twelve Apostles with laughably Dutch faces receiving instruction on a mountain from a Christ whose other name was surely Hans.

Down the center of the hall, leading to a gallery, was a magnificent stairway of marble and lapis lazuli, carpeted with long Bokhara strips so well joined end to end that the whole looked like one piece. And at the top of those stairs Yasmini stood waiting, her golden hair illuminated by glass lamps on either marble column at the stairhead. She was as different from the Gunga Singh of riding boots and turban as the morning is from night—the loveliest, bewitchingest girl in silken gossamer that Tess had ever set eyes on.

"I knew you would come!" she shouted gleefully. "I knew you would get in! I knew you are my friend! Oh, I'm glad! I'm glad!"

She pirouetted a dozen times on bare toes at the top of the stairs, spinning until her silken skirts expanded in a nimbus, then danced down-stairs into Tess's arms, where she clung, panting and laughing.

"I'm so hungry! Oh, I'm hungry! Did you bring the food?"

"I'm ashamed!" Tess answered. "The man set it down outside the door and I left it there."

But Yasmini gave a little shrill of delight, and Tess turned to see that another maid had brought it.

"How many of you are there?"

"Five."

"Thank heaven! I've brought enough for a square meal for a dozen."

"We have eaten a little, little bit each day of the servants' rice, washing it first for hours, until to-day, when two of the servants were taken sick and we thought perhaps their food was poisoned too. Oh, we're hungry!"

Hasamurti, Yasmini's maid, opened the basket on the floor and crowed aloud. Tess apologized.

"I knew nothing about the caste restrictions, but I've put in meat jelly—and bread—and fruit—and rice—and nuts—and milk—and tea—and wine—and sugar——"

Yasmini laughed.

"I am as Western as I choose to be, and only pretend to caste when I see fit. My maids do as I do, or they seek another mistress. Come!"

Hasamurti would have spread a banquet there on the floor, but Yasmini led them up-stairs, holding Tess by the hand, turning to the right at the stairhead into a room all cream and golden, lighted by hanging lamps that shone through disks of colored glass. There she pulled Tess down beside her on to a great soft divan and they all ate together, the maids munching their share while they served their mistress. They devoured the milk, and left the wine, eating, all things considered, astonishingly moderately.

"Now we ought all to go to sleep," announced Yasmini, yawning, and then bubbling with delighted laughter at the expression of Tess's face. "The people outside might wait!"

"Great heavens, child. Do you suppose I can stay here indefinitely?" Tess demanded. "I must be gone in an hour or my husband will murder the guard and force an entrance!"

"I will have just such a husband soon," announced Yasmini. "When I send him one little word, he will cut the throats of thirty men and come to me through flames! Let us try your husband," she added as an afterthought——then laughed again at Tess's expression of dissent, and nodded.

"I, too, will be careful how I risk my husband! Men are but moths in a woman's hands—fragile—but the good ones are precious. Besides, we have no time to-night for sport. I must escape."

Evidently Tess was causing her exquisite amusement. The thought of being an accomplice in any such adventure stirred all her Yankee common sense to its depths, and she had none of the Eastern trick of not displaying her emotions.

"Nonsense, child! Let me go to the commissioner and warn him that you are being starved to death in this place. I will threaten him with public scandal if he doesn't put an end to it at once."

"Pouf!" laughed Yasmini. "Samson sahib would make a nice clumsy accomplice! He would send me to Calcutta, where I should be poisoned sooner or later for a certainty, because Gungadhura would send agents to attend to that. They would wait months and months for their opportunity, and I can not always stay awake.

Meanwhile Samson sahib would claim praise from his government, and they would put some more initials at the end of his name, and promote him to a bigger district with more pay. No! Samson sahib shall have another district surely, but even he in his conceit will not consider it promotion! There will not be room for Samson sahib in Sialpore when I am maharanee!"

"You maharanee? It was you yourself who told me that Gungadhura has lots of children, who all stand between you and the throne. Do you mean——?"

Again the bell-like laugh announced utter enjoyment of Tess's bewilderment.

"No, I will kill nobody. I will not even send snakes in a basket to Gungadhura. That scorpion shall sting himself to death if he sees fit, with a ring of the fire of ridicule all about him and no friends to console him, and no hope—nothing but disappointment and fear and rage! I will kill nobody. Yet I will be maharanee within the month!"

Suddenly she grew deadly serious, her young face darkening as the sky does when a quick cloud hides the sun.

"What is your husband's contract with Gungadhura? May he dig for gold anywhere? He is digging now, isn't he, close to the British fort on the 'island' in our territory—that fort with the flag-staff on it that can be seen from Gungadhura's roof? He is wasting time!"

"He has found a little vein of gold," said Tess, "that will likely lead to a bigger vein."

"He is wasting time! Sita Ram, who has a compass, and who knows all that goes on in Samson sahib's office, sent me word that the little vein of gold runs nearly due north. In another week at the rate the men are digging your husband will be under the fort. That is English territory. The English have nothing to do with Gungadhura's contract. They will take the gold your husband finds and give him nothing. Then Samson sahib would be considered a most excellent commissioner and would surely get promotion! Pouf!"

"Perhaps my husband can make a separate bargain with the English."

"Pouf! Samson sahib is an idiot, but he is not fool enough to give away what would be in his hands already! I myself, hidden beneath your window, heard him give you clear warning on that point! No, there must be another plan. Your husband must dig elsewhere."

"But, my dear, Gungadhura knows already that my husband has found a 'leader.' He is all worked up about it, and goes every day to watch the progress."

"Surely—knowing as well as I do that the vein is leading toward the fort. He goes afterward to the priests, and prays that the vein of gold may turn another way and save him from bankruptcy! Listen! I speak truth! I speak to you woman to woman— womb to womb! I will count myself accursed, and will let a cobra bite me if I tell you now one word that is not true! Do you believe I am going to tell you the truth?"

Tess nodded. Yasmini, by her own admission, would lie deliberately when that suited her; but the truth tells itself, as it were, and there is no mistaking it, except by such as lie invariably, of whom there is a multifarious host.

"If your husband continues digging near the fort he will get nothing, because the English will take it all. If he digs in a certain other place he will get a very great fortune!"

"But, my dear, supposing that is quite true, how shall he convince Gungadhura, after all the outlay and expense of the present operations, that it's best to abandon them and begin all over again in another place?"

Yasmini lay back on the cushions, drew something out from under one of them, and laughed softly, as if enjoying a deep underflow of secret information.

"Gungadhura himself shall insist on it!"

"What? On starting again in a new place?"

Yasmini nodded.

"Only do as I say, and Gungadhura himself shall insist."

"What do you wish me to do?"

Tess was beginning to feel alarmed again. She knew to a rupee how much Gungadhura had been obliged to pay out for the digging. To make herself responsible even in degree for the abandonment of all that outlay would be risky, even if no other construction could be placed on it.

"Has Tom Tripe been told to search your house?"

"Yes, so he says."

"Do you know the cellar of your house?"

"Yes."

"It is dark. Are you afraid to go there?"

"No. Why?"

"Is there a flat stone in a corner of the cellar floor that once had a ring in it but the ring is broken out?"

"Yes."

"Good. Then Sita Ram did not lie to me. Take this." She gave her a little silver tube, capped at either end and sealed heavily with wax. "There is a writing inside it—done in Persian. Hide that under the stone, and let Tom Tripe search the cellar and find it there; but forbid him to remove it."

"If I only knew what you are driving at!" said Tess with a wry smile.

A clumsier conspirator might have lost the game at that point by over-emphasis, for Tess was wavering between point-blank refusal and delay that would give her time to consult her husband. But Yasmini, even at that age, was adept at feeling her way nicely. Again she lay back on the cushion, and this time lit a cigarette, smoking lazily.

"The stake that I am playing for—the stake that I shall surely win," she said after a minute, "is too big to be risked. If you are afraid, let us forget all that I have said. Let us be friends and nothing more."

Tess did not answer. She recognized the appeal to her own pride, and ignored it. What she was thinking of was Gungadhura's beastliness—his attempts to poison Yasmini—his treatment of women generally—his cruelty to animals in the arena—his viciousness; and then, of how much more queenly if nothing else, this girl would likely be than ever Gungadhura could be kingly. It was tempting enough to have a hand in substituting Yasmini for Gungadhura on the throne of Sialpore if the chance of doing it were real.

Yasmini seemed able to read her thoughts, or at all events to guess them.

"When I am maharanee," she said, "there will be an end of Gungadhura's swinishness. Moreover, promises will all be kept, unwritten ones as well as written. Gungadhura's contracts will be carried out. Do you believe me?"

"Yes, I think I believe that."

"Let Tom Tripe find that silver tube in your cellar then. But listen! When Gungadhura comes to your husband and insists on digging elsewhere, let your husband bargain like a huckster! Let him at first refuse. It may be that Gungadhura will let him continue where he digs, and will himself send men to start digging in the other place. In that case, well and good."

"I would prefer that," said Tess. "My husband is a mining engineer. I think he would hate to abandon a true lead for a whim of some one's else."

Yasmini's bright eyes gleamed intelligence. She was only learning in those days to bend people to her own imperious will and to use others' virtues for her own ends as readily as their vices. She recognized the necessity of yielding to Tess's compunctions, more than suspecting that Dick Blaine would color his own views pretty much to suit his wife's in any case. And with a lightning ability peculiar to her she saw how to improve her own plan by yielding.

"That is settled, then," she said lazily. "Your husband shall continue to dig near the fort, if he so wishes. But let him show Samson sahib some specimens of the gold—how little it is—how feeble—how uncertain. Be sure he does that, please. That will be the end of

Gungadhura. And now it is time to escape from here, and for you to help me."

Tess resigned herself to the inevitable. Whatever the consequences, she was not willing to leave Yasmini to starve or be poisoned.

"I'm ready!" she said. "What's the plan?"

"I shall leave all the maids behind. They have food enough for the morning. In the morning, after it is known that I have escaped, word shall be sent to Samson sahib that the women in this palace have nothing but poisoned food to eat. He must beard Gungadhura about that or lose his own standing with the English."

"But how will you escape?"

"Nay, that is not the difficulty. Your husband and Tom Tripe are waiting with the carriage. My part is easy. This is the problem: how will you follow me?"

"I don't understand."

"I must wear your clothes. In the dark I shall get past the guard, making believe that I am you."

"Then how shall I manage?"

"You must do as I say. I can contrive it. Come, the maids and I will make a true Rajputni of you. Only I must study how to walk as you do; please walk along in front of me—that way—follow Hasamurti through that door into my room. I will study how you move your feet and shoulders."

Looking back as she followed Hasamurti, Tess witnessed a caricature of herself that made her laugh until the tears came.

"It is well!" said Yasmini. "This night began in hunger, like the young moon. Now is laughter without malice. In a few hours will be bright dawn—and after that, success!"

AN ELEPHANT INTERLUDE

Watch your step where the elephants sway
Each at a chain at the end of a day,
Hurrumdi-diddlidi-um-di-ay!
Nothing to do but rock and swing,
Clanking an iron picket ring,
Plucking the dust to flirt and fling;
Keep et ceteras out of range,
Anything out of the way or strange
Suits us elephant folk for change—
Various odds and ends appeal
To liven the round of work and meal.
Curious trunks can reach and steal!
Fool with Two-tails if you dare;
Help yourself. But fool, beware!
Whatever results is your affair!
We are the easiest beasts that be,
Gentle and good and affectionate we,
You are the monarchs; we bow the knee,
Big and obese and obedient——um!
Just as long as it suits us——um!
Hurrumti-tiddli-di-um-ti-um!.........."

(Unfortunately at this point Akbar's attention was diverted to another matter, so the rest of his picket-song goes unrecorded.)

CHAPTER EIGHT

"They're elephants and I'm a soldier. The trouble with
you is nerves, my boy!"

THERE was brandy in the place that Tom Tripe
knew of—brandy and tobacco and a smell of elephants.
Dick Blaine, who scarcely ever touched strong liquor,
having had intimate acquaintance with abuse of it in
Western mining camps, had to sit and endure the spectacle of Tom's chief weakness, glass after glass of the
fiery stuff descending into a stomach long since rendered insatiable by soldiering on peppery food in a
climate that is no man's friend. He protested a dozen
times.

"We may need our wits to-night, Tom. Suppose
we both keep sober."

"Man alive, I've been doing this for years.
Brandy and brains are the same in my case. Keep me
without it, and by bedtime I'm an invalid. Give me all
I want of it, and I'm a crafty soldier-man."

Dick Blaine refilled his pipe and watched for an
opportunity. He had heard that kind of argument
before, and had conquered flood and fire with the aid
of the very men who used it, that being the gift (or
whatever you like to call it) that had made him inde-
pendent while the others drew monthly pay in
envelopes.

138

It was a low oblong shed they sat in, with a wide door opening on a side street within four hundred yards of Yasmini's palace gate. It was furnished with a table, two chairs and a cot for Tom Tripe's special use whenever the maharajah's business should happen to keep him on night duty, his own proper quarters being nearly a mile away. Alongside the shed was a very rough stable that would accommodate a horse or two, and the back wall was a mere partition of mud brick, behind which, under a thatched roof, were tethered some of the maharajah's elephants. There were two windows in the wall, through which one could see dimly the great brutes' rumps as they swayed at their pickets restlessly. The smell came through a broken pane, and every once in a while the Blaines' horse, standing ready in the shafts outside with a blanket over him, squealed at it indignantly.

Tom's horse dozed in the rough shed, being used to elephants.

Dick got up once or twice to peer through the window at the brutes.

"Are they tethered fore and aft?" he wondered.

"No," Tom answered. "One hind foot only."

"What's to stop them from turning round and breaking down this rotten wall?"

"Nothing—except that they're elephants. They could break their picket chains if they were minded to, same as I could break Gungadhura's head and lose my job. But I won't do it, and nor will they. They're elephants, and I'm a soldier. The trouble with you is nerves, my boy. Have some brandy. You're worried about your wife, but I tell you she's right as a

trivet. I'd trust my last chance with that little princess. I've done it often. Brandy's the stuff to keep
your hair on. Have some."

The bottle had only been three parts full. Tom
poured out the last of it and set a stone jorum of rum
in readiness on the table over against the wall.

"Wish we had hot water handy," he grumbled.

"Which of the elephants are tethered here?" asked
Dick. "That big one that killed a tiger in the arena
the other day?"

"Yes. Did you see that? Akbar was scarcely
scratched. Quickest thing ever I saw—squealed with
rage the minute they turned 'stripes' loose—chased
him to the wall—downed him with a forefoot and
crushed him into tiger jelly before you could say British Constitution!"

"I guess that tiger had been kept in a cage too
long," said Dick.

"Don't you believe it. He was fighting fit. But
they'd given old Akbar a skin-full of rum, and that
turns him into a holy terror. He's quite quiet other
times."

Dick looked at his watch. Tess had been in the
palace about three hours, and he was confident she
would come away as soon as possible, if for no other
reason than to put an end to his anxiety. She was
likely to appear at the gate at any minute. At any
minute Tom Tripe was likely to attack the jorum, and.
if present symptoms went for anything, it would not
take much of it to make him worse than useless. At
present he was growing reminiscent.

"Once old Akbar had a belly-ache and they gave

him arrak. They didn't catch him for two days! He pulled up his picket-stake and lit out for the horizon, chasing dogs and hens and monkeys and anything else he could find that annoyed him. Screamed like a locomotive. Horrid sight!"

"Where does this road outside lead to?" asked Dick.

"Don't lead anywhere. Blind alley. Why?"

"Oh, nothing."

Dick was examining the wall between the shed they sat in and the stable-place next door. It was much stronger than the mud affair between them and the elephants. Tom Tripe had nearly finished his tumbler-full, and there was madness in the air that night that made a man take awfully long chances.

"Do you suppose a man could lose his way in the dark between here and the palace gate?"

"Not even if he was as drunk as Noah. All he'd have to do 'ud be hold on to the wall and walk forward. The road turns a corner, but the walls are all blind and there's no other way but past the palace. You sit here, though, my boy. No need to try that. Your wife's all right."

"Well, maybe I'd better stay here."

"Sure."

"Do you suppose I could back the dog-cart into the shed where your horse is? I hardly like to leave my horse standing any longer in the open, yet he's better in the shafts in case we want him in a hurry."

"Yes, the door's wide enough."

"Then I'll do it."

"Suit yourself. But take some of that rum before

you go outside. The night air's bad for your lungs.
Help yourself and pass the bottle, as the Queen said to
the Archbishop of Canterbury."

"All right, I will."

Dick poured a little on his handkerchief, thrust the
handkerchief through the broken pane and waved it
violently to spread the smell. It was cheap, immodest
stuff, blatant with its own advertisement. Then he
set the jorum down on the end of the table farthest
from the wall, to the best of his judgment out of reach
from the window.

"Come along, Tom," he said then. "Help me with
the horse."

"What's your hurry? Take a drink first."

"No, let's take one together afterward."

He took Tom by the shoulder and pushed him to
his feet.

"The horse might break away. Come on, man,
hurry!"

Over his shoulder Dick could see a long trunk nosing its way gingerly through the broken pane and
searching out the source of the alluring smell. He
pushed Tripe along in front of him, and together they
backed the dog-cart into the stable-place, making a
very clumsy business of it for three reasons: Tom
Tripe was none too sober: the horse was nearly crazy
with fear of the uncanny brutes just beyond the wall;
and Dick was in too much hurry for reasons of his
own. However, they got horse and cart in backward,
and the door shut before the crash came.

The crash was of a falling mud-brick wall, pushed
outward by the shoulders of a pachyderm that wanted

alcohol. The beast had had it out of all sorts of containers and knew the trick of emptying the last drop. The jorum was about his usual dose.

About two minutes later, while Dick and Tom Tripe between them held a horse in intolerable durance between the shafts, and Tom's horse out of sympathy kicked out at random into every shadow he could reach, the door and part of the wall of Tom's shed fell outward into the pitch dark street as Akbar, eleven feet four inches at the shoulder, strode forward conjecturing what worlds were yet to conquer. The other elephants stood motionless at their pickets. A terrified mahout emerged through the debris like a devil from hell's bunkers, calling to his elephant all the endearing epithets he knew, and cursing him alternately. The horses grew calmer and submitted to caresses, like children and all creatures that have intimate contact with strong men; and presently the night grew still.

"D'you suppose that brute swiped my liquor?" wondered Tom Tripe. "You mind the horses while I look."

But suddenly there was a savage noise of trumpeting up-street, followed by a bark and a yelp of canine terror.

"God!" swore Tom. "That's Trotters coming to fetch us! Akbar's chasing him back this way! Hang on to the horse like ten men! I'll go see!"

He was outside before Dick could remonstrate. Between them they had lashed the dog-cart wheels during the first panic, but even so Dick had his hands full, as the trumpeting drew nearer and the horse went into agonies of senseless fear. It was a fight, nothing less, between thinking man and mere instinctive beast, and eventually Dick threw him with a trick of the reins about his legs, and knelt on his head to keep him down. By the grace of the powers of unexpectedness neither shafts nor harness broke.

Outside in the darkness Tom Tripe peered through brandied eyes at a great shadow that hunted to and fro a hundred yards away, chasing something that was quite invisible, and making enough noise about it to awake the dead.

"Trotters!" he yelled. "Trotters!"

A moment later a smaller shadow came into view at top speed, panting, chased hotly by the bigger one.

"Trotters! Get back where you came from! Back, d'ye hear me! Back!"

Within ten yards of his master the dog stopped to do his thinking, and the elephant screamed with a sort of hunter's ecstasy as he closed on him with a rush. But thought is swift, and obedience good judgment. The dog doubled of a sudden between Akbar's legs, and the elephant slid on his rump in the futile effort to turn after him—then crashed into the wall opposite Tripe's dismantled shed—cannoned off it with a grunt of sheer disgust—and set off up-street, once more in hot pursuit.

"That brute got my good rum, damn him!" said Tom, opening the stable door. "Hello! Horse down? Any harm done? Right-oh! We'll soon have him up again. Better hurry now—Trotters came for us."

So many look at the color,
So many study design,
Some of 'em squint through a microscope
To judge if the texture is fine.
A few give a thought to the price of the stuff,
Some feel of the heft in the hand,
But once in a while there is one who can smile
And—appraising the lot—understand.
                    Look out,
When the seemingly sold understand!
                    All's planned,
For the cook of the stew to be canned
                    Out o' hand,
When the due to be choused understand!

CHAPTER NINE

"It means, the toils are closing in on Gungadhura!"

WITHIN the palace Tess was reveling in vaudeville. In the first place, Yasmini had no Western views on modesty. Whatever her mother may have taught her in that respect had gone the way of all the other handicaps she saw fit to throw into the discard, or to retain for use solely when she saw there was advantage. The East uses dress for ornament, and understands its use. The veil is for places where men might look with too bold eyes and covet. Out of sight of privileged men prudery has no place, and almost no advocates all the way from Peshawar to Cape Comorin.

And Yasmini had loved dancing since the days when she tottered her first steps for her mother's and Bubru Singh's delight. Long before an American converted the Russian Royal Ballet, and the Russian Royal Ballet in return took all the theatre-going West by storm—scandalizing, then amazing, then educating bit by bit—Yasmini had developed her own ideas and brought them by arduous practise to something near perfection. To that her strength, agility and sinuous grace were largely due; and she practised no deceptions on herself, but valued all three qualities for their effect on other people, keeping no light under a bushel.

146

The consciousness of that night's climactic quality raised her spirits to the point where they were irrepressible, and she danced her garments off one by one, using each in turn as a foil for her art until there was nothing left with which to multiply rhythm and she danced before the long French mirrors yet more gracefully with nothing on at all.

Getting Tess disrobed was a different matter. She did not own to much prudery, but the maids' eyes were over-curious. And, lacking, as she knew she did, Yasmini's ability to justify nakedness by poetry of motion, she hid behind a curtain and was royally laughed at for her pains. But she was satisfied to retain that intangible element that is best named dignity, and let the laughter pass unchallenged. Yasmini, with her Eastern heritage, could be dignified as well as beautiful as nature made her. Not so Tess, or at any rate she thought not, and what one thinks is after all the only gage acceptable.

Then came the gorgeous fun of putting on Tess's clothes, each to be danced in as its turn came, and made fun of, so that Tess herself began to believe all Western clothes were awkward, idiotic things—until Yasmini stood clothed complete at last, with her golden hair all coiled under a Paris hat, and looked as lovely that way as any. The two women were almost exactly the same size. Even the shoes fitted, and when Yasmini walked the length of the room with Tess's very stride and attitude Tess got her first genuine glimpse of herself as another's capably critical eyes saw her— a priceless experience, and not so humiliating after all.

They dressed up Tess in man's clothes—a young

Rajput's—a suit Yasmini had worn on one of her wild
excursions, and what with the coiled turban of yellow
silk and a little black mustache adjusted by cunning
fingers she felt as happy as a child in fancy dress.
But she found it more difficult to imitate the Rajput
walk than Yasmini did to copy her tricks of carriage.
For a few minutes they played at walking together up
and down the room before the mirror, applauded by
the giggling maids. But then suddenly came anti-
climax. There was a great hammering at the outer
door, and one of the maids ran down to investigate,
while they waited in breathless silence.

The news the maid brought back was the worst
imaginable. The look-out at the northern corner of
the wall (Yasmini kept watch on her captors as rigor-
ously as they spied on her) had run with the word to
the gateman that Gungadhura himself was coming
with three eunuchs, all four on foot.

Almost as soon as the breathless girl could break
that evil tidings there came another hammering, and
this time Hasamurti went down to answer. Her news
was worse. Gungadhura was at the outer gate
demanding admission, and threatening to order the
guard to break the gate in if refused.

"What harm can he do?" demanded Tess. "He
won't dare try any violence in front of me. Let us
change clothes again."

Yasmini laughed at her.

"A prince on a horse may ride from harm," she
answered. "When princes walk, let other folk 'ware
trouble! He comes to have his will on me. Those
eunuchs are the leash that always hunt with him by

night. They will manhandle you, too, if they once get
in, and Gungadhura will take his chance of trouble
afterward. The guard dare not refuse him."

"What shall we do?" Tess wondered. "Can we
hide?" Then, pulling herself together for the sake of
her race and her Western womanhood: "If we make
noise enough at the gate my husband will come.
We're all right."

"If there are any gods at all," said Yasmini piously,
"they will consider our plight. I think this is a vengeance on me because I said I will leave my maids
behind. I will not leave them! Hasamurti—you and
the others make ready for the street!"

That was a simple matter. In three minutes all
five women were back in the room, veiled from head
to foot. But the hammering at the front door was
repeated, louder than before. Tess wondered whether
to hope that the risaldar of the guard had already
reported to Gungadhura the lady doctor's visit, or to
hope that he had not.

"We will all go down together now," Yasmini
decided, and promptly she started to lead the way
alone. But Hasamurti sprang to her side, and insisted
with tears on disguising herself as her mistress and
staying behind to provide one slim chance for the rest
to escape.

"In the dark you will pass for the memsahib," she
urged. "The memsahib will pass for a man. Wait by
the gate until the maharajah enters, while I stand at
the door under the lamp as a decoy. I will run into the
house, and he will follow with the eunuchs, while the
rest of you slip out through the gate, and run before

the guard can close it. Perhaps one, at least, of the
other maids had better stay with me."

A second maid volunteered, but Yasmini would
have none of that plan. First and last the great out-
standing difference between her and the ordinary run
of conspirators, Western or Eastern, was unwillingness
to sacrifice faithful friends even in a pinch—although
she could be ruthlessness itself toward half-hearted
ones. Both those habits grew on her as she grew older.

By the time they reached the little curtained outer
hall the maids were on the verge of hysteria. Tess had
herself well in control, and was praying busily that her
husband might only be near enough to hear the racket
at the gate. She was willing to be satisfied with that,
and to ask no further favors of Providence, unless that
Dick should have Tom Tripe with him. Outwardly
calm enough, she could not for the life of her remember to stride like a man. Yasmini turned more than
once to rally her about it.

Yasmini herself looked unaccountably meek in the
Western dress, but her blue eyes blazed with fury and
she walked with confidence, issuing her orders in a
level voice. The gateman had come to the door again
to announce that Gungadhura had issued a final warning. Two more minutes and the outer gate should be
burst in by his orders.

"Tell the maharajah sahib that I come in person to
welcome him!" she retorted, and the gateman hurried
back into the dark toward his post.

There were no lights at the outer gate. One could
only guess how the stage was set—the maharajah
hooded lest some enemy recognize him—the eunuchs

behind him with cords concealed under their loose
outer garments—and the guard at a respectful distance
standing at attention.   There was not a maharajah's
sepoy in Sialpore who would have dared remonstrate
with Gungadhura in dark or daylight.

Only as they passed under the yellow light shed by
the solitary lantern on the iron bracket did Tess get an
inkling of Yasmini's plan.   Light glinted on the
wrought hilt of a long Italian dagger, and her smile
was cold—uncompromising—shuddersome.

Tess objected instantly.   "Didn't you promise
you'd kill nobody?   If we'd a pistol we could fire it in
the air and my husband would come in a minute."

"How do we know that Gungadhura hasn't killed
your husband, or shut him up somewhere?" Yasmini
answered, and Tess had an attack of cold chills that
rendered her speechless for a moment.   She threw it
off with a prodigious effort.

"But I've no weapon of any kind, and you can't
kill Gungadhura, three eunuchs and the guard as
well!" she argued presently.

"Wait and see what I will do!" was the only
answer.   "Gungadhura caused my pistols to be stolen.
But the darkness is our friend, and I think the gods—
if there are any gods—are going to assist us."

They walked to the gate in a little close-packed
group, and found the gateman stuttering through the
small square hole provided for interviews with strangers, telling the maharajah for the third or fourth time
that the princess herself was coming.   Gungadhura's
voice was plainly audible, growling threats from the
outer darkness.

"Stand aside!" Yasmini ordered. "I will attend to the talking now."

She went close to the square hole, but was careful to keep her face in shadow at the left-hand side of it.

"What can His Highness, Gungadhura Singh, want with his relative at this strange hour?" she asked.

"Open the gate!" came the answer. He was very close to it—ready to push with his shoulder the instant the bolt was drawn, for black passion had him in hand. But in the darkness he was as invisible as she was.

"Nay, how shall I know it is Gungadhura Singh?"

"Ask the guard! Ho, there! Tell her who it is demands admission!"

"Nay, they might lie to me! The voice sounds strange. I would open for Gungadhura Singh; but I must be sure it is he and no other."

"Look then!" he answered, and thrust his dark face close to the opening.

Even the utterly base have intuition. Nothing else warned him. In the very nick of time he stepped back, and Yasmini's long dagger that shot forward like a stab of lightning only cut the cheek beneath the eye, and slit it to the corner of his mouth.

The blood poured down into his beard and added fury to determination.

"Guards, break in the gate!" he shouted, and Yasmini stood back in the darkest shadow, about as dangerous as a cobra guarding young ones. With her left hand she signed to all six women to hide themselves; but Tess came and stood beside her, minded in that minute to give Gungadhura Western aftermath to reckon with as well as the combined present courage

of two women. Wondering desperately what she
could do to help against armed men she suddenly
snatched one of the long hat-pins that she herself had
adjusted in her own hat on Yasmini's head.

Yasmini hugged her close and kissed her.

"Better than sister! Better than friend!" she
whispered.

Gungadhura had not been idle while he waited for
his message to reach Yasmini, but had sent some of the
guard to find a baulk of timber for a battering-ram.
The butts of rifles would have been useless against
that stout iron.

The gate shook now under the weight of the first
assault, but the guards were handling the timber clum-
sily, not using their strength together. Gungadhura
cursed them, and spent two valuable minutes trying to
show them how the trick should be worked, the blood
that poured into his beard, and made of his mouth a
sputtering crimson mess, not helping to make his
raging orders any more intelligible.

Presently the second crash came, stronger and
more elastic than the first. The iron bent inward, and
it was plainly only a matter of minutes before the bolt
would go. The gateman came creeping to Yasmini's
side, and, with yellow fangs showing in a grin meant
to be affectionate, displayed an Afghan tulwar.

"Ismail!" she said. "I thought you were afraid
and ran to hide!"

"Nay!" he answered. "My life is thine, Princess!
Gungadhura took away all weapons, but this I hid. I
went to find it. See," he grinned, feeling the edge

with his thumb, "it is clean! It is keen! It will cut throats!"

"I will not forget!" Yasmini answered, but the words were lost in the din of the third blow of wood on iron.

The odds began not to look so bad—two desperate women and a faithful Northern fighting man armed with a weapon that he loved and understood, against a wounded blackguard and three eunuchs. Perhaps the guard might look on and not interfere. There was a chance to make a battle royal of it, whose tumult would bring Dick Blaine and Tom Tripe to the rescue. What was the dog doing? Tess wondered whether any animal could be so intelligent after all as Tom pretended his was. Perhaps the maharajah had seen the dog and killed him.

"Listen!" she urged. "Tell your maids to stampede for the street the instant the door breaks in. That will give the guard their work to do to hold them. Meanwhile——"

"Thump!" came the timber on the gate again, and even the hinges shook in their stone setting.

"Listen!" said Yasmini.

There was another noise up-street—a rushing to and fro, and a trumpeting that no one could mistake.

"I said that ——"

"Thump!" came the baulk of timber—not so powerfully as before. There was distraction affecting the team-work. The scream of an elephant fighting mad, and the yelp of a dog, that pierces every other noise, rent the darkness close at hand.

"I said that the gods——"

There came the thud of a very heavy body collid-
ing with a wall, and another blood-curdling scream of
rage—then the thunder of what might have been an
avalanche as part of a near-by wall collapsed, and a
brute as big as Leviathan approached at top speed.

There was another thud, but this time caused by the
baulk of timber falling on the ground, as guard,
eunuchs and Gungadhura all took to their heels.

"*Allah! Il hamdul illah!*" swore the gateman.
(Thanks be to God!)

"I *said* that the gods would help to-night!" Yasmini
cried exultantly.

"O Lord, what has happened to Dick?" groaned
Tess between set teeth.

The thunder of pursuit drew nearer. Possessed by
some instinct she never offered to explain, Yasmini
stepped to the gate, drew back the bolt, and opened it
a matter of inches. In shot Tom Tripe's dog, with his
tongue hanging out and the fear of devils blazing in
his eyes. Yasmini slammed the gate again in the very
face of a raging elephant, and shot the bolt in the
nick of time to take the shock of his impact.

It was only a charge in half-earnest or he would
have brought the gate down. An elephant is a very
short-sighted beast, and it was pitch-dark. He could
not believe that a dog could disappear through a solid
iron gate, and after testing the obstruction for a
moment or two, grumbling to himself angrily, he stood
to smell the air and listen. There was a noise farther
along the street of a stampede of some kind. That was
likely enough his quarry, probably frightening other
undesirables along in front of him. With a scream of

mingled frenzy and delight he went off at once full pelt.

"Oh, Trotters! Good dog, Trotters!" sobbed Tess, kneeling down to make much of him, and giving way to the reaction that overcomes men as well as women. "Where's your master? Oh, if you could tell me where my huband is!"

She did not have long to wait for the answer to that. It took the two men a matter of seconds to get the horse on his feet, and no fire-engine ever left the station house one fraction faster than Dick tooled that dog-cart. The horse was all nerves and in no mood to wait on ceremony, which accounted for a broken spoke and a fragment of the gate-post hanging in the near wheel. They forgot to unlash the wheels before they started, so the dog-cart came up-street on skids, as it were, screaming holy murder on the granite flags— which in turn saved the near wheel from destruction. It also made it possible to rein in the terrified horse exactly in front of the palace gate; another proof that as Yasmini said, the gods of India were in a mood to help that night. (Not that she ever believed the gods are one bit more consequential than men.)

Yasmini drew the bolt, and the gate creaked open reluctantly; the shock of the elephant's shoulder had about ended its present stage of usefulness. Tom Tripe, dismounting from his horse in a hurry and throwing the reins over the dog-cart lamp, was first to step through.

"Where's my dog?" he demanded. "Where's that Trotters o' mine? Did Akbar get him?"

A cold nose thrust in his hand was the answer.

"Oh, so there you are, you rascal! There—lie down!"

That was all the ceremonial that passed between them, but the dog seemed satisfied.

Tess was out through the gate almost sooner than Tom Tripe could enter it. They brushed each other's shoulders as they passed. Up in the dog-cart she and her husband laughed in each other's arms, each at the other's disguise, neither of them with the slightest notion what would happen next, except that Dick knew the dog-cart wheels would have to be unlashed.

"How many people will the carriage hold?" Yasmini called to them, appearing suddenly in the lamplight. And Dick Blaine began laughing all over again, for except for the golden hair she looked so like the wife who sat on his left hand, and his wife so like a Rajput that the humor of the situation was its only obvious feature.

"I must not take my carriage, for they would trace it, and besides, there is too little time. Can we all ride in your carriage? There are six of us."

"Probably. But where to?" Dick answered.

"I will direct. Ismail must come too, but he can run."

It was an awful crowd, for the dog-cart was built for four people at the most, and in the end Tess insisted on riding behind Tom Tripe because she was dressed like a man and could do it easily. Ismail was sent back to close the gate from the inside and clamber out over the top of it. There was just room for a lean and agile man to squeeze between the iron and the stone arch.

"Let the watchmen who feared and hid themselves stay to give their own account to Gungadhura!" Yasmini sneered scornfully. "They are no longer men of mine!"

"Now, where away?" demanded Dick, giving the horse his head. "To my house? You'll be safe there for the present."

"No. They might trace us there."

Yasmini was up beside him, wedged tightly between him and Hasamurti, so like his own wife, except for a vague Eastern scent she used, that he could not for the life of him speak to her as a stranger.

"Listen!" she said excitedly. "I had horses here, there, everywhere in case of need. But Gungadhura sent men and took them all, Now I have only one horse—in your stable. I must get that to-night. First, then, drive my women to a place that I will show you."

Away in the distance they could hear the trumpeting of Akbar, and the shouts of men who had been turned out to attempt the hopeless task of capturing the brute. At each scream the horse trembled in the shafts and had to be managed skilfully, but the load was too heavy now for him to run away with it.

"If that elephant will continue to be our friend and will only run the other way for a distraction, so that we are not seen, one of these days I will give him a golden howdah!" vowed Yasmini.

And Akbar did that very thing. Whoever was awake that night in Sialpore, and was daring enough to venture in the dark streets, followed the line of destruction and excitement, gloating over the broken

property of enemies or awakening friends to make
them miserable with condolences. The dog-cart
threaded through the streets unseen, for even the
scarce night-watchmen left their posts to take part in
the hunt.

Yasmini guided them to the outskirts of the town
in a line as nearly straight as the congenital devious-
ness of Sialpore's ancient architects allowed. There
was not a street but turned a dozen times to the mile.
At one point she bade Dick stop, and begged Tess to
let Tom Tripe take her home, promising to see her
again within the hour. But Tess had recovered her
nerve and was determined to see the adventure
through, in spite of the discomforts of a seat behind
Tom's military saddle.

They brought up at last in front of a low dark
house at the very edge of the city. It stood by itself
in a compound, with fields behind it, and looked prosperous enough to belong to one of the maharajah's
suite.

"The house of Mukhum Dass!" Yasmini announced.

"The money-lender?"

"Yes."

Dick made a wry face, for the man's extortions
were notorious. But Yasmini never paused to cast up
virtue when she needed assistants in a hurry; rather
she was adept at appraising character and bending it
to suit her ends. Ismail, hot and out of breath from
running at the cart-tail, was sent to pound the money-
lender's door, until that frightened individual came
down himself to inquire (with the door well held by a
short chain) what the matter was.

"I lend no money in the night!" was his form of greeting. He always used it when gamblers came to him in the heat of the loser's passion at unearthly hours—and sometimes ended by making a loan at very high interest on sound security. Otherwise he would have stayed in bed, whatever the thunderous importunity.

Yasmini was down at the door by that time, and it was she who answered.

"Nay, but men win lawsuits by gathering evidence! Are title-deeds not legal in the dark?"

"Who are you?" he demanded, reaching backward for a little lamp that hung on the wall behind him and trying to see her face.

"I am the same who met you that morning on the hilltop and purchased silence from you at a price."

He peered through the narrow opening, holding the lamp above his head.

"That was a man. You are a woman."

For answer to that she stood on tiptoe and blew the lamp out. He would have slammed the door, but her foot was in the way.

"By dark or daylight, Mukhum Dass, your eyes read nothing but the names on *hundis* (notes)! Now, what does the ear say? Does the voice tell nothing?"

"Aye, it is the same."

"You shall have that title-deed to-morrow at dawn —on certain terms."

"How do I know?"

"Because I say it—I, who said that Chamu would repay his son's loan,—I, who knew from the first all about the title-deed,—I, who know where it is this

minute,—I, who know the secrets of Jinendra's priest,
—I, whose name stands written on the hundred-rupee
note with which the butler paid his son's debt!"

"The princess! The Princess Yasmini! It was her
name on the note!"

"Her name is mine!"

The money-lender stood irresolutely, shifting his
balance from foot to foot. It was his experience that
when people with high-born names came to him by
night mysteriously there was always profit in it for
himself. And then, there was that title-deed. He had
bought the house cheap, but its present value was five
times what he gave for it. Its loss would mean more
to him than the loss of a wife to some men—as Yasmini knew, and counted on.

"Open the door and let me in, Mukhum Dass! The
terms are these——"

"Nay, we can talk with the door between us."

"Very well, then, lose thy title-deed! Dhulap
Singh, thine enemy, shall have it within the hour!"

She took her foot out from the door and turned
away briskly. Promptly he opened the door wide, and
called after her.

"Nay, come, we will discuss it."

"I discuss nothing!" she answered with a laugh.
"I dictate terms!"

"Name them, then."

"I have here five women. They must stay in
safety in your house until an hour before dawn."

"God forbid!"

"Until an hour before dawn, you hear me? If any

come to inquire for them or me, you must deny all
knowledge."

"That I would be sure enough to do! Shall I have
it said that Mukhum Dass keeps a dozen women in his
dotage?"

"An hour before dawn I will come for them."

"None too soon!"

"Then I will write a letter to a certain man, who, on
presentation of the letter, will hand you the title-deed
at once without payment."

"A likely tale!"

"Was it a likely tale that Chamu would repay his
son's debt?"

"Well—I will take the hazard. Bring them in.
But I will not feed them. And if you fail to come for
them before dawn I will turn them out and it shall be
all over Sialpore that the Princess Yasmini——"

"One moment, Mukhum Dass! If one word of
this escapes your lips for a month to come, you shall go
to jail for receiving stolen money in payment of a debt!
My name was on the money that Chamu paid you with.
You knew he stole it!"

"I did not know!"

"Prove that in court, then!"

"Bring the women in!" he grumbled. "I am no
cackler from the roofs!"

Yasmini did not wait for him to change his mind
but shepherded her scared dependents through the
door, and called for Ismail.

"Did you see these women enter?" she demanded.

"Aye. I saw. Have I not eyes?"

"Stay thou here outside and watch. Afterward,

remember, if I say nothing, be thou dumb as Tom
Tripe's dog. But if I give the word, tell all Sialpore
that Mukhum Dass is a satyr who holds revels in his
house by night. Bring ten other men to swear to it
with thee, until the very children of the streets shout
it after him when he rides his rounds! Hast thou
understood? Silence for silence! But talk for talk!
Hast thou heard, too, Mukhum Dass? Good! Shut
thy door tight, but thy mouth yet tighter! And try
rather to take liberties with hornets than with those
five women!"

Before he could answer she was gone, leaving
Ismail lurking in the shadows. Tess had dismounted
from behind Tom Tripe and climbed up beside her
husband so that there were three on the front seat
again.

"Now, Tom Tripe!" Yasmini ordered, speaking
with the voice of command that Tom himself would
have used to a subordinate. "Do you as the elephant
did, and cause distraction. Draw Gungadhura off the
scent!"

"Hell's bells, deary me, Your Ladyship!" he
answered. "All the drawing I'll do after this night's
work will be my last month's pay, and lucky if I see
that! Lordy knows what the guard'll tell the maharajah, nor what his rage'll add to it!"

"Nonsense! Gungadhura and the guard ran from
the elephant like dust before the wind. The guards
are the better men, and will be back at their post before
this; but Gungadhura must find a discreet physician
to bind a slit face for him! Visit the guard now, and
get their ear first. Tell them Gungadhura wants no

talk about to-night's work. Then come to Blaine sahib's house and search the cellar by lamplight, letting Chamu the butler see you do it, but taking care not to let him see what you see. What you do see, leave where it lies! Then see Gungadhura early in the morning——"

"Lordy me, Your Ladyship, he'll——"

"No, he won't. He'll want to know how much you know about his behavior at the gate. Tell him you know everything, and that you've compelled the guard to keep silence. That ought to reconcile the coward! But if he threatens you, then threaten him! Threaten to go to Samson sahib with the whole story. (But if you do dare really go to Samson sahib, never look me in the face again!) Then tell Gungadhura that you searched the cellar, and what you saw there under a stone, adding that Blaine sahib was suspicious, and watched you, and afterward sealed the cellar door. Have you understood me?"

"I understand there's precious little sleep for me to-night, and hell in the morning!"

"Pouf! Are you a soldier?"

"I'm your ladyship's most thorough-paced admirer and obedient slave!" Tom answered gallantly, his mutton-chop whiskers fairly bristling with a grin.

"Prove it, then, this night!"

"As if I hadn't! Well—all's well, Your Ladyship, I'm on the job! Crib, crupper and breakfast-time, yours truly!"

"When you have finished interviewing Gungadhura, find for Blaine sahib a new cook and a new butler, who can be trusted not to poison him!"

"If I can!"

"Of course you can find them! Tell Sita Ram, Samson sahib's babu, what is wanted. He will find men in one hour who have too much honor, and too little brains, and too great fear to poison any one! Say that I require it of him. Have your understood? Then go! Go swiftly to the guard and stop their tongues!"

Tom whistled his dog and rode off at a canter. Dick gave the horse his head and drove home as fast as the steepness of the hill permitted, Yasmini talking to him nearly all the way.

"You must dismiss Chamu," she insisted. "He is Gungadhura's man, and the cook is under the heel of Chamu. Either man would poison his own mother for a day's pay! Send them both about their business the first thing in the morning if you value your life! Before they go, let them see you put a great lock on the cellar door, and nail it as well, and put weights on it! If men come at any time to pry about the house, ask Samson sahib for a special policeman to guard the place!"

"But what is all this leading to?" demanded Dick. "What does it mean?"

"It means," she said slowly, "that the toils are closing in on Gungadhura!"

"The way I figure it," he answered, "some one else had a pretty narrow shave to-night!"

Yasmini knew better than to threaten Dick, or even to argue with him vehemently, much less give him orders. But each man has a line of least resistance.

"Your wife has told you what Gungadhura attempted?" she asked him.

"Yes, while you were at the money-lender's—something of it."

"If the guard should tell Gungadhura that your wife was in the palace with me and could give evidence against him, what do you suppose Gungadhura would do?"

"Damn him!" Dick murmured.

"There are so many ways—snakes—poison—daggers in the dark——"

"What do you suggest?" he asked her. "Leave Sialpore?"

"Yes, but with me! I know a safe place. She should come with me."

"When?"

"To-night! Before dawn."

"How?"

"By camel. I had horses and Gungadhura took them all, but his brain was too sotted to think of camels, and I have camels waiting not many miles from here! I shall take my horse from your stable and ride for the camels, bringing them to the house of Mukhum Dass. Let your wife meet me there one hour before dawn."

"Dick!" said Tess, with her arm around him. "I want to go! I know it sounds crazy, and absurd, and desperate; but I'm sure it isn't! I want you to let me go with her."

They reached the house before he answered, he, turning it over and over in his mind, taking into reckoning a thousand things.

"Well," he said at last, "once in a while there's the strength of a man about you, Tess. Maybe I'm a lunatic, but have it your own way, girl, have it your own way!"

In odor of sweet sanctity I bloom,
With surplus of beatitude I bless,
I'm the confidant of Destiny and Doom,
I'm the apogee of knowledge more or less.
If I lie, it is to temporize with lying
Lest obliquity should suffer in the light.
If I prey upon the widow and the dying,
They withheld; and I compel them to do right.
I am justified in all that I endeavor,
If I fail it is because the rest are fools.
I'm serene and unimpeachable forever,
The upheld, ordained interpreter of rules.

CHAPTER TEN

"Discretion is better part of secrecy!"

SOME of what follows presently was told to Yasmini afterward by Sita Ram, some of it by Tom Tripe, and a little by Dick Blaine, who had it from Samson himself. The rest she pieced together from admissions by Jinendra's fat priest and the gossip of some dancing girls.

Sir Roland Samson, K. C. S. I., as told already, was a very demon for swift office work, routine pouring off him into the hands of the right subordinates like water into the runnels of a roof, leaving him free to bask in the sunshine of self-complacency. But there is work that can not be tackled, or even touched by subordinates; and, the fixed belief of envious inferiors to the contrary notwithstanding, there are hours unpaid for, unincluded in the office schedule, and wholly unadvertised that hold such people as commissioners in durance vile.

On the night of Yasmini's escape Samson sat sweating in his private room, with moths of a hundred species irritating him by noisy self-immolation against the oil lamp—whose smoke made matters worse by being sucked up at odd moments by the punkah, pulled jerkily by a new man. Most aggravating circumstance of all, perhaps, was that the movement of the punkah flickered his papers away whenever he removed a weight. Yet he could not study them unless he spread them all in front of him; and without the punkah he felt he would die of apoplexy. He had to reach a decision before midnight.

Babu Sita Ram was supposed to be sitting under a punkah in the next room, with a locked door between him and his master. He was staying late, by special request and as a special favor, to copy certain very important but not too secret documents in time for the courier next day. There were just as many insects to annoy him, and the punkah flapped his papers too; but fat though he was, and sweat though he did, his smile was the smile of a hunter. From time to time he paused from copying, stole silently to the door between the offices, gingerly removed a loose knot from a panel, and clapped to the hole first one, and then the other avidious brown eye.

Samson wished to goodness there was some one he dared consult with. There were other Englishmen, of course, but they were all ambitious like himself. He felt that his prospects were at stake. News had reached the State Department (by channels Sita Ram could have uncovered for him) that Gungadhura was intriguing with tribes beyond the northwest frontier.

The tribes were too far away to come in actual touch with Sialpore, although they were probably too wild and childish to appreciate that fact. The point was that Gungadhura was said to be promising them armed assistance from the British rear—assistance that he never would possibly be able to render them; and his almost certain intention was, when the rising should materialize, to offer his small forces to the British as an inexpensive means of quelling the disturbance, thus restoring his own lost credit and double-crossing all concerned. A subtle motive, subtly suspected.

It was no new thing in the annals of Indian state affairs, nor anything to get afraid about; but what the State Department desired to know was, why Sir Roland Samson, K. C. S. I., was not keeping a closer eye on Gungadhura, what did he propose as the least troublesome and quietest solution, and would he kindly answer by return.

All that was bad enough, because a "beau ideal commissioner" rather naturally feels distressed when information of that sort goes over his head or under his feet to official superiors. But he could have got around it. It should not have been very difficult to write a report that would clear himself and give him time to turn around.

But that very evening no less an individual than the high priest of Jinendra had sent word by Sita Ram that he craved the favor of an interview.

"And," had added Sita Ram with malicious delight, "it is about the treasure of Sialpore and certain claims to it that I think he wants to see you."

"Why should he come by night?" demanded Samson.

"Because his errand is a secret one," announced the babu, with a hand on his stomach as if he had swallowed something exquisite.

So Samson was in a quandary, going over secret records getting ready for an issue with the priest. His report had to be ready by morning, yet he hardly dared begin it without knowing what the priest might have in mind; and on his own intricate knowledge of the situation might depend whether or not he could extract, from a man more subtle than himself, information on which to base sound proposals to his government. His reputation was decidedly at stake; and dangerous intrigue was in the air, or else the priest would never be coming to visit him.

Sita Ram kept peeping at him through the knot-hole, as a cook peers at a tit-bit in the oven, to judge whether it is properly cooked yet.

Jinendra's priest had had time for reflection. True to his kidney, he trusted nobody, unlike Yasmini who knew whom to trust, and when, and just how far. It was all over the city that Gungadhura's practises were hastening his ruin, so it was obviously wise not to espouse the maharajah's cause, in addition to which he had become convinced in his own mind that Yasmini actually knew the whereabouts of the Sialpore treasure. But he did not trust Yasmini either, nor did he relish her scornful promise of a mere percentage of the hoard when it should at last be found. He wanted at least the half of it, bargains to the contrary notwithstanding; and he had that comfortable conscience that has soothed so many priests, that argues how the church must be above all bargains, all bonds, all promises. Was there any circumstance, or man, or woman who could bind and circumscribe Jinendra's high priest? He laughed at the suggestion of it.

Samson was the man to see—Samson the man to be
inveigled in the nets. So he sent his verbal message
by the mouth of Sita Ram—a very pious devotee of
Jinendra by Yasmini's special orders; and, disguising
his enormous bulk in a thin cloak, set forth long after
dark in a covered cart drawn by two tiny bulls.

There were two doors to Sita Ram's small office;
two to Samson's large one—three doors in all, because
they shared the connecting one (that was locked just
now) in common. At the first sound of the long-
awaited heavy footsteps on the outer porch Sita Ram
hurried to do the honors, and presently ushered into
Samson's presence the enormous bulk of the high
priest, spreading a clean cloth for him on an easy chair
because the priest's caste put it out of the question for
him to sit on leather defiled by European trousers.

Then, while the customary salaams were taking
place, and the customary questions about health and
other matters that neither cared a fig about, Sita Ram
ostentatiously drew a curtain part-way over the connecting door, and retired by way of the other door and
the passage to remove the knot from its hole.

It was part of Samson's pride, and one of his stout-
est rungs in the ladder of preferment, that he knew
more Indian languages than any other man of his rank
in the service, and knew them well. There were aster-
isks and stars and twiggly marks against his name in
the blue book that would have passed muster as a
secret code, and every one of them betokened passed
examinations in some Eastern tongue. So he was
fully able to meet the high priest on his own ground,
as well as conscious of the advantage he held to begin

with, in that the priest had come to him instead of his
going to the priest.

"Well?" he demanded, cutting the pleasantries
short abruptly as soon as Sita Ram had closed the door.

"I came to speak of politics."

"I listen."

Samson leaned back and scrutinized his visitor with
deliberate rudeness. Having the upper hand he proposed to hold it.

But Jinendra's high priest was no beginner either
in the game of Beggar-my-neighbor. He understood
the value of a big trump to begin with, provided there
is other ammunition in reserve.

"The whereabouts of the treasure of Sialpore is
known!"

"The deuce it is!" said Samson, in good plain English. "Who knows it?" he demanded.

The high priest smiled.

Samson, as was natural, felt that tingling up and
down the spine and quickening of the heart-beats that
announces crisis in one's personal affairs, but concealed
it admirably. It was the high priest's turn to speak.
He waited.

"Half of that treasure belongs to the priesthood of
Jinendra," said the priest at last.

"Since when?"

"Since the beginning."

"Why?"

"We were keepers of the treasure once years ago,
before the English came. There came a time when the
reigning rajah deceived us by a trick, including murder; and ever since the English took control the priests

have had less and less authority. There has been no
chance to—to bring any—to put pressure—to reestab-
lish our rights. Nevertheless, our rights in the matter
were never surrendered."

"What do you mean by that exactly?"

"The English are now the real rulers of Sialpore."

Samson nodded. That was a significant admission,
coming from a Brahman priest.

"They should claim the treasure. But they can not
claim it without knowing where it is. The priests of
Jinendra are entitled to their half."

"You mean you are willing that my government
should take half the treasure, provided the priests of
Jinendra get the other half of it?"

The priest moved his head and his lips in a way that
might be taken to mean anything.

"If you know where the treasure is, dig it up,"
said Samson, "and you shall have your answer!"

Yasmini in the heat of excitement had called Samson an idiot, but he was far from being that, as she
knew as well as any one. He judged in that moment
that if Jinendra's priest knew really where the treasure was, he would never have come to drive a bargain
for the half of it, but would have taken all and said
nothing. On the other hand, it well might be that
Gungadhura's searchers had stumbled on it. In that
case, there was that secret letter from headquarters
hurriedly placed in his top drawer when the priest
came in, that would give good excuse for putting
screws on Gungadhura. A coup d'etat was not beyond
the pale of possibility. As a champion of indiscretion
and a judge of circumstances, he would dare. The

gleam in his eyes betrayed that he would dare, and the priest grew uneasy.

"It is not I who know where the treasure is. I know who knows."

"You mean Gungadhura knows!"

The priest smiled again. The commissioner was not such a dangerous antagonist after all. Samson's eyes betrayed disappointment, and the priest took heart of grace.

"For one-half of the treasure I will tell you who it is that knows. You can take possession of the person. Then——"

"Illegal. By what right could I arrest a person simply because some one else asserts without proof that that person knows where the treasure is?"

"Not arrest, perhaps. But you might protect."

"From whom? From what?"

"Gungadhura suspects. He might use poison—torture—might carry the person off into hiding——"

He paused, for Samson's eyes were again a signal of excitement. He had it! He knew as much as the priest himself did in that instant! There was one particular individual in Sialpore who fitted that bill.

"Nonsense!" he answered. "Gungadhura would be answerable to me for any outrages."

The priest showed a slight trace of dejection, but went forward bravely to defeat.

"There is danger," he said. "If Gungadhura should lay hands on all that money, there would be no peace in Rajputana. I should not bargain away what belongs to the priesthood, but discretion is permitted me; if you will agree with me to-night, I will accept a little less than half of it."

Samson wanted time to think, and he was through with the priest—finished with the interview,—not even anxious to appear polite.

"If you bring me definite information," he said slowly, "and on the strength of that my government should come in possession of the Sialpore treasure, I will promise you in writing five per cent. of it for the funds of the priesthood of Jinendra, the money to be held in trust and administered subject to accounting."

Jinendra's high priest hove his bulk out of the leather chair and went through the form of taking leave, contenting himself, too, with the veriest shell of courtesy—scorn for such an offer scowling from his fat face. Samson showed him to the door and closed it after him, leaving Babu Sita Ram to do the honors outside in the passage.

"I kiss feet!" said the babu. "You must bless me, father. I kiss feet!"

The priest blessed him perfunctorily.

"Is there anything I can do, holy one? Anything a babu such as I can do to earn merit?"

Rolling on his ponderous way toward the waiting bull-cart, the priest paused a moment—eyed Sita Ram as a python eyes a meal—and answered him.

"Tell that woman from me that if she has a plan at all she must unfold it swiftly. Tell her that this Samson sahib is after the treasure for himself; that he invited me to help him and to share it with him. Let her have word with me swiftly."

"What treasure?" asked Sita Ram ingenuously. Having had his ear to the knot-hole throughout the interview, it suited him to establish innocence. The priest could have struck himself for the mistake, and Sita Ram, too, for the impudence.

"Never mind!" he answered. "Tell her what I say. Those who obey and ask no unwise questions oftentimes receive rewards."

Inside the office Samson sat elated, wiping his forehead and setting blotter over writing-paper lest sweat from his wrists make the ink run. It was a bender of a night, but he saw his way to a brilliant stroke of statecraft that would land him on the heights of official approval forever. Heat did not matter. The man at the punkah had fallen asleep, but he did not bother to waken him. Back at the knot-hole, babu Sita Ram watched him scribble half a dozen letters, tearing each up in turn until the last one pleased him. Finally he sealed a letter, and directed it by simply writing two small letters—r. s.—in the bottom left-hand corner.

"Sita Ram!" he shouted then.

The babu let him call three times, for evidence of how hard it was to hear through that thick door. When he came it was round by the other way in a hurry.

"You called, sir?"

"You need not copy any more of those documents to-night, Sita Ram. I shall send a telegram in the morning and keep my report in hand for a day or two. But there's one more little favor I would like to ask of you."

"Anything, sahib! Anything! Am only desirous to please your excellency."

"Do you know a man named Tripe—Tom Tripe—drill-instructor to the Maharajah's Guard?"

"Yes, sahib."

"Could you find him, do you think?"

"To-night, sahib?"

"Yes, to-night."

"Sahib, he is usually drunk at night, and very rough! Nevertheless, I could find him."

"Please do. And give him this letter. Say it is from me. He will know what to do with it. Oh, and Sita Ram——"

"Yes, sahib."

"You will receive two days' extra pay from me, over and above your salary, for to-night's extra work."

"Thank you, sahib. You are most kind—always most generous."

"And—ah—Sita Ram——"

"Sahib?"

"Say nothing, will you? By nothing I mean nothing! Hold your tongue, eh?"

"Certainly, sahib. Aware of the honor of my confidential position, I am always most discreet!"

"What are you doing with that waste-basket?"

"Taking it outside, sahib."

"The sweeper will do that in the morning."

"Am always discreet, sahib. Discretion is better part of secrecy! Better to burn all torn-up paper before daylight always!"

"Very good. You're quite right. Thank you, Sita Ram. Yes, burn the torn paper, please."

So Sita Ram, piecing together little bits of paper got a very good idea of what was in the letter that he carried. The bonfire in the road looked beautiful and gladdened his esthetic soul, but the secret information thrilled him, which was better. He crossed the river, and very late that night he found Tom Tripe, as sober as a judge, what with riding back and forth to the Blaines' house and searching in a cellar and what-not. He gave him the letter, and received a rupee because Tom's dog frightened him nearly out of his wits. Tom swore at the letter fervently, but that was Tom's affair, who could not guess the contents.

Almost exactly at dawn Sita Ram, as sleepy as a homing owl, reached his own small quarters in the densest part of town. He had his hand on the door when another hand restrained him from behind.

"You know me?" said a voice he did not know. A moment later his terrified eyes informed him.

"Mukhum Dass? I owe you nothing!"

"Liar! You have my title-deed! Hand it over before I bring the constabeel!"

"I? Your title-deed? I know nothing of it. What title-deed?"

Mukhum Dass cut expostulation short, and denied himself the pleasure of further threatening.

"See. Here is a letter. Read it, and then hand me over my title-deed!"

"Ah! That is different!" said Sita Ram, pocketing Yasmini's letter, for precaution's sake. "Wait here while I bring it!"

Two minutes later he returned with a parchment in a tin tube.

"Do I receive no recompense?" he asked. "Did I not find the title-deed and keep it safe? Where is the reward?"

"Recompense?" growled Mukhum Dass. "To be out of jail is recompense! The next time you find property of mine, bring it to me, or the constabeel shall have work to do!"

"Dog!" snarled the babu after him. "Dog of a usurer! Wait and see!"

*To cover a trail is less than half the work, for any dog with a nose can smell it out. You should make a false trail afterward to deceive the clever folk.—*EASTERN PROVERB.

CHAPTER ELEVEN

"Say: that little girl you're wanting to run off with is
my wife!"

THE other side to the intrigue developed furiously
up at the Blaines' house on the hillside. Yasmini gave
directions from Tess's bedroom, where Tess hid her
from prying servants, she electing to change clothes
once more—this time into her hostess' riding breeches,
boots and helmet. But she insisted on Tess retaining
the Rajput costume, only allowing a hand-bag to be
packed with woman's things, skirt, blouse and so on.

"If I am seen there must be no mistake about me.
They must swear that I am you! It doesn't matter
who they believe that you are. Above all, Chamu the
butler must not see me. When he is dismissed in the
morning he will tell tales for very spite, and take his
chance of my accusing him of theft; so be sure that he
sees Tom Tripe search the cellar. Then he will confirm to the maharajah afterward that Tripe did search
—and did see something—and that Blaine sahib did
lock the cellar door afterward in anger, and put
weights on it. That is the important thing. Blaine
sahib must drive the carriage again to the house of
Mukhum Dass; and be sure that I am not kept waiting
there—we must start before the dawn breaks! Now

183

give me paper and a pen to write the *chit* (letter) for Mukhum Dass."

There was no ink in the bedroom; Dick took her into the place he called his study, and locked the door, glad of the excuse. He was minded to know more of the intrigue before letting his wife go off again that night on any wild adventure, second thoughts having stirred his caution. He began by offering to lend her money, suspecting that a fugitive princess would need that more than anything. But she replied by drawing out from her bosom a packet containing thousands of rupees in Bank of India notes, and gave him money instead—not much, but she forced it on him.

"For the three beggars. Ten rupees each. Pay it them in silver in the morning. They have been very useful often, and may be so again."

He watched her write the letter and seal the envelope. Then:

"Say," he said, "don't you think you'd be doing right by telling me more of this? I'll say nothing to a soul, but that little girl you're wanting to run off with is my wife, and I'll admit I'm kind o' concerned on her account."

Yasmini met his iron-gray eyes, judged him and found him good.

"I never trusted man yet, not even the husband I shall marry, with all I shall tell you," she answered. "Will you give me silence in return for it?"

"Mum as the grave," he answered. And Dick Blaine kept his word, not even hinting to Tess on the long drive afterward that there had been as much as a question asked or confidence exchanged. And Tess respected the silence, not deceived for a minute by it. He and Yasmini had been longer in that room together than any one-page letter needed, and she was sure there was only one subject they discussed.

Dick brought Yasmini's horse to the gate, not to the door, and she mounted outside in the road for additional precaution. Instantly, then, without a word of farewell she was off like the wind down-hill.

"It'll be all over town to-morrow that I'm dead or dying, if anybody sees her!" Dick told his wife. "They'll swear that was you, Tess, riding full pelt for the doctor!"

Soon after that Tom Tripe came, and made Chamu hold a light for him while he searched the cellar.

"Hold the candle and your tongue too, confound you!" he told the grumbling butler, indignant at being brought from bed.

Dick had already put the silver tube in place. Tom Tripe raised the stone and saw it—uttered a tremendous oath—and dropped the heavy stone back over the hole.

"What are you doing?" Dick demanded from the ladder-head, appearing with a lantern from behind the raised trap.

"Looking for rum!" Tom answered. Then he turned on Chamu. "Did you see what I saw? Speak a word of it, you devil, and I'll tear your throat out! Silence, d'you understand?"

"Come out of there!" Dick ordered angrily. "I'll have to lock this cellar door! I can't have people prospecting down there! I've got reasons of my own for keeping that cellar undisturbed! I'm surprised at you, Tom Tripe, taking advantage of me when my back's turned!"

The minute they were up he put a padlock on the trap, and nailed it down to the beams as well. Then, summoning Tom's aid, he levered and shoved into place on top of it the heavy iron safe in which he kept his specimens and money.

"That'll do for you, Chamu!" he said finally. "I don't care to keep a butler who takes guests into the cellar at this hour of night! You may go. I'll give you your time in the morning."

Chamu showed his teeth, by no means for the first time. It was a favorite method of his for covering up bad service to fall back on his reference.

"Maharajah sahib who is recommending me will not be pleased at my dismissal!"

"You and your maharajah go to hell together!" Dick retorted. "Tell him from me that I won't have inquisitive people in my cellar! Now go; there's nothing more to talk about. Fire the cook, too, as soon as he wakes! Tell him I don't like ground glass in my omelette! Not been any in it? Well, what do I care? I don't want any in it—that's enough! I'm taking no chances. Tell him he's fired, and you two pull your freight together in the morning first thing!"

Ten minutes alone with Yasmini had worked won- ders with Dick Blaine. Given to making up his mind and seeing resolution through to stern conclusions, he was her stout ally from the moment when he unlocked the study door again until the end—a good silent ally too busy, apparently, about his own affairs to be sus- pected. Certainly Samson never suspected his real

share in the intrigue—Samson, the judge of circumstances, indiscretions, men and opportunity.

He sent Tom Tripe packing, with a flea in his ear
for Chamu's benefit, and a whispered word of friendship. Later he drove Tess down-hill in the dog-cart,
first changing his own disguise for American clothes
because the *saises* might be up and about when he
returned at dawn, and for them to see him in the costume of a *sais* would only have added to the risk of
putting Gungadhura's men on the scent of Yasmini.
Saises are almost the most prolific source of rumor,
but he had a means of stilling their tongues.

There was little to say during the dark drive.
They were affectionate, those two, without too many
words when it came to leave-taking, each knowing
the other's undivided love. Tess had money—a
revolver—cartridges—some food—sufficient change
of clothing for a week—sun-spectacles; he reassured
himself twice on all those points.

"If you're camel-sick, fetch it up and carry on," he
advised, "it'll soon pass. Then a hot bath, if you can
get it, before you stiffen. Failing that, oil."

The camels, with Yasmini and her women already
mounted, were kneeling in the darkness outside the
house of Mukhum Dass.

"Come!" called Yasmini. "Hurry!"

Dick kissed his wife—waved his hand to Yasmini
—helped Tess on to the last camel in the kneeling
line—and they were off, the camel-men not needing
to shout to make those Bikaniri racers rise and start.
They were gone like ghosts into the darkness, making

absolutely no noise, before Dick could steady his nervous horse.

Then Ismail wanted to tie Yasmini's abandoned horse to the tail of the dog-cart, but Dick sent him off to stable it somewhere at the other side of town to help throw trackers off the scent. He himself drove home by a very wide circuit indeed, threading his cautious way among the hills toward the gold-diggings, where he drove back and forward several times around the edges of the dump, in order that the *saises* might see the red dirt on the wheels afterward and believe, and tell where he had been.

There was some risk that a panther, or even a tiger might try for the horse in the dark, but that was not the kind of danger that disturbed Dick Blaine much. A pistol at point-blank range is as good as a rifle most nights of the week. He arrived home after daylight with a very weary horse, and ordered the *saises* to wash the wheels at once, in order that the color of the dirt might be impressed on them thoroughly. They were quite sure he had been at the mine all night. Then he paid off Chamu and the cook and sent them packing.

He was looking for the beggars, to pay them, when Tom Tripe's dog arrived and began hunting high and low for Tess. Trotters had something in his mouth, wrapped in cloth and then again in leather. He refused to give it to Dick, defying threats and persuasion both. Dick offered him food, but the dog had apparently eaten—water, but he would not drink.

Then the three beggars came, and watched Dick's efforts with the interest of spectators at a play.

"Messenger!" said Bimbu finally, nodding at the dog. That much was pretty obvious.

"Princess!" he added, seeing Dick was still puzzled.

It flashed across Dick's mind that on the dresser in the bedroom was Tess's hat that Yasmini had worn. Doubtless to a dog's keen nose it smelt of both of them. He ran to fetch it, the dog followed him, eager to get into the house. He offered the hat to the dog, who sniffed it and yelped eagerly.

"Bang goes fifty dollars, then!" he laughed.

He took the hat to Bimbu.

"Can you ride a camel?" he demanded.

The man nodded. "Another would drive it"

"Do you know where to get one?"

Bimbu nodded again.

"Take this hat, so that the dog will follow you, and ride by camel to the home of Utirupa Singh. Here is money for the camel. If you overtake the princess there will be a fabulous reward. If you get there soon after she does there will be a good reward. If you take too long on the way there will be nothing for you but a beating! Go—hurry—get a move on! And don't you lose the dog!"

There are they who yet remember, when the depot's
    forty jaws
Through iron teeth that chatter to the tramping of a
    throng
Spew out the crushed commuter in obedience to laws
That all accord observance and that all agree are
    wrong;
When rush and din and hubbub stir the too responsive
    vein
Till head and heart are conquered by the hustle
    roaring by
And the sign looks good that glitters on the temple
    gate of Gain,—
"There are spaces just as luring where the leagues
    untrodden lie!"

There are they who yet remember 'mid the fever of
    exchange,
When the hot excitement throttles and the millions
    make or break,
How a camel's silent footfall on the ashen desert range
Swings cushioned into distances where thoughts unfet-
    tered wake,
And the memory unbidden plucks an unconverted heart
Till the glamour goes from houses and emotion from
    the street,
And the truth glares good and gainly in the face of
    'change and mart:
"There are deserts more intensive. There are silences
    as sweet!"

CHAPTER TWELVE

"Ready for anything! If I weaken, tie me on the camel!"

THERE are camels and camels—more kinds than there are of horses. The Bishareen of the Sudan is not a bad beast, but compared to the Bikaniri there are no other desert mounts worth a moment's consideration. Fleet as the wind, silent as its own shadow, enduring as the long hot-season of its home, the trained Bikaniri swings into sandy distances with a gait that is a gallop really—the only saddle-beast of all that lifts his four feet from the ground at once, seeming to spurn the very laws of gravity.

They are favored folk who come by first-class Bikaniri camels, for the better sort are rare, hard held to, and only to be bought up patiently by twos and ones. Fourteen of them in one string, each fit that instant for a distance-race with death itself, was perhaps the best proof possible of Yasmini's influence on the country-side. They were gathered for her and held in readiness by men who loved her and detested Gungadhura.

Normally the drivers would have taken a passenger apiece, and seven of the animals would have been ample; but this was a night and a dawn when speed

was nine-tenths of the problem, and Yasmini had
spared nothing—no man, no shred of pains or influence,—and proposed to spare no beast.

They rode in single file, each man with a led camel
ridden by a woman, except that Yasmini directed her
own mount and for the most part showed the way, her
desert-reared guide being hard put to keep his own
animal abreast of her. There is a gift—a trick of riding camels, very seldom learned by the city-born; and
he, or she, who knows the way of it enjoys the
ungrudged esteem of desert men all the way from
China to Damascus, from Peshawar to Morocco. The
camels detect a skilled hand even more swiftly than a
horse does and, like the horse, do their best work for
the rider who understands. So the only sound, except
for a gurgle now and then, and velvet-silent footfalls
on the level sand, was the grunts of admiration of the
men behind. They had muffled all the camel-bells.

When they started the night was deepest purple,
set densely with a mass of colored jewels; even the
whitest of the stars stole color from the rest. But
gradually, as they raced toward the sky-line and the
stars paled, the sky changed into mauve. Then without warning a belt of pale gold shone in the west
behind them, and with the false dawn came the cool
wind like a legacy from the kindly night-gods to
encourage humans to endure the day. A little later
than the wind the true dawn came, fiery with hot
promise, and Tess on the last camel soon learned the
meaning of the cloak Yasmini had made her wear.
Worn properly it covers all the face except the eyes,

leaving no surface for the hot wind to torture, and saving the lips and lungs from being scorched.

In after years, when Yasmini was intriguing for an empire that in her imagination should control the world, she had the telegraph and telephone at times to aid her, as well as the organized, intricate system of British Government to manipulate from behind the scenes; but now she was racing against the wires, and in no mood to appeal for help to a government that she did not quite understand as yet, but intended to fool royally in any case.

The easiest thing Gungadhura could do, and the surest thing he would attempt once word should reach him that she had vanished from Sialpore would be to draw around her a network of his own men. Watchers from the hills and lurkers in the sand-dunes could pass word along of the direction she had taken; and the sequel, if Gungadhura was only quick enough, would depend simply on the loneliness or otherwise of the spot where she could be brought to bay. If there were no witnesses his problem would be simple. But if murder seemed too dangerous, there was the Nesting-place of Seven Swans up in the mountains, as well as other places even lonelier, to which she and Tess could be abducted. Tess might be left, perhaps, to make her own way back and give her own explanation of flight with a maharajah's daughter; but for Yasmini abduction to the hills could only mean one of two things: unthinkable surrender, or sure death by any of a hundred secret means.

So the way they took was wild and lonely, frequented only by the little jackals that eat they alone know what, and watched by unenthusiastic kites that always seemed to be wheeling in air just one last time before flying to more profitable feeding ground. Yet within a thousand paces of the line they took lay a trodden track, well marked by the sun-dried bones of camels (for the camel dies whenever he feels like it, without explanation or regret, and lies down for the purpose in the first uncomfortable place to hand).

Yasmini and the guide between them, first one, then the other assuming the direction, led the way around low hills and behind the long, blown folds of sand netted scantly down by tufted, dry grass, always avoiding open spaces where they might be seen, or hollows too nearly shut in on both sides, where there might be ambush.

Twice they were seen before the sun was two hours high, the first time by a caravan of merchants headed toward Sialpore, who breasted a high dune half a mile away and took no notice; but that would not prevent the whole caravansary in the city's midst from knowing what they had seen, and just how long ago, and headed which way, within ten minutes after they arrived—as, in fact, exactly happened.

The second party to catch sight of them consisted of four men on camels, whose rifles, worn military fashion with a sling, betrayed them as Gungadhura's men. "Desert police" he called them. "Takers of tenths" was the popular, and much more accurate description. The four gave chase, for a caravan in a hurry is always likely to pay well for exemption from delay; and coming nearly at right angles they had all the advantage. It was crime to refuse to halt for them,

for they were semi-military, uniformed police. Yet
their invariable habit of prying into everything and
questioning each member of a caravan would be certain to lead to discovery. They had a signal station on
the hill two miles behind them, to keep them in touch
with other parties, north, south, east and west. It
looked like Yasmini's undoing, for they were gaining
two for one along the shorter course. Tess fingered
the pistol her husband had made her bring, wondering
whether Yasmini would dare show fight (not guessing
yet the limitless abundance of her daring), and wondering whether she herself would dare reply to the fire
of authorized policemen. She did not relish the
thought of being an outlaw with a genuine excuse for
her arrest.

But the four police were oversure, and Yasmini too
quick-witted for them. They took a short cut down
into a sandy hollow, letting their quarry get out of
sight, plainly intending to wait on rising ground about
a thousand yards ahead, where they could foil attempts
to circumvent them and, for the present, take matters
easy.

Instantly Yasmini changed direction, swinging her
camel to the right, down a deep nullah, and leading
full pelt at right angles to her real course. It was ten
minutes before the men caught sight of them again,
and by that time they had nearly drawn abreast, well
beyond reasonable rifle range, and were heading back
toward their old direction, so that the police had lost
advantage, and a stern chase on slower camels was
their only hope but one. They fired half a dozen shots
by way of calling attention to themselves—then

wheeled and raced away toward the signal station on the hill.

Yasmini held her course for an hour after that, until a spur of the hillside and another long fold of the desert shut them off from the signaler's view. There she called a halt, unexpectedly, for the camels did not need it. She was worried about Tess—the one untested link in her chain of fugitives.

"Can you keep on through all the hot day?" she asked. "These other women are as lithe as leopards, for I make them dance. They are better able to endure than cheetahs. But you? Shall I put two women on one camel, and send you back to Sialpore with two men?"

Tess's back ached and she was dizzy, but her own powers had been tested many a time; this was not more than double the strain she had withstood before, and she was aware of strength in reserve, to say nothing of conviction that what Yasmini's maids could do she herself would rather perish than fall short of. There is an element of sheer, pugnacious, unchristian human pride that is said to damn, while it saves the best of us at times.

"Certainly not! I can carry on all day!" she answered.

Yasmini emitted her golden bell-like laugh that expressed such immeasurable understanding and delight in all she understands. (It has over-tones that tell of vision beyond the ken of folk who build on mud.)

"The maids shall knead your muscles for you at the other end," she answered. "Courage is good!

You are my sister! You shall see things that the West knows nothing of! If those thrice-misbegotten Takers of Tenths had not seen us, we would have reached our goal a little after midday. As it is, they have certainly signaled to another party of Gungadhura's spawn somewhere ahead of us, who will be coming this way with eyes open and a lesson in mind for those who disregard their comrades' challenge to halt and be looted! When I am maharanee there shall be a new system of protecting desert roads! But I dare not try conclusions now. We must take a wide circuit and not reach our destination until night falls. Are you willing?"

"Ready for anything!" said Tess. "If I weaken, tie me on the camel!"

"Good! So speaks a woman! One woman of spirit is the master of a dozen men—always!"

They all drank sparingly of tepid water, ate a little of the food each had, and were off again without letting the camels kneel—heading now away from the hills toward a dazzling waste of silver sand, across which the eyes lost all sense of perspective, and all power to separate three objects in a row; a land of mirage and monotony, glittering in places with the aching white of salt deposits.

The heat increased, but the speed never slackened for an instant. Flies emerged from everywhere to fasten on to unprotected skin, and the only relief from them was under the hot cloaks that burned them with the heat absorbed from sun and wind. But even in that ghastly wilderness there were other living things. Now and then a lean leopard stole away from in front of them; and once they saw a man, naked and thinner than a rake, striding along a ridge on heaven knew what errand. There were scorpions everywhere.

Hour after hour, guided by desert-instinct that needs no compass, and ever alert for sky-line watchers, Yasmini and the headman took turns in giving direction, he yielding to her whenever their judgment differed. And whether she was right or not in every instance, she brought them at last to a little desert oasis, where there was brackish water deep down in a sand-hole, and a great rock offered shadow to rest in.

There they lay until the sun declined far enough to lose a little of his power to scorch, and the camels bubbled to one another, thirstless, unwearied, dissatisfied, as the universal way of camels is, kneeling in a circle, rumps outward, each one resentful of the other's neighborhood and, above all, disgruntled at man's tyranny.

"By now," laughed Yasmini, smoking one of Tess's cigarettes in the shadow of the rock, "Gungadhura knows surely that my palace is empty and the bird has flown. Ten dozen different people will have carried to him as many accounts of it, and each will have offered different explanation and advice! I wonder what Jinendra's fat priest has to say about it! Gungadhura will have sent for him. He would hardly ride to the priest through the streets, even in a carriage, with that love-token still raw and smarting with which I marked his face! Two reliable reports will have reached him already as to which direction I have taken. Yet the telegraph will have told him that I have not been seen to cross the border, and he will be wondering—wondering. May he wonder until his brains whirl round and sicken him!"

"What can he do?" suggested Tess.

"Do? He can be spiteful. He will enter my palace and remove the furniture, taking my mother's legacies to his own lair—where I shall recover them all within three weeks—and his own beside! I will be maharanee within the month!"

"Aren't you a wee bit previous?" suggested Tess.

"Not I! I never boast. My mother taught me that. Or when I do boast it is to put men off the scent. I boasted once to Samson sahib when he offered to have me sent to college, telling him I was in the same school as himself and would learn the quicker. He has wondered ever since then what I meant. Krishna!" she laughed impiously. "I wonder what Samson sahib would not give to have me in his clutches at this minute! Have I told you that Gungadhura plots with the Northwest tribes, and that the English know it? No? Didn't I tell you? Samson sahib would give me almost anything I asked, if he knew that it was I who told his government of Gungadhura's plots; he would know then that with my knowledge to guide him he would be more than a match for Gungadhura, instead of a ball kicked this and that way between Gungadhura and the English! Sometimes I almost think he would consent to try to make me maharanee!"

"Why not give him the chance then?"

"For two reasons. The English too often desert their commissioners. My sure way is better than his blundering attempts! The other reason is an even bet-

ter one, and you shall know it soon. I think—I do not
know—I think, and I hope that the fat high priest of
Jinendra is playing me false, and has gone to Samson
sahib to make a bargain with him. Samson sahib will
consent to no bargains with that fat fool, if I am any
judge of hucksters; but he will have his ears on end
and his eyes sore with over-watchfulness from now
forward! Oh, I hope Jinendra's priest has gone to
him! I tried to stir treachery in his mind by brow-
beating him about the bargain that he tried to force
from me!"

"But what are you and the priest and Samson all
bargaining about?" demanded Tess.

"The treasure of Sialpore! But I make no bargains! I, who know where the treasure is! Why
should I offer to share what is mine? I will have a
marriage contract drawn, and you shall be a witness.
That treasure is my dowry. Listen! Bubru Singh my
father died without a son—the first of all that long
line who left no son to follow him. The custom was
that he should tell his son, and none else, the secret of
the treasure. He hated Gungadhura; and, not knowing which the English would choose for his successor,
Gungadhura or another man, he told no one, making
only hints to my mother on his death-bed and saying
that if I, his daughter, ever developed brains enough to
learn the secret of the treasure, then I might also have
wit enough to win the throne and all would be well."

"And you discovered it? How did you discover it?"

"Not I."

"Who then?"

"Your husband did!"

"My husband? Dick Blaine? But that can't be true; he never told me; he tells me everything."

"Perhaps he would have told if he had understood. He hardly understands yet. Only in part—a little."

"Then how in the world——?"

Yasmini's golden laugh cut short the question as she rose to her feet with a glance at the westering sun.

"Let us go. Two hours from now we shall cross the border into another state. Two hours after nightfall our journey is ended. Then the last game begins—the last chukker—and I win!"

Tess wished then that they had never halted! The rest had given her muscles time to stiffen, and her nerves the opportunity to learn how tired they were. As the camels rose jerkily and followed their leader in line at the same fast pace as before she grew sick with the agony of aching bones and the utter weariness of motion repeated again and again without varying or ceasing. Every ligament in her body craved only stillness, but the camel's unaccustomed thrust and sway continued, repeated to infinity, until her nerves grew numb and she was hardly conscious of time, distance, or direction.

Once again there was pursuit, but Tess was hardly conscious of it—hardly realized that shots were fired—clinging to the saddle in the misery of a sickness more weakening and deathly than the sort small boats provide at sea. The sun went down and left her cooler, but not recovered. She knew nothing of boundaries, or of the changing nature of the country-side. It meant nothing to her that they were passing great trees now, and that once they crossed a stream by a

wide stone bridge. The only thought that kept drum-
ming in her mind was that Dick, the ever dependable,
had misinformed her. She had "fetched it up"—a
dozen times. True to his instruction, she had "carried
on." But it did not pass! She felt more sick, more
agonized, more weary every minute.

But at last, because there is an end even to the
motion of a camel, in this world of example instances,
about two hours after nightfall the caravan halted in
the shadow of great trees beside a stone house with a
wall about it. Her camel knelt with a motion like a
landslide, and Tess fell off forward on the ground and
fainted, only snatched away by strong hands in the
nick of time to save her from the camel's teeth.
Uncertain, unforgiving brutes are camels—ungrateful
for the toil men put them to. For an hour after that
she was only dimly conscious of being laid on something soft, and of supple, tireless women's hands that
kneaded her, and kneaded her, taking the weary
muscles one by one and coaxing them back to
painlessness.

So she did not see the dog arrive—Trotters, the
Rampore-Great Dane, cousin to half the mongrel stock
of Hindustan, slobbering on a package that his set
jaws hardly could release; Yasmini, scornful of the
laws of caste and ever responsive to a true friend,
pried it loose with strong fingers. It was she, too, who
saw to the dog's needs—fed him and gave him drink—
removed a thorn from his forefoot and made much of
him. She even gave Bimbu food, with her own hands,
and saw that his driver and camel had a place to rest

in, before she undid the string that bound the leather
jacket of the package.

Bimbu on the camel had led the dog by the short
route and, having nothing to be robbed of, had had
small trouble with policemen on the way.

The first thing Tess was really conscious of when
she regained her senses was a great dog that slum-
bered restlessly beside her own finger-marked, dishev-
eled, dusty, fifty-dollar hat on the floor near by, awak-
ing at intervals to sniff her hand and reassure himself
—then returning to the hat to sleep, and gallop in his
sleep; a rangy, gray, enormous beast with cavernous
jaws that she presently recognized as Trotters.

Then came the maids again, afraid for their very
lives of the dog, but still more mindful of Yasmini's
orders. They resumed their kneading of stiff muscles,
rubbing in oil that smelt of jasmine, singing incanta-
tions while they worked. They lifted the bed away
from the wall, and one of the women danced around
and around it rhythmically, surrounding Tess with
what the West translates as "influence"—the spell that
all the East knows keeps away evil interference.

Last of all by candlelight, Yasmini came, scented
and fresh and smiling as the flower from which she
has her name, dressed now in the soft-hued silken
garments of a lady of the land.

"Where did you get them?" Tess asked her.

"These clothes? Oh, I have friends here. Have
no fear now—there are friends on every side of us."

She showed Tess a letter, pierced in four places by
a dog's eye-teeth.

"This is from Samson sahib. Do you remember

how I prayed that Jinendra's priest might think to play me false? I think he has. Some one has been to Samson sahib. Hear this:

" 'The Princess Yasmini Omanoff Singh,
" 'Your Highness,
" 'Word has reached me frequently of late of pressure brought to bear on you from certain quarters, and hints have been dropped in my hearing that the object of the pressure is to induce you to disclose a secret you possess. Let me assure you that my official protection from all illegal restraint and improper treatment is at your service. Further, that in case your secret is such as concerns vitally the political relations, present or future, of Sialpore the proper person to whom to confide it is myself. Should you see your way to take that only safe course, you may rest assured that your own interests will be cared for in every way possible.
" 'I have the honor to be,
" 'Your Highness' obedient servant,
" 'Roland Samson, K. C. S. I.' "

"That looks fair enough," said Tess. "I dislike Samson for reasons of my own, but——"

"Hah!" laughed Yasmini. "He makes love to you! Is it not so? He would make love to me if I gave him opportunity! What a jest for the gods if I should play that game with him and make him marry me! I could! I could make of Samson a power in India! But the man would weary me with his conceit and his 'orders from higher up' within a week. I can have power without his help! What a royal jest, though, to marry Samson and intrigue with all the jealous English wives who think they pull the strings of government!"

"You'd get the worst of it," laughed Tess.

"Maybe. I shall never try it. I am more of the East than the West. But I will answer Samson. Bimbu shall remain here lest he talk too much, but the dog shall take a letter to Tom Tripe at dawn. Samson knew hours ago that I have flown the nest. He will wonder how Tom Tripe holds communication with me, and so swiftly, and will have greater respect for him—which may serve us later."

"Let me add a letter to my husband then, to tell him I'm safe."

"Surely. But now eat. Eat and be strong. Can you stand? Can you walk? Have the maids put new life in you?"

Tess was astonished at her swift recovery. She was a little stiff—a little weak—a little tired; but she could walk up and down the room with her natural gait and Yasmini clapped her hands.

"I will order food brought. Listen! To-night I am Abhisharika. Do you know what that is—Abhisharika?"

Tess shook her head.

"I go to my lover of my own accord!"

"That sounds more like West than East!"

"You think so? You shall come with me and see! You shall play the part of *cheti* (the indispensable hand-maiden)—you and Hasamurti. You must dress like her. Simply be still and watch, and you shall see!"

Of what use were the gift of gods,
The buoyant sweetness of a virgin state,
The blossomy delight of youth
Ablow with promise of fruit consummate;
What use the affluence of song
And marvel of delicious motion meet
To grace the very revelings of Fawn,
Could she not lay them at another's feet?

CHAPTER THIRTEEN

"I am a king's daughter!"

THAT was a night when the full-moon rose in a sea
of silver, and changed into amber as it mounted in the
sky. The light shone like liquid honey, and the shad-
owed earth was luminous and still. The very deepest
of the shadows glowed with undertones of half-sug-
gested color. Hardly a zephyr moved.

"You see?" said Yasmini. "The gods are our servants! They have set the stage!"

Hand in hand—Yasmini in the midst in spotless
silken white; Tess and Hasamurti draped in black from
head to foot—they left the house by a high teak door
in the garden wall and started down a road half hidden
by lacy shadows. All three wore sandals on bare feet,
and Tess was afraid at first of insects.

"Have no fear of anything to-night," Yasmini
whispered. "The gods are all about us! Wasuki, who
is king of all the snakes, is on our side!"

One could not speak aloud, for the spell of mystery
overlay everything. They walked into the very heart
of silent beauty. Overhead, enormous trees, in which
the sacred monkeys slept, dropped tendrils like long
arms yearning with the love of mother earth. Here
and there the embers of a dying fire glowed crimson,

and the only occasional sound was of sleepy cattle that chewed the cud contentedly—or when a monkey moved above them to change his roost. Once, a man's voice singing by a fireside conjured back for a moment the world's hard illusion; but the stillness and the mystery overcame him too, and all was true again, and wonderful.

Hand in hand they followed the road to its end and turned into a lane between thorn hedges. Now the moon shone straight toward them and there was no shadow, so that the earth was bright golden underfoot —a lane of mellow light on which they trod between fantastic woven walls. At the end of the lane they came into a clearing at a forest-edge, where an ancient ruined temple nestled in the shadow of great trees, its stone front and the seated image of a long-neglected god restored to more than earthly sanctity and peace by the cool, caressing moonlight.

"Jinendra again!" Yasmini whispered. "Always Jinendra! His priests are rascals, but the god himself is kind! When I am maharanee, that temple shall stand whole again!"

In front of the temple, between them and the trees, was a pond edged with carved stone. Lotus leaves floated on the water, and one blue flower was open wide to welcome whoever loved serenity.

Still hand in hand, they crossed the clearing midway to the pond, and there Yasmini bade them stand.

"Draw no nearer. Only stand and watch."

She had a great blue flower in her bosom that heaved and fell for proof of her own emotion. Hasamurti's hand was trembling as she nestled closer, and

Tess felt her own pulsing to quick heart-beats as she clasped the girl's.

Yasmini left them, and walked alone to the very edge of the pond, where she stood still for several minutes, apparently gazing at her own reflection in the moonlit water—or perhaps listening. There was no sign of any one else, nor sound of footfall. Then, as if the reflection satisfied, or she had heard some whisper meant for her and none else, she began to dance, moving very slowly in the first few rhythmic steps, resembling a water-goddess, the clinging silk displaying her young outline as she bent and swayed.

She might have been watching her reflection still, so close she danced to the water's edge with her back turned to the moon. But presently the dance grew quicker, and extended arms that glistened in the light like ivory increased the sinuous perfection of each pose. Still there was nothing wild in it—nothing but the very spirit of the moonlight, beautiful and kind and full of peace. She moved now around the water, in a measured cadence that by some unfathomable witchery of her devising conveyed a thought of maidenhood and modesty. It dawned on Tess, who watched her spell-bound, that there was not one immodest thought in all Yasmini's throng of moods, but only a scorn of all immodesty and its pretensions. And whether that was art, or sheer expression of the truth within her rather than a recognition of the truth without, Tess never quite determined; for it is easier to judge spoken word and unexpected deed than to see the thought behind it. That night Yasmini's mood was simpler and less unseemly than the very virgin dress she wore.

Presently she danced more swiftly, making no sound, so phantom-light and graceful that the rhythm of her movement carried her with scarce a touch to earth. That was strength as well as art, but the art made strength seem spiritual power to float on air. Gaiety grew now into her cadences—the utter joy of being young. She seemed to revel in a sense of buoyancy that could lift her above all the grim deceptions of the world of wrath and iron, and make her, like the moonlight, all-kind, all-conquering. Three times round the pond she leapt and gamboled in an ecstasy of youth undisillusioned.

Then the dance changed, though there was yet in it the heart of gaiety. There moved now in the steps a sense of mystery—a consciousness of close infinity unfolding, far more subtly signified than by the clumsy shift of words. And she welcomed all the mystery—greeted it with outstretched arms—was glad of it, and eager—impetuous to know the new worlds and the ways undreamed of. Minute after minute, rhapsody on rhapsody, she wooed the near, untouchable delights that, like the moonbeams, seem but empty nothing when the drudges seize them for their palaces of mud.

Nor did she woo in vain. There were stanzas in her dance of simple gratitude, as if the spirit of the mystery had found her mood acceptable and dowered her with new ability to see, and know, and understand. Even the two watchers, hand in hand a hundred paces off, felt something of the power of vision she had gained, and thrilled at its wonder.

Borne on new wings of fancy now her dance became a very image of those infinite ideas she had

seen and felt. She herself, Yasmini, was a part of all
she saw—mistress of all she knew—own sister of the
beauty in the moonlight and the peace that filled the
glade. The night itself—moon, sky and lotus-dappled
water—trees—growth and grace and stillness, were
part of her and she of them. Verily that minute she,
Yasmini, danced with the gods and knew them for
what in truth they are—ideas a little lower, a little less
essential than the sons of men.

Then, as if that knowledge were the climax of
attainment, and its ownership a spell that could command the very lips of night, there came a man's voice
calling from the temple in the ancient Rajasthani
tongue.

"Oh, moon of my desire! Oh, dear delight! Oh,
spirit of all gladness! Come!"

Instantly the dance ceased. Instantly the air of
triumph left her. As a flower's petals shut at evening,
fragrant with promise of a dawn to come, she stood
and let a new mood clothe her with humility; for all
that grace of high attainment given her were nothing,
unless she, too, made of it a gift. That night her purpose was to give the whole of what she knew herself
to be.

So, with arms to her sides and head erect, she
walked straight toward the temple; and a man came
out to meet her, tall and strong, who strode like a
scion of a stock of warriors. They met mid-way and
neither spoke, but each looked in the other's eyes, then
took each other's hands, and stood still minute after
minute. Hasamurti, gripping Tess's fingers, caught

her breath in something like a sob, while Tess could think of nothing else than Brynhild's oath:

"O Sigurd, Sigurd,
Now hearken while I swear!
The day shall die forever
And the sun to darkness wear
Ere I forget thee, Sigurd..."

Her lips repeated it over and over, like a prayer, until the man put his arm about Yasmini and they turned and walked together to the temple. Then Hasamurti tugged at Tess, and they followed, keeping their distance, until Yasmini and her lover sat on one stone in the moonlight on the temple porch, their faces clearly lighted by the mellow beams. Then Tess and Hasamurti took their stand again, hand in each other's hand, and watched once more.

It was love-making such as Tess had never dreamed of,—and Tess was no familiar of hoydenish amours; gentle—poetic—dignified on his part—manly as the plighting of the troth of warriors' sons should be. Yasmini's was the attitude of simple self-surrender, stripped of all pretense, devoid of any other spirit than the will to give herself and all she had, and knowledge that her gift was more than gold and rubies.

For an hour they sat together murmuring questions and reply, heart answering to heart, eyes reading eyes, and hand enfolding hand; until at last Yasmini rose to leave him and he stood like a lord of squadroned lances to watch her go.

"Moon of my existence!" was his farewell speech to her.

"Dear lord!" she answered. Then she turned and
went, not looking back at him, walking erect, as one
whose lover is the son of twenty kings. Without a
word she took Tess and Hasamurti by the hand, and,
looking straight before her with blue eyes glowing at
the welling joy of thoughts too marvelous for speech,
led them to the lane—the village street—and the door
in the wall again. The man was still gazing after her,
erect and motionless, when Tess turned her head at the
beginning of the lane; but Yasmini never looked back
once.

"Why did you never tell me his name?" Tess
asked; but if Yasmini heard the question she saw fit
not to answer it. Not a word passed her lips until
they reached the house, crossed the wide garden
between pomegranate shrubs, and entered the dark
door across the body of a sleeping watchman—or a
watchman who could make believe he slept. Then:

"Good night!" she said simply. "Sleep well!
Sweet dreams! Come, Hasamurti—your hands are
cleverer than the other women's."

Daughter of a king, and promised wife of a son of
twenty kings, she took the best of the maids to undress
her, without any formal mockery of excuse. Two of
the other women were awake to see Tess into bed—no
mean allowance for a royal lady's guest.

Very late indeed that night Tess was awakened by
Yasmini's hand stroking the hair back from her forehead. Again there was no explanation, no excuse. A
woman who was privileged to see and hear what Tess
had seen and heard, needed no apology for a visit in
the very early hours.

"What do you think of him?" she asked. "How do you like him? Tell me!"

"Splendid!" Tess answered, sitting up to give the one word emphasis. "But why did you never tell me his name?"

"Did you recognize him?"

"Surely! At once—first thing!"

"No true-born Rajputni ever names her lover or her husband."

"But you knew that I know Prince Utirupa Singh. He came to my garden party!"

"Nevertheless, no Rajputni names her lover to another man or woman—calling him by his own name only in retirement, to his face."

"Why—he—isn't he the one who Sir Roland Samson told me ought to have been maharajah instead of Gungadhura?"

Yasmini nodded and pressed her hand.

"To-morrow night you shall see another spectacle. Once, when Rajputana was a veritable land of kings, and not a province tricked and conquered by the English, there was a custom that each great king held a durbar, to which princes came from everywhere, in order that the king's daughter might choose her own husband from among them. The custom died, along with other fashions that were good. The priests killed it, knowing that whatever fettered women would increase their sway. But I will revive it—as much as may be, with the English listening to every murmur of their spies and the great main not yet thrown. I have no father, but I need none. I am a king's daughter! To-morrow night I will single out my husband, and

name him by the title under which I shall marry him—
in the presence of such men of royal blood as can be
trusted with a secret for a day or two! There are
many who will gladly see the end of Gungadhura!
But I must try to sleep—I have hardly slept an hour.
If a maid were awake to sing to me—but they sleep
like the dead after the camel-ride, and Hasamurti, who
sings best, is weariest of all."

"Suppose I sing to you?" said Tess.

"No, no; you are tired too."

"Nonsense! It's nearly morning. I have slept for
hours. Let me come and sing to you."

"Can you? Will you? I am full of gladness, and
my brain whirls with a thousand thoughts, but I ought
to sleep."

So Tess went to Yasmini's room, and sat beneath
the punkah crooning Moody and Sankey hymns and
darky lullabies, until Yasmini dropped into the land of
dreams. Then, listening to the punkah's regular soft
swing, she herself fell forward on her arms, half-rest-
ing on the bed, half on the chair, until Hasamurti crept
in silently and, laughing, lifted her up beside Yasmini
and left her there until the two awoke near noon, wondering, in each other's arms.

He who is most easily persuaded is perhaps a fool, for the world is full of fools, and it is dangerous to deal with them.   But perhaps he is a man who sees his own advantage hidden in the folds of your proposal; and that is dangerous too.—EASTERN PROVERB.

CHAPTER FOURTEEN

"Acting on instructions from Your Highness!"

IT TICKLED Gungadhura's vanity to have an Englishman in his employ; but Tom Tripe never knew
from one day to another what his next reception would
be. On occasion it would suit the despot's sense of
humor to snub and slight the veteran soldier of a said-
to-be superior race; and he would choose to do that
when there was least excuse for it. On the other hand,
he recognized Tom as almost indispensable; he could
put a lick and polish on the maharajah's troops that no
amount of cursing and coaxing by their own officers
accomplished. Tom understood to a nicety that drift
of the Rajput's martial mind that caused each sepoy
to believe himself the equal of any other Rajput man,
but permitted him to tolerate fierce disciplining by an
alien.

And Tom had his own peculiarities. Born in a
Shorncliffe barrack hut, he had a feudal attitude
toward people of higher birth. As for a prince—there
was almost no limit to what he would not endure from
one, without concerning himself whether the prince was
right or wrong. Not that he did not know his rights;
his limitations were not Prussian; he would stand up
for his rights, and on their account would answer the

maharajah back more bluntly and even offensively than
Samson, for instance, would have dreamed of doing.
But a prince was a prince, and that was all about it.

So, on the morning following the flight of Yasmini
and Tess, Tom, sore-eyed from lack of sleep but with
an eye-opener of raw brandy inside him, and a sense of
irritation due to the absence of his dog, roundly cursed
nine unhappy mahouts for having dared let an elephant
steal his rum—drilled two companies of heavy infantry
in marching order on parade until the sweat ran down
into their boots and each miserable man saw two suns
in the sky where one should be—dismissed them with
a threat of extra parades for a month to come unless
they picked their feet up cleaner—and reported, with
his heart in his throat, at Gungadhura's palace.

As luck would have it, the Sikh doctor was just
leaving. It always suited that doctor to be very
friendly with Tom Tripe, because there were pickings,
in the way of sick certificates that Tom could pass
along to him, and shortcomings that Tom could overlook. He told Tom that the maharajah was in no
mood to be spoken to, and in no condition to be seen.

"Then you go back and tell his highness," Tom
retorted, "that I've got to speak with him! Business is
business!"

The doctor used both hands to illustrate.

"But his cheek is cut with a great gash from here
to here! He was testing a sword-blade in the armory
last night, and it broke and pierced him."

"Hasn't a soldier like me seen wounds before? I
don't swoon away at the sight of blood! He can do
his talking through a curtain if he's minded!"

"I would not dare, Mr. Tripe! He has given orders. You must ask one of the eunuchs—really."

"I thought you and I were friends?" said Tom, with whiskers bristling.

"Always! I hope always! But in this instance—"

Tom folded both arms behind his back, drill-master-on-parade fashion.

"Suit yourself," he answered. "Friendship's friendship. Scratch my back and I'll scratch yours. I want to see his highness. I want to see him bad. You're the man that's asked to turn the trick for me."

"Well, Mr. Tripe, I will try. I will try. But what shall I tell him?"

Tom hesitated. That doctor was a more or less discreet individual, or he would not have been sent for. Besides, he had lied quite plausibly about the dagger-wound. But there are limits.

"Tell him," he said presently, "that I've found the man who left that sword in his armory o' purpose for to injure him! Say I need private and personal instructions quick!"

The doctor returned up the palace steps. Ten minutes later he came down again smiling, with the word that Tom was to be admitted. In a hurry, then, Tom's brass spurs rang on Gungadhura's marble staircase while a breathless major-domo tried to keep ahead of him. One takes no chances with a man who can change his mind as swiftly as Gungadhura habitually did. Without a glance at silver shields, boars' heads, tiger-skins, curtains and graven gold ornaments beyond price, or any of the other trappings of royal luxury, Tom followed the major-domo into a room furnished with one sole divan and a little Buhl-work table. The maharajah, sprawling on the divan in a flowered silk deshabille and with his head swathed in bandages, ignored Tom Tripe's salute, and snarled at the major-domo to take himself out of sight and hearing.

Soldier-fashion, as soon as the door had closed behind him Tom stood on no ceremony, but spoke first.

"There was a fracas last night, Your Highness, outside a certain palace gate." He pronounced the word to rhyme with jackass, but Gungadhura was not in a mood to smile. "An escaped elephant bumped into the gate and bent it. The guard took to their heels; so I've locked 'em all up, solitary, to think their conduct over."

The maharajah nodded.

"Good!" he said curtly.

"I cautioned the relieving guard that if they had a word to say to any one they'd follow the first lot into cells. It don't do to have it known that elephants break loose that easy."

"Good!"

"Subsequently, acting on instructions from Your Highness, I searched the cellar of Mr. Blaine's house on the hill, Chamu the butler holding a candle for me."

"What did *he* see? What did that treacherous swine see?" snapped Gungadhura, pushing back the bandage irritably from the corner of his mouth.

"Nothing, Your Highness, except that he saw me lift a stone and look under it."

"What did *you* see under the stone?"

"A silver tube, all wrought over with Persian patterns, and sealed at both ends with a silver cap and lots o' wax."

"Why didn't you take it, you idiot?"

"Two reasons. Your Highness told me to report to you what I saw, not to take nothing. And Mr. Blaine came to the top of the cellar ladder and was damned angry. He'd have seen me if I'd pinched a cockroach. He was that angry that he locked the cellar door afterward, and nailed it down, and rolled a safe on top of it!"

"Did he suspect anything?"

"I don't know, Your Highness."

"What did you tell him?"

"Said I was looking for rum."

"Doubtless he believed that; you have a reputation! You are an idiot! If you had brought away what you saw under that stone, you might have drawn your pension to-day and left India for good!"

Tom made no answer. The next move was Gungadhura's. There was silence while a gold clock on the wall ticked off eighty seconds.

"You are an idiot!" Gungadhura broke out at last. "You have missed a golden opportunity! But if you will hold your tongue—absolutely—you shall draw your pension in a month or two from now, with ten thousand rupees in gold into the bargain!"

"Yes, Your Highness." (A native of the country would have begun to try to bargain there and then. But there are more differences than one between the ranks of East and West; more degrees than one of dissimulation. Tom gravely doubted Gungadhura's prospect of being in position to grant him a pension, or any other favor, a month or two from then. A native of the country would have bargained nevertheless.)

"Keep that guard confined for the present. You have my leave to go."

Tom saluted and withdrew. He was minded to spit on the palace steps, but refrained because the guard would surely have reported what he did to Gungadhura, who would have understood the act in its exact significance.

As he left the palace yard he passed a curtained two-wheeled cart drawn by small humped bulls, and turned his head in time to see the high priest of Jinendra heave his bulk out from behind the curtains and wheezily ascend the palace steps.

"A little ghostly consolation for the maharajah's sins!" he muttered, as he headed toward his own quarters for another stiff glass of brandy and some sleep. He felt he needed both—or all three!

"If it's true there's no hell, then I'm on velvet!" he muttered. "But I'm a liar! A liar by imputation—by suggestion—by allegation—by collusion—and in fact! Now, if I was one o' them Hindus I could hire a priest to sing a hymn and start me clean again from the beginning. Trouble is, I'm a complacent liar! I'll do it again, and I know it! Brandy's the right oracle for me!"

But there was no consolation, ghostly or otherwise, being brought to Gungadhura. Jinendra's fat high priest, short-winded from his effort on the stairs, with aching hams and knees that trembled from exertion, was ushered into a chamber some way removed from that in which Tom Tripe had had his interview. The maharajah lay now with his head on the lap of Patali, his favorite dancing girl, in a room all scent and cushions and contrivances. (That was how Yasmini learned about it afterward.)

It was against all the canons of caste and decency to accord an interview to any one in that flagrant state of impropriety—to a high priest especially. But it amused Gungadhura to outrage the priest's alleged asceticism, and to show him discourtesy (without in the least affecting his own superstitious scruples in the matter of religion.) Besides, his head ached, and he liked to have Patali's resourcefulness and wit to reenforce his own tired intuition.

The priest sat for several minutes recovering breath and equipoise. Then, when the pain had left his thighs and he felt comfortable, he began with a bomb.

"Mukhum Dass the money-lender has been to me to give thanks, and to make a meager offering for the recovery of his lost title-deed! He has it back!"

Gungadhura swore so savagely that Patali screamed.

"How did he find it? Where?"

Mukhum Dass had told the exact truth, as it happened, but the priest had drawn his own conclusions from the fact that it was Samson's babu who returned the document. He was less than ever sure of Gungadhura's prospects, suspecting, especially since his own night-interview with the commissioner, that some new dark plot was being hatched on the English side of the river. Having no least objection to see Gungadhura in the toils, he did not propose to tell him more than would frighten and worry him.

"He said that a hand gave him the paper in the dark. It was the work of Jinendra doubtless."

"Pah! Thy god functions without thee, then! That is a wondrous belly-ful of brains of thine! Do you know that the princess has fled the palace?"

Jinendra's priest feigned surprise.

"Is it not as clear as the stupidity on thy fat face that the ten-times casteless hussy is behind this? Bag of wind and widows' tenths! Now I must buy the house on the hill from Mukhum Dass and pay the brute his price for it!"

"Borrowing the money from him first?" the priest suggested with a fat smirk. None guessed better than he how low debauch had brought the maharajah's private treasury.

"Go and pray!" growled Gungadhura. "Are thy temple offices of no more use than to bring thee here twitting me with poverty? Go and lay that belly on the flags, and beat thy stupid brains out on the altar step! Jinendra will be glad to see thy dark soul on its way to Yum (the judge of the dead) and maybe will reward me afterward! Go! Get out here! Leave me alone to think!"

The priest went through the form of blessing him, taking more than the usual time about the ceremony for sake of the annoyance that it gave. Gungadhura was too superstitious to dare interrupt him.

"Better tell that Mukhum Dass to sell me the house cheap," said the maharajah as a sort of afterthought. Patali had been whispering to him. "Tell him the gods would take it as an act of merit."

"Cheap?" said the priest over his shoulder as he

reached the door. "I proposed it to him." (That was not exactly true. He had proposed that Mukhum Dass should give the title to the temple as an act of grace.) "He answered that what the gods have returned to him must be doubly precious and certainly entrusted to his keeping; therefore he would count it a deadly sin to part with the title now on any terms!"

"Go!" growled Gungadhura. "Get out of here!"

After the priest had gone he talked matters over with Patali, while she stroked his aching head. Whoever knows the mind of the Indian dancing girl could reason out the calculus of treason. They are capable of treachery and loyalty to several sides at once; of sale of their affections to the highest bidder, and of death beside the buyer in his last extremity, having sold his life to a rival whom they loathe. They are the very priestesses of subterfuge—idolators of intrigue—past-mistresses of sedition and seduction. Yet even Patali did not know the real reason why Gungadhura lusted for possession of that small house on the hill. She believed it was for a house of pleasure for herself.

"Persuade the American gold-digger to transfer the lease of it," she suggested. "He is thy servant. He dare not refuse."

But Gungadhura had already enough experience of Richard Blaine to suspect the American of limitless powers of refusal. He was superstitious enough to believe in the alleged vision of Jinendra's priest, that the clue to the treasure of Sialpore would be found in the cellar of that house, where Jengal Singh had placed it; impious enough to double-cross the priest, and to use any means whatever, foul preferred, to get possession of the clue. But he was sensible enough to know that Dick Blaine could not be put out of his house by less than legal process. Patali, watching the expression of his eyes, mercurially changed her tactics.

"To-day the court is closed," she said. "To-morrow Mukhum Dass will go to file his paper and defeat the suit of Dhulap Singh. He will ride by way of the ghat between the temple of Siva and the place where the dead Afghan kept his camels. He must ride that way, for his home is on the edge of town."

But Gungadhura shook his head. He hardly dared seize Mukhum Dass or have him robbed, because the money-lender was registered as a British subject, which gave him full right to be extortionate in any state he pleased, with protection in case of interference. He could rob Dick Blaine with better prospect of impunity. Suddenly he decided to throw caution to the winds. Patali ceased from stroking his head, for she recognized in his eyes the blaze of determination, and it put all her instincts on the defensive.

"Pen, ink and paper!" he ordered.

Patali brought them, and he addressed the envelope first, practising the spelling and the none too easily accomplished English.

"Why to him?" she asked, watching beside his shoulder. "If you send him a letter he will think himself important. Word of mouth——"

"Silence, fool! He would not come without a letter."

"Better to meet him, then, as if by accident and——"

"There is no time! That cursed daughter of my

uncle is up to mischief. She has fled. Would that
Yum had her! She went to Samson days ago. The
English harass me. She has made a bargain with the
English to get the treasure first and ruin me. I need
what I need swiftly!"

"Then the house is not for me?"

"No!"

He wrote the letter, scratching it laboriously in a
narrow Italian hand; then sealed and sent it by a messenger. But Patali, sure in her own mind that her
second thoughts had been best and determined to have
the house for her own, went out to set spies to keep a
very careful eye on Mukhum Dass and to report the
money-lender's movements to her hour by hour.

In less than an hour Dick Blaine arrived by dog-
cart in answer to the note, and Patali did her best to
listen through a keyhole to the interview. But she was
caught in the act by Gungadhura's much neglected
queen, and sent to another part of the palace with a
string of unedifying titles ringing in her ears.

There was not a great deal to hear. Dick Blaine
was perfectly satisfied to let the maharajah search his
cellar. He was almost suspiciously complaisant, making no objection whatever to surrendering the key and
explaining at considerable length just how it would be
easiest to draw the nails. He would be away from
home all day, but Chamu the butler would undoubtedly
admit the maharajah and his men. For the rest, he
hoped they would find what they were looking for,
whatever that might be; and he sincerely hoped that
the maharajah had not hurt his head seriously.

Asked why he had nailed the cellar door down, he

replied that he objected to unauthorized people nosing about in there.

"Who has been in the cellar?" asked Gungadhura.

"Only Tom Tripe."

"Are you sure?"

"Quite. Until that very evening I always kept the cellar padlocked. It's a Yale lock. There's nobody in this man's town could pick it."

"Well——thank you for the permission."

"Don't mention it. I hope your head don't hurt you much. Good morning."

Dick little suspected, as he drove the dog-cart across the bridge toward the club, chuckling over the quick success of Yasmini's ruse, that he himself had set the stage for tragedy.

He who sets a tiger-trap
      (Hush! and watch! and wait!)
Can't afford a little nap
Hidden where the twigs enwrap
Lest—it has occurred—mayhap
A jackal take the bait.
So stay awake, my sportsman bold,
And peel your anxious eye,
There's more than tigers, so I'm told,
To test your cunning by!

CHAPTER FIFTEEN

"Me for the princess!"

IT IS not always an entirely simple matter in India to dismiss domestic servants. To begin with it was Sunday; the ordinary means of cashing checks were therefore unavailable, and Dick Blaine had overlooked the fact that he had no money of small denominations in the house. It was hardly reasonable to expect Chamu and the cook to leave without their wages.

Then again, Sita Ram had not yet sent new servants to replace the potential poisoners; and Chamu had put up a piteous bleating, using every argument, from his being an orphan and the father of a son, down to the less appealing one that Gungadhura would be angry. In vain Dick reassured him that he and cook and maharajah might all go to hell together with his, Dick Blaine's, express permission. In vain he advised him to put the son to work, and be supported for a while in idleness. Chamu lamented noisily. Finally Dick compromised by letting both servants remain for one more day, reflecting that they could not very well tamper with boiled eggs; lunch and dinner he would get at the English club across the river; for breakfast on Monday he would content himself again with boiled eggs, and biscuits out of an imported tin, after which he would cash a check and send both the rascals packing.

So the toast that Chamu brought him he broke up and threw into the garden, where the crows devoured it without apparent ill-effect; he went without tea, and spent an hour or so after breakfast with a good cigar and a copy of a month-old Nevada newspaper. That religious rite performed, he shaved twice over, it being Sunday, and strolled out to look at the horses and potter about the garden that was beginning to shrivel up already at the commencement of the hot weather.

"If I knew who would be maharajah of this state from one week to the next," he told himself, "I'd get a contract from him to pipe water all over the place from the hills behind."

He was sitting in the shade, chewing an unlit cigar, day-dreaming about water-pressure and dams and gallons-per-hour, when Gungadhura's note came and he ordered the dog-cart at once, rather glad of something to keep him occupied. As he drove away he did not see Mukhum Dass lurking near the small gate, as it was not intended that he should. Mukhum Dass, for his part, did not see Pinga, the one-eyed beggar with his vertical smile, who watched him from behind a rock, for that was not intended either. Pinga himself was noticed closely by another man.

The minute Dick was out of sight Mukhum Dass entered the small gate in the wall, and called out for Chamu brazenly. Chamu received him at the bottom of the house-steps, but Mukhum Dass walked up them uninvited.

"The cellar," he said. "I have come to see the cellar. There is a complaint regarding the foundations. I must see."

"But, sahib, the door is locked."

"Unlock it."

"I have no key."

"Then break the lock!"

"The cellar door is nailed down!"

"Draw the nails!"

"I dare not! I don't know how! By what right should I do this thing?"

"It is my house. I order it!"

"But, sahib, only yesterday Blaine sahib dismissed me in great anger because I permitted another one as much as to look into the cellar!"

If the tale Yasmini told him on the morning of her first visit to Tess had not been enough to determine Mukhum Dass, now, with the lost title-deed recovered, the conviction that Gungadhura wanted the place for secret reasons, and Chamu's objections to confirm the whole wild story, he became as set on his course and determined to wring the last anna out of the mystery as only a money-lender can be.

"With what money did you repay to me the loan that your son obtained by false pretenses?" he demanded.

"I? What? I repaid the loan. I have the receipt. That is enough."

"On the receipt stands written the number of the bank-note. I have kept the bank-note. It was stolen from the Princess Yasmini. Do you wish to go to jail? Then open that cellar door!"

"Sahib, I never stole the note!" wept Chamu. "It was thrust into my *cummerbund* from behind!"

But Mukhum Dass set his face like a flint, and the wretched Chamu knew nothing about the law against compounding felonies. Wishing he had had curiosity enough himself to search the cellar thoroughly before the door was nailed down, he finally yielded to the money-lender's threats and between them, with much sweating and grunting, they pushed and pulled the safe from off the trap. Then came the much more difficult task of drawing nails without an instrument designed for it. Dick Blaine kept all his tools locked up.

"There is an outside door to the cellar, behind the house," said Chamu.

"But that is of iron, idiot! and bolts on the inside with a great bar resting in the stonework. Are there no tools in the garden?"

Chamu did not know, and the money-lender went himself to see. There Pinga with the vertical smile saw him choose a small crow-bar and return into the house with it. Pinga passed the word along to another man, who told it to a third, who ran with it hot-foot to Gungadhura's palace.

Once inside the house again Mukhum Dass lost no time, arguing to himself most likely that with the secret of the treasure of Sialpore in his possession it would not much matter what damage he had done. He would be able to settle for it. He broke the hasp of the door, and levered up the trap, splintering it badly and breaking both hinges in the process, while Chamu watched him, growing green with fear.

Then he ordered a lamp and went alone into the

cellar, while Chamu, deciding that a desperate situation called for desperate remedies, went up-stairs on
business of his own. It took Mukhum Dass about two
minutes to discover the loose stone—less than two more
to raise it—and about ten seconds to see and pounce on
the silver tube. He was too bent on business to notice
the man with the vertical smile peering down at him
through the trap. Pinga escaped from the house after
seeing the money-lender hide the tube inside his
clothes, and less than a minute later a lean man ran
like the wind to Gungadhura's palace to confirm the
first's report.

With a wry face at the splintered trap-door, and a
shrug of his shoulders of the kind he used when clients
begged in tears for extra time in which to pay, Mukhum Dass looked about for Chamu with a sort of half-
notion of giving him a small bribe. But Chamu was
not to be seen. So he left the house by the way he had
come, mounted his mule where he had left it in a hollow down the road, and rode off smiling.

Ten minutes later Chamu and the cook both left by
the same exit. Chamu had with him, besides his own
bundle of belongings, a revolver belonging to Dick
Blaine, two bracelets belonging to Tess, a fountain-pen
that he had long had his heart on, plenty of note-paper
on which to have a writer forge new references, a half-
dozen of Dick's silk handkerchiefs and a turquoise tie-
pin. The revolver alone, in that country in those days,
would sell for enough to take him to Bombay, where
new jobs with newly arrived sahibs are plentiful. The
cook, not having enjoyed the run of the house, had
only a few knives and a pound of cocoa. They quar-

reled all the way down-hill as to why Chamu should
and should not defray the cook's traveling expenses.

A little later, in the ghat between Siva's temple and
the building where the dead Afghan used to keep his
camels, Mukhum Dass, smiling as he rode, was struck
down by a knife-blow from behind and pitched off his
mule head-foremost. The mule ran away. The
money-lender's body was left lying in a pool of blood,
with the clothing torn from it; and it was considered
by those who found the body several hours afterward
and drove away the pariah dogs and kites, that the
fact of his money having been taken deprived the murder of any unusual interest.

Late that evening Dick Blaine, returning from a
desultory dinner at the club across the river, very
nearly fell into the trap-door, for the hamal had run
away too, thinking he would surely be accused of all
the mischief, and no lamps were lit.

"Well!" he remarked, striking a match to look
about him, "dad-blame me if that isn't a regular small
town yegg's trick! You'd think after I gave Gungadhura the key and all, he'd have the courtesy to use it
and draw the nails! His head can't ache enough to
suit me! Me for the princess! If I'd any scruples,
believe me, bo, they're vanished—gone—vamoosed!
That young woman's going to win against the whole
darned outfit, English, Indian and all! Me for her!
Chamu! Where's Chamu? Why aren't the lamps lit?"

He wandered through the house in the dark in
search of servants, and finally lit a lamp himself,
locked all the doors and went to bed.

The buildings rear immense, horizons fade
And thought forgets old gages in the ecstasy of view.
The standards go by which the steps were made.
On which we trod from former levels to the new.
No time for backward glance, no pause for breath,
Since impulse like a bowstring loosed us in full flight
And in delirium of speed none aim considereth
Nor in the blaze of burning codes can think of night.
The whirring of sped wheels and horn remind
That speed, more speed is best and peace is waste!
They rank unfortunate who lag behind
And only they seem wise who urge, and haste and
      haste.
New comforts multiply (for there is need!)
Each ballot adds assent to law that crowds the days.
None pause. None clamor but for speed—more speed!
And yet—there was a sweetness in the olden ways.

CHAPTER SIXTEEN

"And since, my Lords, in olden days——"

TROTTERS, fed on chopped raw meat by advice of Tess, and brushed by Bimbu for an hour to get the stiffness out of him, was sent off in the noon heat with a double message for his master, one addressed to Samson, one to Dick Blaine, and both wrapped in the same chewed leather cover, that the dog might understand. The mongrel in him made him more immune to heat than a thoroughbred would have been. In any case, he showed nothing but eagerness to get back to Tom Tripe, and, settling the package comfortably in his jaws, was off without ceremony at a steady canter.

"If all my friends were like that one," said Yasmini, "I would be empress of the earth, not queen of a little part of Rajputana! However, one thing at a time!"

It was hardly more than a village that Tess could see through the jalousies of her bedroom windows. The room was at a corner, so that she had a wide view in two directions from either deep window-seat. There were all the signs of Indian village life about her—low, thatched houses in compounds fenced with thorn and prickly pear,—temples in between them,—trades and handicrafts plied in the shade of ancient trees,— squalor and beauty, leisure, wealth, poverty and lord-

237

liness all hand in hand. She could see the backs of elephants standing in a compound under trees, and there were peacocks swaggering everywhere, eating the same offal, though, as the unpretentious chickens in the streets. Over in the distance, beyond the elephants, was the tiled roof of a great house glinting in strong sunlight between the green of enormous pipal trees; and there were other houses, strong to look at but not so great, jumbled together in one quarter where a stream passed through the village.

Yasmini came and sat beside her in the window-seat, as simply dressed in white as on the night before, with her gold hair braided up loosely and an air of reveling in the luxury of peace and rest.

"That great house," she said, peering through the jalousies, "is where the ceremony is to be to-night. My father's father built it. This is not our state, but he owned the land."

"Doesn't it belong to Gungadhura now?" Tess asked.

"No. It was part of my legacy. This house, too, that we are in. Look, some of them have come on elephants to do me honor. Many of the nobles of the land are poor in these days; one, they tell me, came on foot, walking by night lest the ill-bred laugh at him. He has a horse now. He shall have ten when I am maharanee!"

"Won't the English get to hear of this?" Tess asked.

Yasmini laughed.

"Their spies are everywhere. But there has been great talk of a polo tournament to be held on the Eng-

lish side of the river at Sialpore. The English
encourage games, thinking they keep us Rajputs out of
mischief—as indeed is true. This, then, is a conference to decide which of our young bloods shall take
part in the tournament, and who shall contribute
ponies. The English lend one another ponies; why
not we? The spies will report great interest in the
polo tournament, and the English will smile
complacently."

"But suppose a spy gets in to see the ceremony?"
Tess suggested.

Yasmini's blue eyes looked into hers and there was
a Viking glare behind them, suggestive of the wintry
fjords whence one of her royal ancestresses came.

"Let him!" she said. "It would be the last of him!"

Tess considered a while in silence.

"When is the tournament to be?" she asked presently. "Won't the English think it strange that the
conference about men and ponies should be put off
until so late?"

"They might have," Yasmini answered. "They are
suspicious of all gatherings. But a month ago we
worked up a dispute entirely for their benefit. This is
supposed to be a last-hour effort to bring cohesion out
of jealousy. The English like to see Rajputs quarrel
among themselves, because of their ancient saw that
says 'Divide and govern!' I do not understand the
English altogether—yet; but in some ways they are
like an open book. They will let us quarrel over polo
to our heart's content."

There is something very close to luxury in following the thread of an intrigue, sitting on soft cushions

with the sunlight sending layers of golden shafts
through jalousies into a cool room; so little of the
strain and danger of it; so much of its engagement.
Tess was enjoying herself to the top of her bent.

"But when the ceremony is over," she said, "and
you yourself have proclaimed Prince Utirupa king of
Sialpore, there will still remain the problem of how to
make the English recognize him. There is Gungadhura, for instance, to get out of the way; and Gungadhura's sons—how many has he?"

"Five, all whole and well. But the dogs must suffer for their breeding. Who takes a reverter's colt to
school into a charger? The English will turn their
eyes away from Gungadhura's stock."

"But Gungadhura himself?"

"Is in the toils already! Say this for the English:
they are slow to reach conclusions—slower still to
change their policy; but when their mind is made up
they are swift! Gungadhura has been sending messages to the Northwest tribes. How do I know? You
saw Ismail, my gateman? His very brother took the
letters back and forth!"

"But why should Gungadhura risk his throne by
anything so foolish?"

"He thinks to save it. He thinks to prove that the
tribes began the dickering, and then to offer his army
to the English—Tom Tripe and all! Patali put him up
to it. Perhaps she wants a necklace made of Hill-
men's teeth—who knows? Gungadhura went deeply
into debt with Mukhum Dass, to send money to the
Mahsudis, who think more of gold than promises.
The fool imagines that the English will let him levy

extra taxes afterward to recoup himself. Besides, there would be the daily expenses of his army, from which he could extract a lakh or two. Patali yearns for diamonds in the fillings of her teeth!"

"Did you work out all this deep plot for yourself?" Tess asked.

"I and the gods! The gods of India love intrigue. My father left me as a sort of ward of Jinendra, although my mother tried to make a Christian of me, and I always mistrusted Jinendra's priest. But Jinendra has been good. He shall have two new temples when I am maharanee."

"And you have been looking for the treasure ever since your father died?"

"Ever since. My father prophesied on his death-bed that I should have it in the end, but all he told to help me find it was a sort of conundrum. 'Whoever looks for flowers,' he said, 'finds happiness. Who looks for gold finds all the harness and the teeth of war! A hundred guard the treasure day and night, changing with the full moon!' So I have always looked for flowers, and I am often happy. I have sent flowers every day to the temple of Jinendra."

"Who or what can the hundred be, who guard the treasure day and night?" Tess wondered.

"That is what puzzled me. At first, because I was very young, I thought they must be snakes. So I made friends with the snakes, learning how to handle even cobras without fear of them. Then, when I had learned that snakes could tell me nothing, but are only Widyadharas—beautiful lost fairies dreadfully afraid of men, and very, very wishful to be comforted, I began to think the hundred must be priests. So I made friends with the priests, and let them teach me all their knowledge. But they know nothing! They are parasites! They teach only what will keep men in their power, and women in subjection, themselves not understanding what they teach! I soon learned that if the priests were treasure-guards their charge would have been dissipated long ago! Then I looked for a hundred trees, and found them! A hundred pipal trees all in a place together! But that was only like the first goal in the very first chukker of the game—as you shall learn soon!"

"Then surely I know!" said Tess excitedly. "In the grounds of the palace across the river, that you escaped from the night before you came to see me, there is quite a little forest of pipals."

"Nine and sixty and the roots of four," Yasmini answered, her eyes glowing as if there were fire behind them. "The difficulty is, though, that they don't change with the full moon! Pipal trees grow on forever, never changing, except to grow bigger and bigger. They outlive centuries of men. Nevertheless, they gave me the clue, not only to the treasure but to the winning of it!"

The afternoon wore on in drowsy quiet, both of the girls sleeping at intervals—waited on at intervals by Hasamurti with fruit and cooling drinks—Yasmini silent oftener than not as the sun went lower, as if the details of what she had to do that night were rehearsing themselves in her mind. No amount of questioning by Tess could make her speak of them again, or tell any more about the secret of the treasure. At that

age already she knew too well the virtue and fun of
unexpectedness.

They ate together very early, reclining at a low
table heaped with more varieties of food than Tess
had dreamed that India could produce; but ate sparingly because the weight of what was coming
impressed them both. Hasamurti sang during the
meal, ballad after ballad of the warring history of
Rajasthan and its royal heroines, accompanying herself on a stringed instrument, and the ballads seemed
to strike the right chord in Yasmini's heart, for when
the meal finished she was queenly and alert, her blue
eyes blazing.

Then came the business of dressing, and two maids
took Tess into her room to bathe and comb and scent
and polish her, until she wondered how the rest of the
world got on without handmaidens, and laughed to
think that one short week ago she had never had a
personal attendant since her nurse. Swiftly the luxurious habit grows; she rather hoped her husband
might become rich enough to provide her a maid
always!

And after all that thought and trouble and attention
she stood arrayed at last as no more than a maid herself—true, a maid of royalty; but very simply dressed,
without a jewel, with plain light sandals on her stock-
inged feet, and with a plain veil hanging to below her
knees—all creamy white. She admitted to herself that
she looked beautiful in the long glass, and wished that
Dick could see her so, not guessing how soon Dick
would see her far more gorgeously arrayed.

Yasmini, when she came into the room, was a pic-

ture to take the breath away,—a rhapsody in cream
and amber, glittering with gems. There were diamonds sparkling on her girdle, bosom, ears, arms; a
ruby like a prince's ransom nestled at her throat; there
were emeralds and sapphires stitched to the soft texture of her dress to glow and glitter as she moved;
and her hair was afire with points of diamond light.
Coil on coil of huge pearls hung from her shoulders
to her waist, and pearls were on her sandals.

"Child, where in heaven's name did you get them
all?" Tess burst out.

"These? These jewels? Some are the gifts of
Rajput noblemen. Some are heirlooms lent for the
occasion. This—and this"—— she touched the ruby
at her throat and a diamond that glittered at her breast
like frozen dew—— "he gave me. He sent them by his
brother, with an escort of eight gentlemen. But you
should wear jewels, too."

"I have none—none with me."

"I thought of that. I borrowed these for you."

With her own hands she put opals around Tess's
neck that glowed as if they were alive, and then bracelets on her right arm of heavy, graven gold; then
kissed her.

"You look lovely! I shall need you to-night! No
other human guesses how I need you! You and Hasamurti are to stand close to me until the end. The
other maids will take their place behind us. Now we
are ready. Come."

Outside in the dark there were torches flaring, and
low gruff voices announced the presence of about fifty
men. Once or twice a stallion neighed; and there was

another footfall, padded and heavy, in among the stamping of held horses.

The night was hot, and full of that musty mesmeric quality that changes everything into a waking dream. The maids threw dark veils over them to save their clothing from the dust kicked up by a crowd, and perhaps, too, as a concession to the none-so-ancient, but compelling custom that bids women be covered in the streets.

Yasmini took Tess by the hand and walked out with her, followed closely by Hasamurti and the other women, between the pomegranates to the gate in the garden wall. From that moment, though, she stood alone and never touched hand, or sought as much as the supporting glances of her women until they came back at midnight.

A watchman opened the gate and, Yasmini leading, they passed through a double line of Rajput noblemen, who drew their sabers at some one's hoarse command and made a steel arch overhead that flashed and shimmered in the torchlight. Beyond that one order to draw sabers none spoke a word. Tess looked straight in front of her, afraid to meet the warrior eyes on either hand, lest some one should object to a foreigner in their midst on such a night of nights.

In the road were three great elephants standing in line with ladders leaning against them. The one in front was a tusker with golden caps and chains on his glistening ivory, and a howdah on his back like a miniature pagoda—a great gray monster, old in the service of three Rajput generations, and more conscious of his dignity than years. Yasmini mounted him, followed by Tess and Hasamurti, who took their place behind her in the howdah, one on either side, Hasamurti pushing Tess into her proper place, after which her duty was to keep a royal fan of ostrich plumes gently moving in the air above Yasmini's head.

The other women climbed on to the elephant behind, and the third one was mounted by one man, who looked like a prince, to judge by the jewels glittering in his turban.

"His brother!" Hasamurti whispered.

Then again a hoarse command broke on the stillness. Horses wheeled out from the shadow of the wall, led by *saises,* and the Rajput gentry mounted. Ten of them in line abreast led the procession, while some formed a single line on either hand, and ten brought up the rear. Men with torches walked outside the lines. But no one shouted. No one spoke.

Straight down the quiet road under the majestic trees, with the monkeys, frightened by the torchlight, chattering nervously among the branches,—to the right near the lane Yasmini used the night before, and on toward the shadowy bulk of the great house in the distance the elephant trod loftily, the swing and sway of his back suggesting ages of past history, and everlasting ages more to come. The horses kicked and squealed, for the Rajput loves a mettled mount; but nothing disturbed the elephant's slow, measured stride, or moved the equanimity of his mahout.

Villagers came to the walls, and stood under the roadside trees to smile and stare. Every man and child salaamed low as the procession passed, and some followed in the dust to feast their curiosity until the

end of it; but not a voice was raised much above a
whisper, except where once or twice a child cried
shrilly.

"Why the silence?" Tess asked in a whisper, and
without turning her head Yasmini answered:

"Would you have the English know that I was
hailed as maharanee through the streets? Give them
but leave and they would beat the tomtoms, and dance
under the trees. These are all friends here."

The great house was surrounded by a high wall,
but a gate was flung wide open to receive them and
the procession never paused until the leading elephant
came to a halt under a portico lit by dozens of oil
lamps. Standing on the porch were four women,
veiled, but showing the glint of jewels and the sheen
of splendid dresses underneath; they were the first
that night to give tongue in acclamation, raising a hubbub of greeting with a waving of slim hands and arms.
They clustered round Yasmini as she climbed down
from the elephant, and led her into the hall with arms
in hers and a thousand phrases of congratulation and
glad welcome.

"Four queens!" Hasamurti whispered.

Tess and Hasamurti followed, side by side, not
down the main hall, but to the left, into a suite of
rooms reserved for women, where they all removed
their veils and the talking and laughter began anew.
There were dozens of other women in there—about
half as many ladies as attendants, and they made more
noise than a swarm of Vassar freshmen at the close of
term.

The largest of the suite of rooms was higher than

the rest by half a dozen steps. At its farther end
was a gilded door, on either side of which, as far as
the walls at each end, was a panel of very deeply
carved wood, through the interstices of which every
whisper in the durbar hall was audible when the
women all were still, and every man and movement
could be seen. Yasmini took her stand close to the
gilded door, and Tess and Hasamurti watched the
opportunity to come beside her—no very easy matter
in a room where fifty women jockeyed for recognition
and a private word.

But there came a great noise of men's voices in the
durbar hall, and of a roll-call answered one by one,
each name being written in a vellum book, that none
might say afterward he was present, who was not, and
none might escape responsibility. The women grew
silent as a forest that rustles and shivers in the night
wind, and somebody turned down the lights, so that it
was easier to see through the carved panel, and not so
easy to be seen. Immediately beyond the panel was a
dais, or wide platform, bare of everything except a carpet that covered it from end to end. A short flight of
steps from the center of it led to the durbar floor
below.

The durbar floor was of polished teak, and all the
columns that supported the high roof were of the same
wood, carved with fantastic patterns. From the center
hung a huge glass chandelier, its quivering pendants
multiplying the light of a thousand candles; and in
every corner of the hall were other chandeliers, and
mirrors to reflect the light in all directions.

Grouped in the center of the hall were about two

hundred men, all armed with sabers,—men of every
age, and height and swarthiness, from stout, blue-
bearded veterans to youths yet in their teens,—dressed
in every hue imaginable from the scarlet frock-coat,
white breeches and high black boots of a risaldar-
major to the jeweled silken gala costume of the dan-
diest of Rajput's youth.   There was not a man present
who did not rank himself the equal of all reigning
kings, whatever outward deference the exigency of
alien overrule compelled.   This was a race that, like
the Poles, knew itself to have been conquered because
of subdivision and dissension in its ranks; no lack of
courage or of martial skill had brought on their subjection.   Not nearly all their best were there that night
—not even any of the highest-placed, because of jealousy and the dread of betrayal; but there was not a
priest among them, so that the chance was high that
their trust would be well kept.

These were the pick of Rajputana's patriots—the
men who loved the old ways, yet admitted there was
virtue in an adaptation of the new.   And Yasmini, with
a gift for reading men's hearts that has been her secret
and her source of power first and last, was reviving an
ancient royal custom for them, to the end that she
might lead them in altogether new ways of her own
devising.

The roll-call ended, a veteran with a jeweled aigrette in his turban stood apart from the rest with his
back toward the dais steps and made a speech that was
received in silence, though the women peering through
the panel fluttered with excitement, and the deep
breathing in the durbar hall sounded like the very far-

off murmur of a tide. For he rang the changes on
the ancient chivalry of Rajasthan, and on the sanctity
of ancient custom, and the right they had to follow
what their hearts accounted good.

"And as in ancient days," he said, "our royal
women chose their husbands at a durbar summoned by
the king; and because in ancient times, when Rajasthan was a land of kings indeed and its royal women,
as the endless pages of our history tell, stood proved
and acclaimed as fit to govern, and defend, and die
untarnished in the absence of their lords; therefore we
now see fit to attend this durbar, and to witness and
give sanction. Once again, my Lords, a royal daughter of a throne of Rajasthan shall choose her husband
in the sight of all of us let come of it what may!"

He ceased, and the crowd burst into cheers. Yasmini translated his speech afterward to Tess. He said
not a word of Gungadhura, or of the throne of Sialpore, leaving that act of utter daring to the woman who
was, after all, the leader of them all that night.

Now all eyes were on the dais and the door behind
it. In the inner room the women stirred and whispered, while a dozen of them, putting on their veils
again, gathered around Yasmini, waiting in silence for
her to give the cue. She waited long enough to whet
the edge of expectation, and then nodded. Hasamurti
opened the door wide and Yasmini stepped forth,
aglitter with her jewels.

"Ah-h-h!" was her greeting—the unbidden, irrepressible, astonished gasp of mixed emotion of a crowd
that sees more wonder than it bargained for.

The twelve princesses took their place beside her

on the dais, six on either side. Immediately behind
her Tess and Hasamurti stood. Yasmini's other maids
arranged themselves with their backs to the gilded
door. She, Tess and Hasamurti were the only women
there unveiled.

She stood two minutes long in silence, smiling
down at them while Tess's heart-beats drummed until
she lost count, Tess suspecting nervousness because of
her own nerves, and not so wildly wrong.

"You're not alone," she whispered. "You've a
friend behind you—two friends!"

Then Yasmini spoke.

"My Lords." The word "Bahadur" rolled from
her golden throat like chords of Beethoven's overture
to Leonori. "You do our olden customs honor. True
chivalry had nearly died since superstition and the ebb
and flow of mutual mistrust began to smother it in
modern practises. But neither priest nor alien could
make it shame for maidenhood to choose which way
its utmost honor lies. Ye know your hearts' delight.
Goodness, love and soundless fealty are the attributes
your manhood hungers for. Of those three elements
is womanhood. And so, as Shri—goddess of all good
fortune—comes ever to her loved one of her own
accord and dowers him with richer blessing than he
dreamed, true womanhood should choose her mate and,
having chosen, honor him. My Lords, I choose, in
confidence of your nobility and chivalry!"

Pausing for a minute then, to let the murmur of
assent die down, and waiting while they stamped and
shuffled into three long lines, she descended the steps
alone, moving with a step so dignified, yet modest,

that no memory of past events could persuade Tess it was artistry. She felt—Tess was sure of it, and swore to it afterward—in her heart of hearts the full spiritual and profound significance of what she did.

Beginning at the left end of the first line, she passed slowly and alone before them, looking each man in the eyes, smiling at each one as she passed him. Not a man but had his full meed of attention and the honor due to him who brings the spirit of observance and the will to help another man succeed.

Back along the second line she went, with the same supreme dignity and modesty, omitting not even the oldest veteran, nor letting creep into her smile the veriest suggestion of another sentiment than admiration for the manliness by whose leave she was doing what she did. Each man received his smile of recognition and the deference due his pride.

Then down the third line, yet more slowly, until Tess had cold chills, thinking Utirupa was not there! One by one she viewed them all, until the last man's turn came, and she took him by the hand and led him forth.

At that the whole assembly milled into a mob and reformed in double line up and down the room. The same voice that had thundered in the darkness roared again and two hundred swords leapt from their scabbards. Under an arch of blazing steel, in silence, Yasmini and her chosen husband came to the dais and stood facing the assembly hand in hand, while the swords went back to their owners' sides and once more the crowd clustered in the center of the hall.

There was a movement in among them then. Some

servants brought in baskets, and distributed them at about equal intervals amid the forest of booted legs. When the servants had left the hall, Yasmini spoke.

"My Lords, in the presence of you all I vow love, honor, fealty and a wife's devotion to the prince of my choosing—to my husband who shall be—who now is by Gandharva ceremony; for I went to him of my own free will by night! My Lords, I present to you——"

There was a pause, while every man present caught his breath, and the women rustled like a dove-cot behind the panel.

"——Gunga Khatiawara Dhuleep Rhakapushi Utirupa Singh—Maharajah of Sialpore!"

Two hundred swords sprang clear again. The chandeliers rattled and the beams shook to the thunder of two hundred throats.

"Rung, Ho!" they roared.

"Rung Ho!"

"Rung Ho!" bringing down their right feet with a stamp all together that shook the building.

Then the baskets were cut open by the swords' points and they flung flowers at the dais, swamping it in jasmine and sweet-smelling buds, until the carpet was not visible. The same black-bearded veteran who had spoken first mounted the dais and hung garlands on Yasmini and her prince, and again the hall shook to the roar of acclamation and the sharp ringing of keen steel.

But Yasmini had not finished all she had to say. When the shouting died and the blades returned to scabbards, her voice again stirred their emotions, strangely quiet and yet reaching all ears with equal resonance, like the note of a hidden bell.

"And since, my Lords, in olden days it happened often that a Rajput woman held and buttressed up her husband's throne, honoring him and Rajputana with her courage and her wit, and daring even in the arts of war, so now: this prince shall have his throne by woman's wit. Before another full moon rises he shall sit throned in the palace of his ancestors; and ye who love royal Rajasthan shall answer whether I chose wisely, in the days to come!"

They answered then and there to the utmost of their lungs. And while the hall resounded to the crash and clangor of applause she let go Utirupa's hand, bowed low to him, and vanished through the gilded door in the midst of her attendant women.

For two hours after that she was the center of a vortex of congratulation—questions—whisperings—laughter and advice, while the women flocked about her and she introduced Tess to them one by one. Tess, hardly understanding a word of what was said to her, was never made so much of in her life, sharing honors with Yasmini, almost as much a novelty as she—a Western woman, spirited behind the *purdah* by the same new alchemy that made a girl of partly foreign birth, and so without caste in the Hindu sense of it, revive a royal custom with its antecedents rooted in the very rocks of time. It was a night of breathless novelty.

There were the inevitable sweetmeats—the inevitable sugared drinks. Then the elephants again, and torches under the mysterious trees, with a sabered escort plunging to the right and left. The same torch-lit faces peering from the village doors and walls; and at last the gate again in the garden wall, and a bolt shot home, and silence. Then:

"Did I do well?" Yasmini asked, leaning at last on Tess. "Oh, my sister! Without you there to lend me courage I had failed!"

How about the door? Did somebody lock it?
"I," said the Chairman, "had the key in my pocket."
Who shut the windows? "I," said the vice.
"I shut the window, it seemed to me wise."
"I," said the clerk, "looked under the table
And out on the balcony under the gable."
Then who let the secret out? Who overheard?
Maybe a mouse, or the flies, or a bird!

CHAPTER SEVENTEEN

"Suppose I lock the door?"

TOM TRIPE felt like a new man, and his whiskers crackled with self-satisfaction. For one thing, his dog Trotters was back again—sore-footed, it was true, and unable at present to follow him on his rounds; and rather badly scratched where a leopard must have missed his spring on the moonlit desert; but asleep in the stable litter, on the highroad to recovery.

Tom had ridden that morning, first to Dick Blaine up at the gold mine, because he was a friend and needed good news of his wife; then across the bridge to Samson, straightening out the crumpled letter from Yasmini as he rode, and chuckling to himself at the thought of mystifying the commissioner. And it all worked out the way he hoped, even to the offer of a drink—good brandy—Hennesey's Three Star.

"How did you manage it?" asked Samson. "The princess has disappeared. There's a rumor she's over the border in the next state. Gungadhura has seized her palace and rifled it. How did you get my letter to her, and her answer so swiftly?"

"Ah, sir," said Tom Tripe mischievously, "we in the native service have our little compensations—our little ways and means!"

257

That was better than frankincense and myrrh, to mystify a genuine commissioner! Tom rode back to his quarters turning over the taste of brandy in his mouth—he had made a martial raid on Samson's tantalus—and all aglow with good humor.

Not so Samson. The commissioner was irritable, and more so now that he opened the scented letter Tom had brought. It was deuced curt, it seemed to him, and veiled a sort of suggested laughter, if there was anything insinuative in polite phrases.

"The Princess Yasmini Omanoff Singh," it ran, "hastens to return thanks for Sir Roland Samson's kind letter. She is not, however, afraid of imprisonment or of undue pressure; and as for her secret, that is safe as long as the river runs through the state of Sialpore."

Not a word more. He frowned at the letter, and read and reread it, sniffing at the scent and holding up the paper to the light, so that Sita Ram very nearly had a chance to read it through the knot-hole in the door. The last phrase was the puzzler. It read at first like a boast—like one of those picturesque expressions with which the Eastern mind enjoys to overstate its case. But he reflected on it. As an Orientalist of admitted distinction he had long ago concluded that hyperbole in the East is always based on some fact hidden in the user's mind, often without the user's knowledge. He had written a paper on that very subject, which the Spectator printed with favorable editorial comment; and Mendelsohn K. C. had written him a very agreeable letter stating that his own experience in criminal cases amply bore out the theory. He rang the desk bell for Sita Ram.

"Get me the map of the province."

Sita Ram held it by two corners under the draughty punkah while Samson traced the boundaries with his finger. It was exactly as he thought: without that little palace and its grounds, the state of Sialpore would be bounded exactly by the river. Take away the so-called River Palace with the broad acres surrounding it, and the river would no longer run through the state of Sialpore. That would be the end, then, of the safety of the secret. There was food for reflection there.

What if the famous treasure of Sialpore were buried somewhere in the grounds of the River Palace! Somewhere, for instance, among those gigantic pipal trees.

He folded the map and returned it to Sita Ram.

"I'm expecting half a dozen officers presently. Show them in the minute they come. And—ah—you'd better lock that middle door."

Sita Ram dutifully locked the door on Samson's side, and drew the curtain over it. There was a small hole in the curtain, of peculiar shape—moths had been the verdict when Samson first noticed it, and Sita Ram had advised him to indent for some preventive of the pests; which Samson did, and the hole did not grow any greater afterward.

Samson had had to call a conference, much though he disliked doing it. The rules for procedure in the case of native states included the provision of an official known as resident, whose duty was to live near the native ruler and keep a sharp eye on him. But

Samson, prince of indiscretion, had seen fit three months before to let that official go home to England on long leave, and to volunteer the double duty in his absence. The proposal having economic value, and there being no known trouble in Sialpore just then, the State Department had consented.

The worst of that was that there was no one now in actual close touch with Gungadhura. The best of it was that there was none to share the knowledge of Samson's underlying scheme—which was after all nothing but to win high laurels for himself, by somewhat devious ways, perhaps, but justified in his opinion in the circumstances. And the very worst of it was that good form and official precedent obliged him to call a conference before recommending certain drastic action to his government. Having no official resident to consult, he had to go through the form of consulting somebody; and the more he called in, the less likelihood there was of any one man arrogating undue credit to himself.

They were ushered in presently by Sita Ram. Ross, the principal medical officer came first; it was a pity he ranked so high that he could not be overlooked, but there you were. Then came Sir Hookum Bannerjee, judge of the circuit court—likely to have a lot to say without much meaning in it, and certainly anxious to please. Next after him Sita Ram showed in Norwood, superintendent of police; one disliked calling in policemen, they were so interfering and tactless, but Norwood had his rights. Then came Topham, acting assistant to Samson, loaned from another state to replace young Wilkinson, home on sick leave, and

full-back on the polo team—a quiet man as a rule,
anxious to get back to his own district, and probably
reasonably safe. Last came Lieutenant-Colonel Willoughby de Wing—small, brusk and florid—acting in
command of the 88th Sikh Lancers, and preferring
that to any other task this side of heaven or hell;——
"Nothing to do with politics, my boy,—not built that
way—don't like 'em—never understood 'em anyhow.
Soldiering's my business."

It was well understood it was to be a secret conference. The invitations had been marked "Secret."

"Suppose I lock the door," suggested Samson by
way of additional reminder; and he did that, resuming
his chair with an expression that permitted just the
least suggestion of a serious situation to escape him.
But he was smiling amiably, and his curled mustache
did not disguise the corners of a wilful mouth.

"There is proof conclusive," he began, "——I've
telegrams here that you may see in confidence,——that
Gungadhura has been trafficking with Northwest
tribes. He has sent them money, and made them
promises. There isn't a shade of doubt of it. The
evidence is black. The question is, what's to be done?"

They passed the telegrams from hand to hand,
Norwood looking rather supercilious. (The police
could handle espionage of that sort so much better.)
But it was the youngest man's place to speak first.

"Depose him, I suppose, and put his young son in
his place," suggested Topham. "There's plenty of
precedent."

The doctor shook his head.

"I know Gungadhura. He's a bad strain. It's physiological. I've made a study of these things, and I'm as certain as that I sit here that any son of Gungadhura's would eventually show the same traits as his sire. If you can get rid of Gungadhura, get rid of his whole connection by all means."

"What should be done with the sons, then?" asked Sir Hookum Bannerjee, father of half a dozen budding lawyers.

"Oh, send 'em to school in England, I suppose," said Samson. "There's precedent for that too. But there's another point. Mukhum Dass the money-lender has been foully murdered, struck down by a knife from behind by some one who relieved him of his money. Either a case of simply robbery, or else—"

"Or else what?" Colonel Willoughby de Wing screwed home his monocle. *"That's* as obvious as twice two. That rascal Mukhum Dass was bound to die violently sooner or later. He was notoriously the worst usurer and title-jumper on this side of India. He charged me once a total of eighty-five per cent. for a small loan—and legally, too; kept within the law! I know him!"

"On the other hand," said Samson, "I've been informed that the cellar of the house at present occupied by those Americans on the hill—the gold-miner, you know—Blaine—was burgled last Sunday morning. Blaine himself complained to me. It seems that he had given Gungadhura leave to search the cellar, at Gungadhura's request, for what purpose Blaine professes not to know. Blaine himself, you may remember, lunched and dined at the club last Sunday and gave three of us a rather costly lesson in his national

game of poker. It took place while he was with us at
the club. He has been able to discover, by cross-exam-
ining some witnesses—beggars, I believe, who haunt
the house,—that Mukhum Dass got to the place ahead
of Gungadhura, burgled the cellar, removed something
of great value to Gungadhura, and went off with it.
On the way home he was murdered."

"The murder of Mukhum Dass was known very
soon afterward, of course, to the police," said Norwood. "But we can't do anything across the river
without orders. Why didn't Mr. Blaine bring his complaint and evidence to me?"

"Because I asked him not to!" answered Samson.
"We're mixed up here in a political case."

"Damn all politics!" growled Willoughby de Wing.

"If it can be proved that Gungadhura murdered
Mukhum Dass, or caused him to be murdered, I should
say arrest him, try the brute and hang him!" said
Topham. "Confound these native princes that take
law into their own hands!"

"I should say, let's prove the case if we can," said
Samson, "and use that for an extra argument to force
Gungadhura's abdication. No need to hang him. If
he'd killed a princess, or an Englishman, we'd be
obliged to take extreme measures; but, as De Wing
says, Mukhum Dass was an awful undesirable. If we
hanged Gungadhura, we'd almost *have* to put one of
his five sons on the throne to succeed him. If he abdi-
cates, we can please ourselves. I think I can persuade
him to abdicate—if Norwood, for instance, knows of
any way to gather secret evidence about that murder—

secret, you understand me, Norwood. We need that
for a sword of Damocles."

"Who's to succeed him in that case?" asked Ross,
the P. M. O.

"I shall recommend Utirupa Singh," said Samson,
with his eyes alert.

Ross nodded.

"Utirupa is one of those men who make me think
the Rajput race is not moribund."

"A good clean sportsman!" said Topham. "Plays
a red-hot game of polo, too!"

"Pays up his bets, moreover, like a gentleman!"
said Colonel Willoughby de Wing.

"I feel sure," said Sir Hookum Bannerjee, seeing
he was expected to say something, "that Prince Utirupa Singh would be acceptable to the Rajputs themselves, who are long weary of Gungadhura's way.
But he is not married. It is a pity always that a reigning prince should be unmarried; there are so many
opportunities in that case for intrigue, and for
mistakes."

"Gad!" exclaimed Willoughby de Wing, dropping
his monocle. "What a chance to marry him to that
young Princess Whatshername—you know the one I
mean—the one that's said to masquerade in men's
clothes and dance like the devil, and all that kind of
thing. I know nothing of politics, but—what a
chance!"

"God forbid!" laughed Samson. "That young
woman is altogether too capable of trouble without a
throne to play with! I suspect her, as it happens, of

very definite and dangerous intentions along another line connected with the throne of Sialpore. But I know how to disappoint her and stop her game. I intend to recommend—for the second time, by the way—that she, also, should be sent to Europe for a proper education! But the point I'm driving at is this: are we agreed as to the proper course to take with Gungadhura?"

They nodded.

"Then, as I see it, there's no desperate hurry. Norwood will need time to gather evidence; I'll need specific facts, not hearsay, to ram down Gungadhura's throat. I'll send a wire to the high commissioner and another to Simla, embodying what we recommend, and—what do you say to sending for a battery or two?"

"Good!" said Willoughby de Wing. "A very good thought indeed! I know nothing of politics, except this; that there's nothing like guns to overawe the native mind and convince him that the game's up! Let's see—who'd come with the guns? Coburn, wouldn't he? Yes, Coburn. He's my junior in the service. Yes, a very good notion indeed. Ask for two batteries by all means."

"I'll tell them not to hurry," said Samson. "It's hot weather. They can make it in easy stages."

"By jove!" said Topham. "They'll be here in time for the polo. Won't they beef!"

"Talking of polo, who's to captain the other side? Is it known yet?" asked De Wing.

"Utirupa," answered Topham. "There was never any doubt of that. We've got Collins to captain us,

and Latham and Cartwright, besides me.   We'll give
him the game of his life!"

"That settles quite an important point," said Samson.   "The polo tournament—after it, rather—is the
time to talk to Utirupa.   If we keep quiet until then—
all of us, I mean—there'll be no chance of the cat
jumping before the State Department pulls the string.
I feel sure, from inside information, that Headquarters
would like nothing known about this coup d'état until
it's consummated.   Explanations afterward, and the
fewer the better!   Have a drink anybody?"

In the outer office beyond the curtain Sita Ram
cautiously refitted the knot into its hole, and sat down
to write hurriedly while details were fresh in mind.
Ten minutes afterward, when the conference had
broken up in small-talk, he asked permission to absent
himself for an hour or two.   He said he had a debt to
pay across the river, to a man whose wife was ill.

One hour and a half later by Sita Ram's wrist
watch, Ismail, an Afridi gate-keeper at present apparently without a job, started off on a racing camel full-
pelt for the border, with a letter in his pocket addressed
to a merchant by way of ostensible business, and ten
rupees for solace to the Desert Police.   Tucked away
in the ample folds of his turban was a letter to Yasmini, giving Sita Ram's accurate account of what had
happened at the secret conference.

Safe rules for defeating a rascal are three,
And the first of them all is appear to agree.
The second is boggle at points that don't matter,
Hold out for expense and emolument fatter.
The third is put wish-to-seem-wise on the shelf
And keep your eventual plan to yourself.
Giving heed to the three with your voice and eyes level
You can turn the last trick by out-trumping the devil.

CHAPTER EIGHTEEN

"Be discreet, Blaine—please be discreet!"

MEANWHILE, Gungadhura was not inactive, nor without spies of his own, who told him more or less vaguely that trouble was cooking for him in the English camp. A letter he expected from the Mahsudi tribe had not reached him. It was the very letter he had hoped to show to Samson in proof of Mahsudi villainy and his own friendship; but he rather feared it had fallen into secret service hands, in which case he might have a hard time to clear himself.

Then there was the murder of Mukhum Dass. He had not been able to resist that opportunity, when Patali reported to him what Mukhum Dass had been seen to make away with. And now he had the secret of the treasure in his possession—implicit directions, and a map! He suspected they had been written by some old priest, or former rajah's servant, in the hope of a chance for treachery, and hidden away by Jengal Singh with the same object. There were notes on the margins by Jengal Singh. The thing was obviously genuine.

But the worst of it was Patali knew all about it now, and that cursed idiot Blaine had complained to Samson of burglary, after he learned that the cellar door was broken open by the money-lender. Why hadn't he come to himself, he wondered, and been satisfied with a string of promises? That would have been the courteous thing to do. Instead of that, now Samson's spies were nosing about, and only the gods knew what they might discover. The man who had done the murder was safely out of the way—probably in Delhi by that time, or on his way there; but that interfering ass Norwood might be awake for once, and if the murderer should happen to get caught, and should confess—as hired murderers do sometimes—it would need an awful lot of expert lying and money, too, to clear himself.

With funds—ample extravagant supplies of ready cash, he felt he could even negotiate the awkward circumstance that he himself was deeply in debt to Mukhum Dass at the time of the murder. Money and brains combined can accomplish practically anything. Delhi and Bombay and Calcutta were full of clever lawyers. The point was, he must hurry. And he did not dare trust any one with knowledge of his secret, except Patali, who had wormed out some and guessed the rest, because of the obvious risk of Samson getting wind of it through spies and so forestalling him. He felt he had Samson's character estimated nicely.

Arguing with himself—distracted between fear on one hand, and Patali's importunity on the other, he reached the conclusion that Dick Blaine was his only safe reliance. The American seemed to have an obsession for written contracts, and for enforcing the last letter of them. Well and good, he would make another contract with Dick Blaine, and told Patali so, she agreeing that the American was the safest tool to use.

She saw herself already with her arms up to the shoulders in the treasure of Sialpore.

"The American has few friends," she said. "He smokes a pipe, and thinks, and now that they say his wife has gone away there is less chance than ever of his talking."

"He will need to be paid," said Gungadhura.

"There will be plenty to pay him with!" she answered, her eyes gleaming.

So Gungadhura, with his face still heavily bandaged, drove in a lumbering closed carriage up the rough track to the tunnel Dick had blasted in the hillside. The carriage could not go close to the tunnel-mouth, because the track was only wide enough just there for the dump-carts to come and go. So he got out and walked into the tunnel unattended. Dick was used to seeing him about the works in any case and never objected to explaining things, several times over on occasion.

He found Dick superintending the careful erection of a wall of rock and cement, and he thought for an instant that the American looked annoyed to see him there. But Dick assumed his poker expression the moment afterward, and you couldn't have guessed whether he was glad or sorry.

"You block the tunnel?" the maharajah asked.

"The vein's disappeared," said Dick. "The rock's all faulty here this and that way. I'm shoring up the end to keep the roof from falling down on us, and next I'm going to turn sharp at right angles and try to find the end of the vein where it broke off."

"You are too near the fort in any case," said the maharajah. "No use driving under the fort."

"What do you propose I *should* do?" Dick answered a trifle testily.

"Dig elsewhere."

"What, and scrap this outlay?"

"Yes. I have a reason. A particular—eh—reason."

Dick nodded, poker face set solid.

The maharajah paused. His advantage was that his face was all smothered in the bandages, and the dim light in the tunnel was another good ally. His back, too, was toward the entrance, so that the American's chance of reading between the words was remarkably slight. Dick's back was against the uncompleted masonry.

"Could I—eh—count on you for—eh—very absolute silence?"

"I talk like that parrot in the story," Dick answered.

"You—eh—know a little now of Sialpore, Mr. Blaine. You—eh—understand how easily—eh—rumors get about. A little—eh—foundation and—eh—upside-down pyramids of fancy—eh? You comprehend me?"

"Sure, I get you."

"Eh—you have a good working party."

"Fine!" said Dick. "Just about broke in. Got the gang working pretty well to rights at last."

"Would you—eh—it would take a long time to get such another party of laborers—eh—trained to work well and swiftly?"

"Months!" said Dick. "Unless you've got tame wizards up your sleeve."

"Eh—I was wondering—eh—whether you would be content to—eh—take your working party and—eh —do a little work for me elsewhere?"

"I'm right set on puzzling out this fault in the reef," Dick answered promptly. "My contract reads——"

"For compensation, of course," said Gungadhura. "You would be adequately—eh—there could be a contract drawn."

"I wouldn't cancel this one—not for hard cash," Dick retorted.

"No, no. I do not ask that. It would—eh—not be necessary."

"Well, then, what's the proposal?"

Dick settled himself back against the masonry, crossed his feet, and knocked out ashes from his pipe. The maharajah walked twice, ten yards toward the entrance and back again.

"How long would it take you—eh—to—eh—what was it you said?——to puzzle out this fault?"

"No knowing."

"A short—eh—additional delay will hardly matter?"

"Not if I kept the gang in harness. 'Twouldn't pay to let the team-work slide. Costs too much in time and trouble to break 'em in again."

"Then—eh—will you go and dig for me elsewhere?"

"On what terms?"

"The same terms."

"You pay all expenses and—what am I to dig for?"
"Gold!"

"Do I get my percentage of the gross of all gold won?"

"Yes. But because this is a certainty and—eh—I pay all expenses—eh—of course, in—eh—return for secrecy you—eh—should be well paid, but—eh—a certain stated sum should be sufficient, or a much smaller percentage."

"Suppose we get down to figures?" Dick suggested.

"Fifty thousand rupees, or one per cent."

"At my option?"

Gungadhura nodded. Dick whistled.

"There'd have to be a time limit. I can't stay and dig forever for a matter of fifty thousand dibs."

Gungadhura grew emphatic at that point, using both clenched fists to beat the air.

"Time limit? There must be no time lost at all! Have you promised to be silent? Have you promised not to breathe one little word to anybody?——Not to your own wife? Not to Samson?——Above all not to Samson? Then I will tell you."

Gungadhura glanced about him like a stage conspirator.

"Go on," said Dick. "There's nobody here knows English except you and me."

"You are to dig for the treasure of Sialpore! The treasure of my ancestors!"

"Fifty thousand dibs—*or* one per cent. at my option, eh? Make it two per cent., and draw your contract!"

"Two per cent. is too much!"

"Get another man to dig, then!"

"Very well, I make it two per cent. But you must hurry!"

"Draw your contract. Time limit how long?"

"Two weeks—three weeks—not more than a month at the very utmost! You draw the contract in English, and I will sign it this afternoon. You must begin to dig to-morrow at dawn!"

"Where?"

"In the grounds of the River Palace—across the river—beginning close to the great pipal trees."

"They're all outside the palace wall. How in thunder can I keep secret about that?"

"You must begin inside the palace wall, and tunnel underground."

"Dirt's all soft down there," said Dick. "We'll need to prop up as we go. Lots of lumber. Cost like blazes. Where's the lumber coming from?"

"Cut down the pipal trees!"

"Man—we'd need a mill!"

"There is no lumber—not in such a hurry."

"What'll we do then? Can't have accidents."

"Pah! The lives of a few coolies, Mr. Blaine——"

"Nothing doing, Maharajah sahib! Murder's not my long suit."

"Then pull the palace down and use the beams!"

"You'd have to put that in writing."

"Include it in the contract then! Now, have we agreed?"

"I guess so. If I think of anything else I'll talk it over with you when I bring the contract round this afternoon."

"Good. Then I will give you the map."

"Better give it me now, so I can study it."

"The—eh—risk of that is too great, Mr. Blaine!"

"Seems to me your risk is pretty heavy as it is," Dick retorted. "If I was going to spill your secret, I could do it now, map or no map!"

Three times again Gungadhura paced the tunnel, torn between mistrust, impatience and anxiety. At last he thrust his bandaged face very close to Dick's and spoke in a level hard voice, smiling thinly.

"Very well, Mr. Blaine. I will entrust the map to you. But let me first tell you certain things—certain quite true things. Every attempt to steal that treasure has ended in ill-luck! There have been many. All the conspirators have died—by poison—by dagger—by the sword—by snake-bite—by bullets—they have all died—always! Do you understand?"

Dick shuddered in spite of himself.

"Then take the map!"

Gungadhura turned his back and fumbled in the folds of his semi-European clothing. He produced the silver tube after a minute, removed the cap from one end, and shook out a piece of parchment. There was a dull crimson stain on it.

"The blood of a man who tried to betray the secret!" said Gungadhura. "See—the knife of an assassin pierced the tube, and blood entered through the hole. It happened long ago."

But he did not pass the tube to Dick that he might examine the knife mark.

"These notes on the edge of the map are probably in the hand of Jengal Singh, who stole it. He died of snake-bite more than a year ago. They are in Persian; he notes that four of the trees are dead and only their roots remain; therefore that measurements must allow for that. You must find the roots of the last tree, Mr. Blaine, and measure carefully from both ends, digging afterward in a straight line from inside the palace wall by compass. Is it clear?"

"I guess so. Leave it with me and I'll study it."

The maharajah kept the tube and left the parchment in Dick's hands.

"This afternoon, then?"

"This afternoon," said Dick.

When he had gone, Dick resumed the very careful building of the masonry, placing the last stones with his own hands. Then he went out into the sunlight, to sit on a rock and examine the parchment with a little pocket magnifying-glass that he always carried for business purposes. He studied it for ten minutes.

"It's clever," he said at last. "Dashed clever. It 'ud fool the Prince of Wales!" (Dick had astonishing delusions as to the supposed omniscience of the heir to the throne of England.) "The ink looks old, and it's not metallic ink. The parchment's as old as Methuselah—I'll take my oath on that. There's even different ink been used for the map and the margin notes. But that's new blood or my name's Mike! That blood's not a week old! Phew! I bet it's that poor devil Mukhum Dass! Now—let's figure on this: Mukhum Dass burgled my house, and was murdered about an hour afterward. I think—I can't swear, because he didn't let me hold it, but I *think* that tube in Gungadhura's hand was the very identical one that

I hid under the cellar floor—that Mukhum Dass stole
—and that the maharajah now carries in his pocket.
This map has blood on it. What's the inference?"

He filled his pipe and smoked reflectively.

"The inference is, that I'm accessory after the fact
to the money-lender's murder, unless"——

He finished the pipe, and knocked the ashes out.

"——unless I break my promise, and hand this
piece of evidence over to Norwood. I guess he's arch-
high-policeman here."

As if the guardian angel of Dick's conscience was
at work that very minute to torment him, there came
the sound of an approaching horse, and Samson turned
the corner into view.

"Oh, hullo, Blaine! How's the gold developing?"

"So-so. Have they found the murderer of Mukhum Dass yet?"

Samson dropped his reins to light a cigar, and took
his time about it.

"Not exactly."

"Hum! You either exactly find the murderer, or
you don't!"

"We've our suspicions."

"Leading anywhere?"

"Too soon to say."

"If I was to offer to put you next to a piece of
pretty evidence, how'd that suit you?"

Samson had to relight the cigar, in order to get
opportunity to read Dick's face before he answered.

"I don't think so, Blaine, thank you—at least not at
present. If you've direct evidence of an eye-witness,
of course——"

"Nothing like that," said Dick.

"Well, I'll be candid with you, Blaine. We know quite well who the murderer is. At the right moment we shall land on him hammer and tongs. But you see —we need to choose the right moment, for political reasons. Now—technically speaking—all evidence in criminal cases ought to go to the police, and the police might act too hastily—you understand me?"

"If you know who the man is, of course," said Dick, "there's nothing more I need do."

"Except to be discreet, Blaine! Please be discreet! We shall get the man. Don't doubt it! You and your wife have set us all an example here of minding nobody's business except your own. I'd be awfully obliged if you'd keep yourself as far as possible out of this mess. Should we need any further evidence than we've got already, I'd ask you for it, of course."

"Suits me all right," said Dick. "I'm mum."

"Thanks awfully, Blaine. Can I offer you a cigar? I'm on my way to take a look at the fort. Seems like an anachronism, doesn't it, for us to keep an old-fashioned fort like this so near our own border in native territory. Care to come with me? Well, so long then —see you at the club again, I suppose?"

Samson rode on.

"A narrow squeak that!" said Dick to himself, stowing away the map that he had held the whole time in his right hand in full view of the commissioner.

THE EAST TO COLUMBIA

Sister Columbia, wonderful sister,
Weariless wings on aerial way!
Tell us the lore of thy loftiness, sister,
We of the dark are astir for the day!
Give us the gift of thy marvelous wings,
Spell us the charm that Columbia sings!

Oversea sister, affluent sister,
Queen inexclusive, though out of our reach!
How is thy genius ever unruffled?
What is the talisman altitudes teach?
Measureless meed of ability thine,
What is the goal of thy heart's design?

How shall we learn of it? How shall we follow?
Heavy the burden of earth where we lie!
Only a glimpse of thy miracle stirs us,
Stay in our wallow and teach us to fly!
How shall we spring to Columbia's call?
Oh, that thy wings could unweary us all!

CHAPTER NINETEEN

"I am as simple as the sunlight!"

TESS was in something very near to paradise, if paradise is constant assuaging of the curiosity amid surroundings that conduce to idleness. There were men on that country-side in plenty who would not have dared admit a Western woman into their homes; but even those could hardly prevent wives and daughters from visiting Yasmini in the perfectly correct establishment she kept. And there were other men, more fearless of convention, who were willing that Tess, if veiled, should cross their private thresholds.

So there followed a round of visits and return calls, of other marvelous rides by elephant at night, because the daytime was too hot for comfort, and oftener, long drives in latticed carriages, with footmen up behind and an escort to ride before and swear at the lethargic bullock-men—carriages that bumped along the country roads on strange, old-fashioned springs.

Yasmini was welcome everywhere, and, in the cautious, tenfold guarded Eastern way, kept open house. The women reveled in her free ideas and in the wit with which she heaped scorn on the priest-made fashions that have kept all India in chains for centuries, mocking the priests, as some thought, at the risk of blasphemy.

Almost as much as in Yasmini's daring they took ingenuous delight in Tess, persuading Yasmini to interpret questions and reply or, very rarely, bringing with them some duenna who had a smattering of English.

All imprisoned folk, and especially women in the shuttered zenanas of the East, develop a news-sense of their own that passes the comprehension of free-ranging mortals. They were astonishingly well informed about the outer world—even the far-flung outer world, yet asked the most childish questions; and only a few of them could have written their own names,—they who were titled ladies of a land of ancient chivalry.

"Wait until I am maharanee!" Yasmini said. "The women have always ruled India. Women rule the English, though the English hate the thought of it and make believe otherwise. With the aid of women I will change the face of India,—the women and the gods!"

But she was careful of her promises, holding out no prospects that would stir premature activity among the ranks she counted on.

"Promise the gods too much," she said, "and the gods overwhelm you. They like to serve, which is their business, not to have you squandering on them. Tell the women they are rulers, and they will start to destroy their empire by making public what is secret! If you tell the men that the women rule them, what will the men do?"

"Shut them up all the closer, I suppose," suggested Tess.

"Is that what they ever did? No. They will choose for them certain offices they can not fill because of inexperience, and put the noisiest women in them, and make mock of them, and laugh! Not for a long time yet must India know who rules her!"

"Child, where did you learn all your philosophy?" Tess asked her, one night when they were watching the stars from the bedroom window-seat.

"Oh, men taught me this and that thing, and I have always reversed it and believed the opposite. Why do men teach? To make you free, or to bind you to their own wheel? The English teach that English ways are good for the world. I answer that the world has been good to England and the English would like to keep it so! The pundits say we should study the philosophies. They made me study, hours and hours when I was little. Why? To bind me to the wheel of their philosophy, and keep me subject to them! I say philosophy is good for pundits, as a pond is good for frogs; but shall I be a frog, too, and croak about the beauties of the mud? The priests say we should obey them, and pray, and make offerings, and keep the religious law. I say, that religion is good for priests, which is why they cherish it, and add to it, and persuade foolish women to believe it! As for the gods, if they are anything they are our servants!"

"Your husband is going to have an interesting time," laughed Tess.

Yasmini's blue eyes suddenly turned soft and serious.

"Do you think I can not be a wife?" she asked. "Do you suppose there is no mother-love in me? Do you think I do not understand how a man needs cherishing? Do you think I will preach to my husband, or oppose his plans? No! I will do as the gods do when the priests are asleep! I will let him go his own way, and will go with him, never holding back; and little by little he will learn that I have understanding. Little by little he will grow into knowledge of the things I know—and he will be a very great man!"

There were no visits whatever from Utirupa, for the country-side would have been scandalized. Only, flowers came every day in enormous quantities; and there was a wealth of horses, carriages, jewels and armed men at his bride's disposal that proved he had not forgotten her existence or her needs. She had claimed marriage to him by Gandharva rite, and he had tacitly consented, but she was not ready yet to try conclusions with the secret, octopus influence of the priests; and there was another reason.

"If it should get to Samson's ears that he and I are married, that would be the end of his chance of the throne of Sialpore! Samson is English of the English. He would oppose to the end the nomination of a maharajah, whose wife has notions of her own—as I am known to have! They like him—my husband— because he plays good polo, and will bet with them, and can play cricket; and because he seems to follow no special line of politics. But if it were known he had a clever wife—me for wife—they would have none of him! I shall be a surprise for them when the die is cast!"

Tess was in almost daily communication with Dick, for, what with Tom Tripe and Sita Ram and about a dozen other sworn accomplices, Yasmini had messages coming and going all the time. Camels used to arrive long after dark, and letters were brought in, smelly with the sweat of loyal riders who had hidden them from too inquisitive police. Most of them carried back a scribbled word for Dick. But he said nothing about the treasure in his curt, anonymous, unsigned replies, being nervous about sending messages at all. Only, when in one letter he mentioned digging in another place, and Tess read the sentence aloud, Yasmini squealed with delight. The next day her own advices confirmed the hint, Sita Ram sending a long account of new developments and adding that "Samson sahib is much exercised in mind about it."

"All goes well!" Yasmini belled in her golden voice. "Samson has seen the hidden meaning of my letter! If I had told him bluntly where the treasure is, he would have laughed and forgotten it! But because he thinks he reads the secret of my mind, he flatters himself and falls into the trap! Now we have Samson caught, and all is well!"

"It would be a very canny person who could read the secret of your mind, I should say!" laughed Tess.

"I am as simple as the sunlight!" Yasmini answered honestly. "It is Samson who is dark, not I."

Yasmini began making ready for departure, giving a thousand orders to dependents she could trust.

"At the polo game," she asked Tess, "when the English ask questions as to where you have been, and what you saw, what will you tell them?"

"Why not the truth? Samson expressly asked me
to cultivate your acquaintance."

"Splendid! Tell them you traveled on camel-back
by night across the desert with me! By the time they
have believed that we will think of more to add to it!
We return by elephant to Sialpore together, timing our
arrival for the polo game. There we separate. You
watch the game together with your husband. I shall
be in a closed carriage—part of the time. I shall be
there *all* the time, but I don't think you will see me."

"But you say they have rifled your palace. Where
will you sleep?" Tess asked.

"At your house on the hill!"

"But that is in Gungadhura's territory. Aren't you
afraid of him?"

"Of Gungadhura? I? I never was! But now
whoever fears him would run from a broken snake. I
have word that the fool has murdered Mukhum Dass
the money-lender. You may trust the English to draw
his teeth nicely for him after that! Gungadhura is like
a tiger in a net he can not break!"

"He might send men to break into the house,"
Tess argued.

"There will be sharper eyes than any of his
watching!"

But Tess was alarmed at the prospect. She did
not mind in the least what the English might have to
say about it afterward; but to have her little house the
center of nocturnal feuds, with her husband using his
six-shooters, and heaven only knew what bloodshed
resulting, was more of a prospect than she looked forward to.

"Sister," said Yasmini, taking her by both hands. "I must use your house. There is no other place."

No one could refuse her when her deep blue eyes grew soft and pleading, let alone Tess, who had lived with her and loved her for a week.

"Very well," she answered; and Yasmini's eyes softened and brightened even more.

"I shall not forget!"

Getting ready was no child's play. It was to be a leisurely procession in the olden style, with tents, servants, and all the host of paraphernalia and hangers-on that that entails; not across the desert this time, but around the edge of it, the way the polo ponies went, and out of Gungadhura's reach. For, however truly Yasmini might declare that she was not afraid of Gungadhura (and she vowed she never boasted), she was running no unnecessary risks; it takes a long time for the last rats to desert a sinking ship, (the obstinate go down with it), and just as long for the last assassins to change politics. She was eager to run all the risks when that was the surest strategy, but cautious otherwise.

The secret of her safety lay in the inviolable privacy surrounding woman's life in all that part of India— privacy that the English have respected partly because of their own inherent sense of personal retirement, partly because it was the easiest way and saved trouble; but mainly because India's women have no ostensible political power, and there is politics enough without bringing new millions more potential agitators into light. So word of her life among the women did not travel swiftly to official ears, as that of a male intriguer would certainly have done. Utirupa was busy all day long with polo, and the Powers that Be were sure of it, and pleased. What Gungadhura knew, or guessed, was another matter; but Gungadhura had his own hands full just then.

So they formed part of a procession that straggled along the miles, of elephants, camels and groups of ponies, carts loaded with tents, chattering servants, parties of Rajput gentlemen, beggars, hangers-on, retainers armed with ancient swords, mountebanks, several carriage-loads of women, who could sing and dance and were as particular about their veiling as if Lalun were not their ancestress, the inevitable faquirs, camel-loads of entertainers, water-carriers, sheep, asses, and bullock-drawn, squeaking two-wheeled carts aburst with all that men and animals could eat. Three days and nights of circus life, as Tess described it afterward to Dick.

Yasmini and Tess rode part of the way on an elephant, lying full-length in the hooded howdah with a view of all the country-side, starting before dawn and resting through the long heat of the day. But monotony formed no part of Yasmini's scheme of life, and daring was the very breath she breathed. Most of the time they rode horseback together, disguised as men and taking to the fields whenever other parties drew too close. But sometimes Yasmini left Tess on the elephant, and mingled freely with the crowd, her own resourcefulness and intimate knowledge of the language and the customs enough protection.

Nights were the amazing time. A great camp spread out under ancient trees—bonfires glowing everywhere, and native followers squatted around them,—long, whinnying horse-lines—elephants, great gurgling shadows, swaying at their pickets—shouting, laughter, music,—and, over all, soft purple darkness and the stars.

For it was something more than a mere polo tournament that they were traveling to. It had grown out of a custom abolished by the government, of traveling once a year to Sialpore to air and consider grievances —a custom dating from long before the British occupation, when the princes of the different states were all in rival camps and that was about the only opportunity to meet on reasonably friendly terms. In later years it had looked like developing into a focus of political solidity; so some ingenious commissioner had introduced the polo element, eliminating, item after item, all the rest. Then the date had been changed to the early hot weather, in order to reduce attendance; but the only effect that had was to keep away the English from outlying provinces. It was the one chance that part of Rajputana had to get together, and the Rajputs swarmed to the tournament—along the main trunk road that the English had reconstructed in early days for the swifter movement of their guns. (It did not follow any particular trade route, although trade had found its way afterward along it.)

Yasmini saw Utirupa every night, she apparently as much a man as he in turban and the comfortable Rajput costume—shorter by a head, but as straight-standing and as agile. Tess and Hasamurti used to watch them under the trees, ready to give the alarm in case of interruption, sometimes near enough to catch the murmured flow of confidence uniting them in the secrecy of sacred, unconforming interviews. It was common knowledge that Yasmini was in the camp, but she was always supposed to be tented safely on the outskirts, with her women and a guard of watchful servants all about her. There was no risk of an affront to her in any case; it was known that Utirupa would attend to that.

Each night between the bonfires there was entertainment—men who walked tight-ropes, wrestlers, a performing horse, ballad-singers and, dearest delight of all, the tellers of Eastern tales, who sat with silent rings of men about them and reeled off the old, loved, impossible adventures of the days when the gods walked with men on earth—stories of miracles and love and derring-do, with heroes who could fight a hundred men unscathed, and heroines to set the heart on fire.

Then off again before sunrise in the cool amid the shouting and confusion of a breaking camp, with truant ponies to be hunted, and everybody yelling for his right of road, and the elephants sauntering urbanely through it all with trunks alert for pickings from the hay-carts. They were nights and days superbly gorgeous, all-entertaining, affluent of humor.

Then on the third day, nearing Sialpore toward evening they filed past two batteries of Royal Horse Artillery, drawn up on a level place beside the road to let them by—an act of courtesy not unconnected with its own reward. It is never a bad plan to let the possibly rebellious take a long look at the engines of enforcement.

"Ah!" laughed Yasmini, up in the howdah now beside Tess on the elephant, "the guns of the gods! I *said* the gods were helping us!"

"Look like English guns to me," Tess answered.

"So think the English, too. So thinks Samson, who sent for them. So, too, perhaps Gungadhura will think when he knows the guns are coming! But I know better. I never promise the gods too much, but let them make me promises, and look on while they perform them. I tell you, those are the *guns of the gods!*"

A bad man ruined by the run of luck
May shed the slime—they've done it,
    Times and again they've done it.
That turn to aspiration out of muck
Is quick if heart's begun it,
    If heart's desire's begun it.
But 'ware revenge if greater craft it is
That jockeyed him to recognize defeat,
Or greater force that overmastered his—
Efficiency more potent than deceit
    That craved his crown and won it!
Safer the she-bear with her suckling young,
Kinder the hooked shark from a yardarm hung,
More rational a tiger by the hornets stung
Than perfidy outcozened.   Shun it!

CHAPTER TWENTY

"Millions! Think of it! Lakhs and crores!"

THE business of getting a maharajah off the
throne, even in a country where the overlords are nervous, and there is precedent, is not entirely simple,
especially when the commissioner who recommends it
has a name for indiscretion and ambition. The government of conquered countries depends almost as much
on keeping clever administrators in their place as on
fostering subdivision among the conquered.

So, very much against his will, Samson was obliged
to go to see a high commissioner, who is a very
important person indeed, and ram home his arguments
between four walls by word of mouth. He did not
take Sita Ram with him, so there is a gap in the story
at that point, partly bridged by Samson's own sketchy
account of the interview to Colonel Willoughby de
Wing, overheard by Carlos de Sousa Braganza the
Goanese club butler, and reported to Yasmini at third
hand.

There were no aeroplanes or official motor-cars at
that time to take officials at outrageous speed on urgent business. But Samson's favorite study in his spare
time was Julius Cæsar, who usually traveled long distances at the rate of more than a hundred miles a day,

and was probably short-winded from debauch into the
bargain. What the great Julius could do, Samson
could do as well; but in spite of whip and spur and
post, ruthless robbery of other people's reserved
accommodation, and a train caught by good luck on the
last stage, it took him altogether seven valuable days
and nights. For there was delay, too, while the high
commissioner wired to Simla in code for definite permission to be drastic.

The telegram from the secretary of state pointed
out, as Samson had predicted that it would, the desir-
ability of avoiding impeachment and trial if that were
possible, in view of the state of public unrest in India
and the notorious eagerness of Parliament at home to
interfere in Indian affairs.

"Get him to abdicate!" was the meat of the long
message.

"Can you do it?" asked the high commissioner.

"Leave that to me!" boasted Samson. "And now
this other matter. These 'islands' as they're called.
It's absurd and expensive to continue keeping up a
fort inside the maharajah's territory. There's no military advantage to us in having it so near our border.
And there are totally unnecessary problems of administration that are entailed by the maharajah administer-
ing a small piece of territory on our side of the river.
I've had a contract drawn for your approval—Sir
Hookum Bannerjee drew it, he's a very able lawyer—
stipulating with Utirupa, in consideration of our recognition of himself and his heirs as rulers of the State
of Sialpore, that he shall agree to exchange his palace

and land on our side of the river against our fort on his side. What do you think of it?"

"It isn't a good bargain. He ought to give us more than that in the circumstances, against a fort and— and all that kind of thing."

"It's a supremely magnificent bargain!" retorted Samson. "Altogether overlooking what we'll save in money by not having to garrison that absurd fort, it's the best financial bargain this province ever had the chance of!"

"How d'ye mean?"

Samson whispered. Even those four solid walls were not discreet enough.

"The treasure of Sialpore is buried in the River Palace grounds! Millions! Think of it—Millions! Lakhs and crores!"

The high commissioner whistled.

"That 'ud mean something to the province, wouldn't it! Show me your proofs."

How Samson got around the fact that he had no actually definite proofs, he never told. But he convinced the high commissioner, who never told either, unless to somebody at Simla, who buried the secret among the State Department files.

"I'll wire Simla," said the high commissioner presently, "for permission to authorize you to set your signature to that contract on behalf of government. The minute I get it I'll wire you to Sialpore and confirm by letter. Now you'd better get back to your post in a hurry. And don't forget, it would be difficult in a case like this to err on the side of silence, Samson. Who'll have to be told?"

"Nobody but Willoughby de Wing. I'll have to ask him for troops to guard the River Palace grounds. There's a confounded American digging this minute in the River Palace grounds by arrangement with Gungadhura. He'll have to be stopped, and I'll have to make some sort of explanation."

"What's an American doing in Sialpore?"

"Prospecting. Has a contract with Gungadhura."

"Um-m-m! We'll have Standard Oil in next! Better point out to Utirupa that contracts with foreigners aren't regarded cordially."

"That's easily done," said Samson. "Utirupa is nothing if not anxious to please."

"Yes, Utirupa is a very fine young fellow—and a good sportsman, too, I'm told."

"There is no reason why Utirupa should recognize the contract between Gungadhura and the American. It was a private contract—no official sanction. If Gungadhura isn't in position to continue it——"

"Exactly. Well—good-by. I'll look forward to a good report from you."

By train and horse and tonga Samson contrived to reach Sialpore on the morning before the day set for the polo tournament. He barely allowed himself time to shave before going to see Dick Blaine, and found him, as he expected, at the end of the tunnel nearly a hundred yards long that started from inside the palace wall and passed out under it. The guards at the gate did not dare refuse the commissioner admission. So far, Dick had not begun demolition of the palace, but had dragged together enough lumber by pulling down sheds and outhouses. He was not a destructive-minded man.

"Will you come outside and talk with me?" Samson shouted, amid the din of pick and shovel work.

"Sure."

Dick's poker face was in perfect working order by the time they reached the light. But he stood with his back to the sun and let Samson have the worst of the position.

"You're wasting time and money, Blaine. I've come to tell you so."

"Now—that's good of you."

"Your contract with Gungadhura is not worth the paper it's written on."

"How so?"

"He will not be maharajah after noon to-day!"

"You don't mean it!"

"That information is confidential. but the news will be out by to-morrow. The British Administration intends to take over all the land on this side of the river. That's confidential too. Between you and me, our government would never recognize a contract between you and Gungadhura. I warned you once, and your wife a second time."

"Sure, she told me."

"Well. You and I have been friends, Blaine. I'd like you to regard this as not personal. But——"

"Oh, I get you. I'm to call the men off? That it?"

"You've only until to-morrow in any case."

"And Gungadhura, broke, to look to for the pay-roll! Well—as you say, what's the use?"

"I'd pay your men off altogether, if I were you."

"They're a good gang."

"No doubt. We've all admired your ability to make men work. But there'll be a new maharajah in a day or two, and, strictly between you and me, as one friend to another, there'll be a very slight chance indeed of your getting a contract from the incoming man to carry on your mining in the hills. I'd like to save you trouble and expense."

"Real good of you."

"Er—found anything down there?" Samson nodded over his shoulder toward the tunnel mouth.

"Not yet."

"Any signs of anything?"

"Not yet."

Samson looked relieved.

"By the way. You mentioned the other day something about evidence relating to the murder of Mukhum Dass."

"I did."

"Was it anything important?"

"Maybe. Looked so to me."

"Would you mind giving me an outline of it?"

"You said that day you knew who murdered Mukhum Dass?"

"Yes. When I got in this morning there was a note on my desk from Norwood, the superintendent of police, to say that they've arrested your butler and cook, and the murderer of Mukhum Dass all hiding together near a railway station. The murderer has squealed, as you Americans say. They often do when they're caught. He has told who put him up to it."

"Guess I'll give you this, then. It's the map out of

the silver tube that Mukhum Dass burgled from my
cellar. Gungadhura gave it to me with instructions to
dig here. You'll note there's blood on it."

Samson's eyes looked hardly interested as he took
it. Then he looked, and they blazed. He put it in his
inner pocket hurriedly.

"Too bad, Blaine!" he laughed. "So you even had
a map of the treasure, eh? Another day or two and
you'd have forestalled us! I suppose you'd a contract
with Gungadhura for a share of it?"

"You bet!"

"Well—it wasn't registered. I doubt if you could
have enforced it. Gungadhura is an awful rascal."

"Gee!" lied Dick. "I never thought of that! I
had my other contract registered all right—in your
office—you remember?"

"Yes. I warned you at the time about Gungadhura."

"You did. I remember now. You did. Well, I
suppose the wife and I'll be heading for the U. S. A.
soon, richer by the experience. Still—I reckon I'll
wait around and see the new maharajah in the saddle,
and watch what comes of it."

"You've no chance, Blaine, believe me!"

"All right, I'll think it over. Meanwhile, I'll whistle off these men."

The next man Samson interviewed was Willoughby
de Wing.

"Let me have a commissioner's escort, please," he
demanded. "I'm going to see Gungadhura now!
You'd better follow up with a troop to replace the
maharajah's guards around his palace. We can't put
him under arrest without impeaching him; but—make

it pretty plain to the guard they're there to protect a
man who has abdicated; that no one's to be allowed
in, and nobody out unless he can explain his business.
Then, can you spare some guards for another job? I
want about twenty men on the River Palace at once.
Caution them carefully. Nobody's to go inside the
grounds. Order the maharajah's guards away! It's a
little previous. His officers will try to make trouble
of course. But an apology at the proper time will
cover that."

"What's the new excitement?" asked the colonel.
"More murders? More princesses out at night?"

"This is between you and me. Not a word to a
living soul, De Wing!" Samson paused, then whispered: *"The treasure of Sialpore!"*

"What——in the palace?"

"In the grounds! There's a tunnel already half-
dug, leading toward it from inside the palace wall.
I've proof of the location in my pocket!"

"Gad's teeth!" barked Willoughby de Wing. "All
right, I'll have your escort in a jiffy. Have a whisky
and soda, my boy, to stiffen you before the talk with
Gungadhura!"

A little less than half an hour later Samson drove
across the bridge in the official landau, followed by an
officer, a jemadar, a naik and eight troopers of De
Wing's Sikh cavalry. Willoughby de Wing drove in
the carriage with him as a witness. They entered the
palace together, and were kept waiting so long that
Samson sent the major-domo to the maharajah a second time with a veiled threat to repeat, said slowly:

"Say the business is urgent and that I shall not be

held responsible for consequences if he doesn't see me at once!"

"Gad!" swore De Wing, screwing in his monocle. "I'd like a second whisky and soda! I suppose there's none here. I hate to see a man broke—even a blackguard!"

Gungadhura received them at last, seated, in the official durbar room. The bandages were gone from his face, but a strip of flesh-colored court-plaster from eye to lip gave him an almost comical look of dejection, and he lolled in the throne-chair with his back curved and head hung forward, scowling as a man does not who looks forward to the interview.

Samson cleared his throat, and read what he had to say, holding the paper straight in front of him.

"I have a disagreeable task of informing Your Highness that your correspondence with the Mahsudi tribe is known to His Majesty's Government."

Gungadhura scowled more deeply, but made no answer.

"Amounting as it does to treason, at a time when His Majesty's Government are embarrassed by internal unrest, your act can not be overlooked."

Gungadhura made a motion as if to interrupt, but thought better of it.

"In the circumstances I have the honor to advise Your Highness that the wisest course, and the only course that will avoid impeachment, is abdication."

Gungadhura shook his head violently.

"I can explain," he said. "I have proofs."

Samson turned the paper over—paused a moment —and began to read the second sheet.

"It is known who murdered Mukhum Dass. The assassin has been caught, and has confessed."

Gungadhura's eyes that had been dull, and almost listless hitherto, began to glare like an animal's.

"I have here——" Samson reached in his pocket, "a certain piece of parchment—a map in fact—that was stolen from the body of Mukhum Dass. Perhaps Your Highness will recognize it. Look!"

Gungadhura looked, and started like a man stung. Samson returned the map to his pocket, for the maharajah almost looked like trying to snatch it; but instead he collapsed in his chair again.

"If I abdicate——?" he asked, as if his throat and lips could hardly form the words.

"That would be sufficient. The assassin would then be allowed to plead guilty to another charge there is against him, and the matter would be dropped."

"I abdicate!"

"On behalf of His Majesty's Government I accept the abdication. Sign this, please."

Samson laid a formal written act of abdication on the table by the throne. Gungadhura signed it. Willoughby de Wing wrote his signature as witness. Samson took it back and folded it away.

"Arrangements will be made for Your Highness to leave Sialpore to-morrow morning, with a sufficient escort for your protection. Provision will be made in due course for your private residence elsewhere. Be good enough to hold yourself and your family in readiness to-morrow morning."

"But my son!" exclaimed Gungadhura. "I abdicate in favor of my son!"

"In case of abdication by a reigning prince, or deposition of a reigning prince," said Samson, "the Government of India reserves the right to appoint his successor, from among eligible members of his family if there be any, but to appoint his successor in any case. There is ample precedent."

"And my son?"

"Will certainly not be considered."

Gungadhura glanced about him like a frenzied man, and then lay back in a state of near-collapse. Samson and De Wing both bowed, and left the room.

"Poor devil!" said De Wing, "I'm sorry for him."

"Would you be a good fellow," said Samson, "and send off this wire for me? There—I've added the exact time of the abdication. I've got to go now and summon a durbar of Gungadhura's state officers, and tell them in confidence what's happened. I shall hint pretty broadly that Utirupa is our man, and then ask them which prince they'd like to have succeed."

"Good!" said De Wing. "Nothing like tact! Why not meet me at the club for a whisky and soda afterward?"

Inside the durbar hall Gungadhura sat alone for just so long as it took the sound of the closing door to die away. Then another door, close behind the throne chair opened, and Patali entered. She looked at him with pity on her face, and curiosity.

"That American sold you," she said after a minute.

"Eh?"

"I say, that American sold you! He sold you, and the map, and the treasure to the English!"

"I know it! I know it!"

"If I were a man——"

She waited, but he gave no sign of manhood.

"If I were a man I know what I would do!"

"Peace, Patali! I am a ruined man. They will all desert me as soon as the news is out. They are deserting now; I feel it in my bones. I have none to send."

"Send? It is only maharajahs who must send. *Men* do their own work! I know what I would do to an American or any other man, who sold me!"

The king sent his army and said, "Lo, I did i̇. Consider my prowess and my strategy!" But the gods laughed.—EASTERN PROVERB.

CHAPTER TWENTY-ONE

"The guns of the gods!"

VERY shortly after dawn on the morning of the polo game Yasmini left the Blaines' house on business of her own. The news of Gungadhura's abdication was abroad already, many times multiplied by each mouth until two batteries of guns had become an army corps. But what caused the greatest excitement was the news, first of all whispered, then confirmed, that Gungadhura himself was missing.

That disturbing knowledge was the factor that prevented Yasmini from returning to her own rifled palace and making the best of it; for it would take time to hedge the place about properly with guards. There was simply no knowing what Gungadhura might be up to. She judged it probable that he had seen through her whole plot in the drear light of revelation that so often comes to stricken men, and in that case her own life was likely in danger every second he was still at liberty. But she sent word to Utirupa, too, to be on the alert. And she saw him herself that morning, in her favorite disguise of a *rangar zemindari*, which is a Rajput landowner turned Muhammadan. The disguise precluded any Hindu interference, and Muhammadans on that country-side, who might have questioned her, were scarce.

The polo did not take place until late afternoon, because of the heat, but the grounds were crowded long before the time by a multi-colored swarm in gala mood, whom the artillerymen, pressed into service as line-keepers, had hard work to keep back of the line. There was a rope around three sides of the field, but it broke repeatedly, and in the end the gunners had to be stationed a few feet apart all down the side opposite the grand-stand to keep the crowd from breaking through.

There were carriages in swarms, ranging from the spider-wheel gig of a British subaltern to the four-in-hand of Rajput nobility—kept pretty carefully apart, though. The conquerors of India don't mix with the conquered, as a rule, except officially. And there were half a dozen shuttered carriages that might have contained ladies, and might not; none knew.

It was a crowd that knew polo from the inside outward, and when the ponies were brought at last and stood in line below the grand-stand, each in charge of his *sais,* there grew a great murmur of critical approval; for the points of a horse in Rajputana are as the lines of a yacht at Marblehead, and the marks of a dog in Yorkshire; the very urchins know them. The Bombay side of India had been scoured pretty thoroughly for mounts for that event. The Rajputs had on the whole the weight of money, and perhaps the showiest ponies, but the English team, nearly all darker in color as it happened, except for one pie-bald, looked trained up to the last notch and bore the air of knowing just what to expect, that is as unmistakable in horses as in men.

Tom Tripe was there with his dog. Trotters had
the self-imposed and wholly agreeable task of chasing
all unattached dogs off the premises. But Tom Tripe
himself was keeping rather in the background, because
technically, as a servant of Gungadhura, he was in a
delicate position. A voice that he could swear he
almost recognized whispered to him in the crowd that
the English were going to forbid the next maharajah
to have any but employees of his own race. And a
laugh that he could pick out of a million greeted his
change of countenance. But though he turned very
swiftly, and had had no brandy since morning to
becloud his vision, he failed to see his tormentor.

Tess and Dick drove down in ample time, as they
had imagined, and found hard work to squeeze the
dog-cart in between the phalanxes of wheels already
massed on the ground. When they went to the grand-
stand it was to find not a seat left in the rows reserved
for ordinary folk; so Samson, who arrived late too,
magnificent in brand-new riding-boots, invited them
to sit next him in front.

The ground was in perfect condition—a trifle
hard, because of the season, but flat as a billiard table
and as fast as even Rajputs could desire. A committee
of them had been going over it daily for a week past,
recommending touches here, suggesting something
there, neglecting not an inch, because the finer stick-
work of the Rajput team would be lost on uneven
ground; and the English had been sportsmen enough
to accommodate them without a murmur.

When a little bell rang and the teams turned out
for the first chukker in deathly silence, it was evident

at once what the Rajput strategy would be. They had brought out their fastest ponies to begin with, determined to take the lead at the start and hold it.

One could hear the crowd breathe when the whistle blew; for in India polo is a game to watch, not an opportunity for small talk. Instantly the ball went clipping toward the English goal, to be checked by Topham at full-back, who sent it out rattling to the right wing. But the Rajput left-wing man, a young cousin of Utirupa, cut in like an arrow. The ball crossed over to the right wing, where Utirupa took it, galloping down the line on a chestnut mare that had the speed of wind. Topham, racing to intercept the ball, missed badly; a second later the Rajput center thundered past both men and scored the goal, amid a roar from the spectators, less than a minute from the start.

"Dick!" Tess exclaimed. "You ought to be ashamed of me! I'm rooting for the Rajputs against my own color!"

"So'm I!" he answered. "I wish to glory there was some one here to bet with!"

Samson overheard.

"Which way do you want to bet?" he asked.

"A thousand on the Rajputs."

"Thousand what?"

"Dollars. Three thousand rupees."

"Confound it, you Americans are all too rich! Never mind, I'll take you."

"A bet!" Dick answered, and both men wrote it down.

About nine words were said by the captain of the

English team as they rode back to the center of the field, and when the ball was in play again there was no more of the scattering open play that suited the other side, but a close, short-hitting, chop-and-follow method that tried ponies' tempers, and a scrimmage every ten yards that made all unavailing the Rajputs' speed and dash. Whenever a stroke of lightning wrist-work sent the ball clipping down-field Topham returned it to the center and the scrimmage began all over again. The first chukker ended in mid-field, with the score 1-0.

Both sides brought out fresh ponies for the second, and the Rajputs tried again to score with their favorite tactics of long-hitting and tremendous speed. But the English were playing dogged-does-it, and Topham on the pie-bald at full back was invincible. Nothing passed him. Nor were the English slow. Three times they seized opportunity in mid-field and rode with a burst of fiery hitting toward the Rajput goal. Three times the gunners down the line began to yell. The English team were getting together, and the Rajputs a little wild. But the chukker ended with the same score, 1-0.

"How d'you feel about it now?" asked Samson, looking as calm as the English habitually do whenever their pulse beats furiously.

"I'd like to bet too!" Tess laughed, leaning across.

"What—the same sized bet?"

"No, a hundred."

"Dollars?"

"Rupees!" she laughed. "I'm not so rich as my husband."

"Can't refuse a lady!" Samson answered, noting

the bet down. "I shall be a rich man to-night. They play a brilliant game, those fellows, but we always beat them in the end."

"How do you account for that?" Dick asked, suspecting what was coming.

"Oh, in a number of ways, but chiefly because they lack team-loyalty among themselves. They're all jealous of one another, whereas our fellows play as a unit."

As if in confirmation of Samson's words the Rajput team seemed rather to go to pieces in the third chukker. There was the same brilliant individual hitting, and as much speed as ever, but the genius was not there. In vain Utirupa took the ball out of a scrimmage twice and rode away with it. He was not backed up in the nick of time, and before the end of the third minute the English scored.

"You'd better go and hedge those bets," laughed Samson when the chukker ended. "There are plenty of the native gentry over yonder who'd be delighted to gamble a fortune with you yet!"

Dick scarcely heard. He was watching Utirupa, who stood by the pony-line where a *sais* was doing something to a saddle girth. A rangar came up to the prince and spoke to him—a slim, young-looking man, a head the shorter of the two, with a turban rather low over his eyes, and the loose end of it, for some reason, across the lower half of his face. Dick nudged Tess, and she nodded. After that Utirupa appeared to speak in low tones to each member of his own team.

"I beg your pardon. What was that you said?" asked Dick.

"I say you'd better hedge those bets."

"I'll double with you, if you like!"

"Good heavens, man! I've wagered a month's pay already! Go and bet with Willoughby de Wing or one of the gunner officers."

The rangar disappeared into the crowd before the teams rode out for the fourth encounter, and Tess, who had made up her mind to watch the shuttered carriages that stood in line together in a roped enclosure of their own, became too busy with the game. Something had happened to the Rajputs. They no longer played with the gallery-appealing smash-and-gallop fury that won them the first goal, although their speed held good and the stick-work was marvelous. But they seemed more willing now to mix it in the middle of the field, and to ride off an opponent instead of racing for the chance to shine individually. It became the English turn to drive to the wings and try to clear the ball for a hurricane race down-field; and they were not quite so good at those tactics as the other side were.

All the rest of that game until the eighth, chukker after chukker, the Rajputs managed to reverse the usual procedure, obliging the English team to wear itself out in terrific efforts to break away, tiring men and ponies in a tight scramble in which neither side could score.

"It looks like a draw after all," said Samson. "Bets off in that case, I suppose? Disappointing game in my opinion."

" 'Tisn't over yet," said Dick.

The Rajputs were coming out for the last chukker with their first and fastest ponies that had rested through the game; and they were smiling. Utirupa had said something that was either a good joke or else vastly reassuring. As a matter of fact he had turned them loose at last to play their old familiar game again, and from the second that the ball went into play the crowd was on tiptoe, swaying this and that way with excitement.

In vain the English sought to return to the scrim-mage play; it was too late. The Rajputs had them rattled. Topham at full-back on the pie-bald was a stone wall, swift, hard-hitting and resourceful, but in vain. Swooping down the wings, and passing with the dextrous wrist-work and amazing body-bends that they alone seem able to accomplish, they put the English team on the defensive and kept them there. Once, at about half-time, by a dash all together the English did succeed in carrying the ball down-field, but that was their last chance, and they missed it. In the last two minutes the Rajputs scored two goals, the last one driven home by Utirupa himself, racing ahead of the field with whirling stick and the thunder of a neck-and-neck stampede behind him.

"That'll be your month's pay!" laughed Dick. "I hope you won't starve for thirty days!"

The crowd went mad with delight, and swarmed on to the ground, shouting and singing. Samson got up, looking as if he rather enjoyed to lose three thou-sand rupees in an afternoon.

"If you'll excuse me," he said, "I'll go and shake hands with Utirupa. He deserves congratulation. It was head-work won that game."

"I wonder what *she* said to him at the end of the third chukker," Tess whispered to Dick.

Samson found Utirupa giving orders to the *saises*, and shook hands with him.

"Good game, Utirupa! Congratulate you. By the way: there's going to be a meeting on important business in my office half an hour from now. When you've had a tub and a change, I wish you'd come and join us. We want a word with you."

"Where are the gunners going to?" asked Tess. "The men who kept the line—look! They're all trooping off the ground in the same direction."

"Dunno," said her husband. "Let's make for the dog-cart and drive home. If we hang around Samson'll think we're waiting for that money!"

Half an hour after that, Utirupa presented himself at Samson's office in the usual neat Rajput dress that showed off his lithe figure and the straightness of his stature. There was quite a party there to meet him— Samson, Willoughby de Wing, Norwood, Sir Hookum Bannerjee, Topham (still looking warm and rather weary after the game)—and outside on the open ground beyond the compound wall two batteries of horse-guns were drawn up at attention. But if Utirupa felt surprise he did not show it.

"To make a short story of a long one, Prince Utirupa," Samson began at once, "as you know, Gungadhura abdicated yesterday. The throne of Sialpore is vacant, and you are invited to accept it. I have here the required authority from Simla."

Utirupa rose from his chair, and bowed.

"I am willing to accept," he answered quietly. His face showed no emotion.

"There is one stipulation, though," said Samson. "We are tired of these foolish 'islands'—our territory in yours and yours in ours. There's a contract here. As your first official act—there's no time like the present—we want you to exchange the River Palace, on this side of the river, for out fort on your side."

Utirupa said never a word.

"It's not a question of driving a bargain," Samson went on. "We don't know what the palace may be worth, or what is in it. If there is any valuable furniture you'd like removed, we'll waive that point; but on the terms of the contract we exchange the fort, with the guns and whatever else is there except the actual harness and supplies of the garrison, against the land and palace and whatever it contains except furniture."

Utirupa smiled—perhaps because the guns in that fort were known to date from before the Mutiny.

"Will you agree?"

"I will sign," said Utirupa. And he signed the contract there and then, in presence of all those witnesses. Ten minutes later, as he left the office, the waiting batteries fired him a fourteen-gun salute, that the world might know how a new maharajah occupied the throne of Sialpore.

Meanwhile, up at the house on the hill Tess and Dick found Yasmini already there ahead of them, lying at her ease, dressed as a woman of women, and smoking a cigarette in the window-seat of the bedroom Tess had surrendered to her.

"What was it you said to him after the third chukker?" was the first question Tess asked.

"You recognized me?"

"Sure. So did my husband. What did you say to him?"

"Oh, I just said that if he hoped to win he must play the game of the English, and play it better, that was all. He won, didn't he? I didn't stay to the end. I knew he would win."

Almost as they spoke the fourteen-gun salute boomed out from across the river, and echoed from the hills.

"Ah!" said Yasmini. "Listen! The guns of the gods! He is maharajah now."

"But what of the treasure?" Tess asked her. "Dick told me this morning that the English have a guard all round the River Palace, and expect to dig the treasure up themselves."

"Perhaps the English need it more than he and I do," Yasmini answered.

That evening Tom Tripe turned up, and Yasmini came down-stairs to talk with him, Trotters remaining outside the window with his ash-colored hair on end and a succession of volcanic growls rumbling between flashed teeth.

"What's the matter with the dog, that he won't come in?" asked Tess.

"Nothing, ma'am. He's just encouraging himself. He stays here to-night."

"Trotters does? Why?"

"It's known all over Sialpore that her ladyship's staying here, and Gungadhura's at large somewhere.

You're well guarded; that's been seen to, but Trotters stays for double inner-guard. One or two men might go to sleep. Gungadhura might pass them a poisoned drink, or physic their rations in some way. And then, they're what you might call fixed point men—one here, one there, with instructions they'll be skinned alive and burned if they leave their exact position. Trotters has a roving commission, to nose and snarl whenever he's minded. You can't poison him, for he won't eat from strangers. You can't see to knife him in the dark, because he's ash-colored and moves too swift. And if Gungadhura comes an' shoots at where Trotters' eyes gleam—well—Mr. Dick Blaine is liable to wake up an' show his highness how Buffalo Billy imitates a Gatling gun! The house is safe, but I thought I'd come and mention it."

"When will my palace be ready?" Yasmini asked.

"To-morrow or the next day, Your Ladyship. There wasn't so much taken out after all, though a certain amount was stolen. The first orders the new maharajah gave were to have your palace attended to; and some of the stolen stuff is coming in already; word went out that if stuff was returned there'd be nothing said, but if it weren't returned there'd be something brand-new in the line of trouble for all concerned. The priests have been told to pass the word along. 'No obedience from priests, no priests at the coronation ceremony!'——It's my belief from about two hours' observation that we've got a maharajah now with guts, if you'll excuse my bad French, please, ma'am."

"What does it matter to you, Tom, whether he is

good or not?" Yasmini asked mischievously. "Isn't there a rumor that the English won't allow any but the native-born instructors after this?"

"Ah, naughty, naughty!" he laughed, shaking a gnarled forefinger. "I thought it was your voice in the crowd. Your Ladyship 'ud like to have me all nervous, wouldn't you? Well—if Tom Tripe was out of a job to-morrow, the very first person he'd apply to for a new one would be the Princess Yasmini; and she'd give it him!"

"What have you in your hand?" Yasmini asked.

"Gungadhura's turban that he wore the night when Akbar chased him down the street."

Yasmini nodded, understanding instantly.

Five minutes later, after a rousing stiff night-cap, Tom took his leave. They heard his voice outside the window:

"Trotters!"

The dog's tail beat three times on the veranda.

"Take a smell o' this!"

There was silence, followed by a growl.

"If he comes,—kill him! D'ye understand? Kill him! There—there's the turban for you to lie on an' memorize the smell! Kill him! Ye understand?"

A deep growl was the answer, and Tom Tripe marched off toward the stables for his horse, whistling *Annie Rooney*, lest some too enthusiastic watcher knife him out of a shadow.

"When I am maharanee," said Yasmini, "Tom Tripe shall have the title of sirdar, whether the English approve of it or not!"

The Creator caused flowers to bloom in the desert and buried jewels in the bosom of the earth. That is lest men should grow idle, wallowing in delights they have, instead of acquiring merit in the search for beauty that is out of reach.—EASTERN PROVERB.

CHAPTER TWENTY-TWO

"Making one hundred exactly."

TECHNICALLY, Yasmini was as much maharanee of
Sialpore as she would ever be, the moment that the
fourteen-gun salute boomed out across the river. For
the English do not recognize a maharanee, except as
courtesy title. The reigning prince is maharajah, and,
being Hindu, can have one wife or as many as he
pleases. Utirupa and Yasmini claimed to have married themselves by Gandharva rite, and, had she chosen, she could have gone to live with him that minute.

But that would not have paid her in the long run.
The priests, for instance, whom she despised with all
her character, would have been outraged into life-long
enmity; and she knew their power.

"It is one thing," she told Tess, "to determine to
be rid of cobras; but another to spurn them with your
hand and foot. They bite!"

Then again, it would not have suited her to slip
quietly into Utirupa's palace and assume the reins of
hidden influence without the English knowing it. She
proposed taking uttermost advantage of the *purdah*
custom that protects women in India from observation
and makes contact between them and the English
almost impossible. But she intended, too, to force the

319

Indian Government into some form of recognition of her.

"If they acknowledge me, they lock swords with every woman in the country. Let them deny me afterward, and all those swords will quiver at their throats! A woman's sword is subtler than a man's."

(That was the secret of her true strength in all the years that followed. It was never possible to bring her quite to bay, because the women pulled hidden strings for her in the sphere that is above and below the reach of governments.)

So she moved back into her own palace, where she received only Tess of all the Anglo-Saxon women in India.

"Why don't you keep open house to English women, and start something?" Tess asked her. But Yasmini laughed.

"My power would be gone. Do you fight a tiger by going down on all-fours with him and using teeth and claws? Or do you keep your distance, and use a gun?"

"But the English women are not tigresses."

"If they were, I would laugh at them. Trapping tigers is a task the jungle coolies can attend to well! But if I admit the English women into my palace, they will come out of curiosity. And out of pity, or compassion or some such odious emotion they will invite me to their homes, making an exhibition of me to their friends. Should I be one of them? Never! Would they admit other Indian women with me? Certainly; any one I cared to recommend. They would encourage us to try to become their social equals, as they would call it, always backing away in front of us and beckoning, we striving, and they flattered. No! I will reverse that. I will have the English women striving to enter *our* society! They shall wake up one day to discover there is something worth having that is out of reach. *Then* see the commotion! Watch the alteration *then!* To-day they say, when they trouble to think of us at all, 'Come and visit us; our ways are good; we will not hurt you; come along,' as the children call to a kitten in the street. *Then* they will say, 'We have this and that to offer. We desire your good society. Will you admit us if we bring our gifts?' That will be another story, but it will take time."

"More than time," Tess answered. "Genius."

"I have genius. That is why I know too much to declare war on the priests. I shall have a proper wedding, and priests shall officiate, I despising them and they aware of it. That will be their first defeat. They shall come to my marriage as dogs come to their mistress when she calls—and be whipped away again if they fawn too eagerly! They will not dare refuse to come, because then war would be joined, and I might prove to people how unnecessary priests are. But they are more difficult to deal with than the English. A fat hypocrite like Jinendra's high priest is like a carp to be caught with a worm, or an ass to be beaten with a stick; but there are others—true ascetics—lusting for influence more than a belly-ful, caring nothing for the outside of the power if they hold the nut—nothing for the petals, if they hold the seed. Those men are not easy. For the present I shall seem to play into their hands, but they know that I despise them!"

So great preparations were made for a royal wedding. And when Samson heard that Yasmini was to be Utirupa's bride he was sufficiently disgusted, even to satisfy Yasmini, who was no admirer of his. Sita Ram's account of Samson's rage, as he explained the circumstance to Willoughby de Wing, was almost epic.

"Damn the woman! And damn him! She's known for a trouble-maker. Simla will be asking me why on earth I permitted it. They'll want to know why I didn't caution Utirupa and warn him against that princess in particular. She's going to parade through the streets under my very nose and in flat defiance of our government, just at the very time when I've gone on record as sponsor for Utirupa. I've assured them he wouldn't do an ill-advised thing, and I specifically undertook to see that he married wisely. But it was too early yet to speak to him about it. And here he springs this offense on me! It's too bad—too bad!"

"You'll be all right with Simla," said Willoughby de Wing. "Dig up the treasure and they'll recommend you for the K. C. B., with the pick of all the jobs going!"

"They don't give K. C. B.'s to men in my trade," Samson answered rather gloomily. "They reserve them for you professional butchers."

He was feeling jumpy about the treasure, and dreaming of it all night long in a way that did not make the waking fears more comfortable. A whole company of sappers had been sent for; and because of the need of secrecy for the present, a special appropriation had had to be made to cover the cost of lumber for the tunnel that Dick began, and that the sappers finished. They had dug right up to the pipal trees, and half-killed them by tunneling under their roots along one side; but without discovering anything so far, except a few old coins. (The very ancient golden mohur in the glass case marked "Sialpore" in the Allahabad Museum is one of them.) Now they were going to tunnel down the other side and kill the ancient trees completely.

Being a man of a certain courage, Samson had it in mind—perhaps—to send the map to an expert for an opinion on it. Only, he hated experts; they were so bent always on establishing their own pet theory. And it was late—a little late for expert opinions on the map. The wisest way was to keep silent and continue digging, even if the operation did kill ancient landmarks that one could see—from across the river, for instance.

And, of course, he could not refuse to recognize the wedding officially and put on record the name, ancestry and title of the maharajah's legal first wife. Nor could he keep away, because, with amazingly shrewd judgment, Yasmini had contrived the novelty of welding wedding and coronation ceremony and festival in one. Instead of two successive outbursts of squandering, there would be only one. It was economic progress. One could not withhold approval of it. He must go in person, smile, give a valuable present (paid for by the government, of course), and say the proper thing.

One modicum of consolation did ooze out of the rind of Samson's situation. It would have been no easier, he reflected, to say the right thing at the right

time at the coronation ceremony, especially to the right
people, if that treasure should already have been dug
up and reposing in the coffers of the Indian Government.   After a certain sort of bargain, one's tongue
feels unpleasant in one's cheek.

Sialpore, however, was much more taken up with
preparations for the colossal coronation-wedding feast
than with Samson's digging.   Yasmini went on her
palace roof each day to see how the trees leaned this
and that way, as the earth was mined from under them.
And Tom Tripe, standing guard on the bastion of the
fort to oversee the removal of certain stores and fit-
tings before the English should march out finally and
the maharajah's men march in, could see the destruction of the pipal trees too.   So, for that matter, could
Dick Blaine, on the day when he took some of the
gang and blocked up the mouth of the mine on the hill
with cemented masonry—to prevent theft; and cursed
himself afterward for being such a fool as to brick up
his luncheon basket inside the tunnel, to say nothing of
all the men's water bottles and some of their food and
tools.   But nobody else in Sialpore took very much
notice of Samson's excavation, and nobody cared about
Dick's mine.

Every maharajah always tries to make his wedding
and coronation ceremonies grander, and more extravagant and memorable than anybody's else have been
since history began; and there are plenty whose interest it is to encourage him, and to help him do it;
money-lenders, for instance.   But Utirupa not only
had two magnificent ceremonies to unite in one, but
Yasmini to supply the genius.   The preparations made

the very priests gasp (and they were used to orgies of
extravagance—taught and preached and profited by
them in fact.)

Once or twice Tess remonstrated, but Yasmini
turned a scornfully deaf ear.

"What would you have us do instead? Invest all
the money at eight per cent., so that the rich traders
may have more capital, and found an asylum where
Bimbu, Umra and Pinga may live in idleness and be
rebuked for mirth?"

"Bimbu, Umra and Pinga might be put to work,"
said Tess. "As for mirth, they laugh at such unseemly
things. They could be taught what proper humor is."

"Have they not worked?" Yasmini asked. "Has
one man got into your house, without you, or the guard
set to watch you, knowing it? Could any one have
done it better? Did it not have to be done? As for
humor—have they not enjoyed the task? Has it not
been a sweeter tale in their ears than the story-teller's
at the corner, because they have told it to themselves
and acted a part in it?"

"Well," said Tess, "you can't convince me! There
are institutions that could be founded with all that
money you and your husband are going to spend on
ceremony, that would do good."

"Institutions?" Yasmini's eyes grew ablaze with
blue indignant fire. "There were institutions in this
land before the English came, which need attention
before we worry ourselves over new ones. Play was
one of them, and I will revive it first! The people
used to dance under the trees by moonlight. Do they
do it now? It is true they used to die of famine in the

bad years, growing much too fat in good ones, and
the English have changed that. But I will give them
back the gladness, if I can, that has been squeezed out
by too many 'institutions!'"

"You would rather see Bimbu, Umra and Pinga
happy, than prosperous and well-clothed?"

"Which would you rather?" Yasmini asked her.
"You shall see them well clothed in a little while.
Just wait."

There were almost endless altercations with the
priests. Utirupa himself was known to have profound Sikh tendencies—a form of liberalism in religion that produced almost as much persecution at one
time as Protestantism did in Europe. To marry a
woman openly who had no true claim to caste at all, as
Yasmini, being the daughter of a foreigner, had not,
was in the eyes of the priests almost as great an
offense as Yasmini's father's, who crossed the *kali pani*
(ocean) and married abroad in defiance of them. So
the priests demanded the most elaborate ritual of puri-
fication that ingenuity could devise, together with
staggering sums of money. Utirupa's eventual threat
to lead a reform movement in Rajputana brought them
to see reason, however, and they eventually compromised, with a stipulation that the public should not be
told how much had been omitted.

There was feasting in the streets for a week before
the great inauguration ceremony. Tables were set in
every side-street, where whoever cared to might eat his
fill of fabulous free rations. Each night the streets
were illuminated with colored lights, and fireworks
blazed and roared against the velvet sky at intervals,

dowering the ancient trees and temple-tops with momentary splendor.

All day long there were performances by acrobats, and songs, and story-telling whenever there was room for a crowd to gather. Faquirs as gruesome and fantastic as the side-shows at a Western fair flocked in to pose and be gaped at, receiving, besides free rations and tribute of small coin, gratification to their vanity in return for the edifying spectacle.

There were little processions, too, of princes arriving from a distance to be present on the great day, their elephants of state loaded with extravagant gifts and their retainers vying with peacocks in efforts to look splendid, and be arrogant, and claim importance for their masters. Never a day but three or four or half-a-dozen noble guests arrived; and nobody worked except those who had to make things easy for the rest; and they worked overtime.

One accustomed spectacle, however, was omitted. Utirupa would have none of the fights between wild animals in the arena that had formed such a large part of Gungadhura's public amusement. But there was ram-fighting, and wrestling between men such as Sialpore had never seen, all the best wrestlers from distant parts being there to strive for prizes. Hired dancers added to the gaiety at night, and each incoming nobleman brought nautch girls, or acrobats, or trained animals, or all three to add to the revelry. And there was cock-fighting, and quail-fighting, of course, all day long and every day, with gambling in proportion.

When the day of days at last arrived the city seemed full of elephants. Every compound and avail-

able walled space had been requisitioned to accommodate the brutes, and there were sufficient argumenta-
tive mahouts, all insisting that their elephants had not
enough to eat, and all selling at least half of the provided ration, to have formed a good-sized regiment.
The elephants' daily bath in the river was a sight
worth crossing India to see. There was always the
chance, besides, that somebody's horses would take
fright and add excitement to the spectacle.

Up in the great palace Utirupa feasted and enter-
tained his equals all day long, and most of the night.
There was horse-racing that brought the crowd out in
its thousands, and a certain amount of tent-pegging
and polo, but most of the royal gala-making was hidden from public view. (Patali, for instance, reckless
of Gungadhura's fall and looking for new fields to
conquer, provided a nautch by herself and her own
trained galaxy of girls that would not have done at all
in public.)

Yasmini kept close in her own palace. She, too,
had her hands full with entertaining, for there were
about a dozen of the wives of distant princes who had
made the journey in state to attend the ceremony and
watch it from behind the durbar grille—to say nothing
of the wives of local magnates. But she herself kept
within doors, until the night before the night of full
moon, the day before the ceremony.

That night she dressed as a rangar once more, and
rode in company with Tess and Dick, with Ismail the
Afridi running like a dog in the shadows behind them,
to the fort on the hill that the English had promised to
evacuate that night. They never changed the garrison

in any case except by night, because of the heat and
the long march for the men; and as near the full moon
as possible was the customary date.

As they neared the fort they could see Tom Tripe,
with his huge dog silhouetted on the bastion beside
him, standing like Napoleon on the seashore keeping
vigil. From that height he could oversee the blocked-
up mouth of Dick's mine, and in the bright moonlight
it would have been difficult for any one to approach
either mine or fort without detection; for there was
only one road, and Dick's track making a detour from
it—both in full view.

He caught sight of them, and Dick whistled, the
dog answering with a cavernous howl of recognition.
Tom disappeared from the bastion, and after about ten
minutes turned up in the shadow where they waited.

"Come to watch the old march out and the new
march in?" he asked. "I'll stand here with you, if I
may. They're due."

"Is everything ready?" asked Yasmini.

"Yes, Your Ladyship. They've been ready for an
hour, and fretful. There's a story gone the rounds
that the fort is haunted, and if ever a garrison was
glad to quit it's this one! Let's hope the incoming garrison don't get wind of it. A Sepoy with the creeps
ain't dependable. Hullo, here they come!"

There came a sound of steady tramping up-hill,
and a bugle somewhere up in the darkness announced
that the out-going garrison had heard it and were
standing to arms. Presently Utirupa rode into view
accompanied by half a dozen of his guests, and followed by a company from his own army, officered by

Rajputs. If he knew that Yasmini was watching from the shadow he made no sign, but rode straight on uphill. The heavy breathing of his men sounded through the darkness like the whispering of giants, and their steady tramp was like a giant's footfall; for Tom Tripe had drilled them thoroughly, even if their weapons were nearly as old-fashioned as the fort to which they marched.

After an interminable interval there came another bugle-blast above them, and the departing garrison tramped within ear-shot.

"Now count them!" Yasmini whispered, and Tess wondered why.

They were marching down-hill as fast as they could swing—a detachment of Punjabi infantry under the command of a native *subahdar,* with two ammunition mules and a cartful of their kits and personal belongings—all talking and laughing as if regret were the last thing in their minds.

"Ninety-seven," said Tess, when the last had passed down-hill.

"Did you count the man beside the driver on the cart?"

"Yes."

"There was one sick man in a *dhoolie.* Did you count him?"

"No."

"Ninety-eight, then. Tom!"

"Your Ladyship?"

"Weren't there some English officers?"

"Two. A captain and a subaltern. They left late this afternoon."

"Making?" said Yasmini.

"Exactly a hundred," answered Tess.

"Let us go now," said Yasmini. "We must be up at dawn for the great day. I shall expect you very early, remember. Tom! You may ride back with us. His highness will mount the guard in person. You're to come to my palace. I've a present waiting for you."

It is better to celebrate the occasion than to annoy the gods with pretended virtue and too many promises.
—EASTERN PROVERB.

CHAPTER TWENTY-THREE

Three amber moons in a purple sky.

THE day of the great inauguration ceremony
dawned inauspiciously for somebody. For one thing,
the blasting powder laid ready by the sappers under
the pipal trees for explosion the day following, blew
up prematurely. Some idiot had left a kerosene lamp
burning in the dug-out, probably, and a rat upset it;
or some other of the million possibilities took place.
Nobody was killed, but a dozen pipal trees were blown
to smithereens, and the ghastly fact laid bare for all
to see that in the irregular chasm that remained there
was not a symptom of the treasure—as Samson was
immediately notified.

So Samson had to attend the ceremony with that
disconcerting knowledge up his sleeve. But that was
not all. The night signaler, going off duty, had
brought him a telegram from the high commissioner
to say that all available military bands were to be lent
for the day to the maharajah, and that as many British officers as possible, of all ranks, were to take part
in the procession to grace it with official sanctity.

That was especially aggravating because it had
reached his ears that the Princess Yasmini intended
to ride veiled in the procession, and to sit beside her

333

husband in the durbar hall unveiled. He was therefore going to be obliged to recognize her more or less
officially as consort of the reigning prince. Simla did
not realize that, of course; but it was too late to wire
for different instructions. He had a grim foreboding
that he himself would catch it later on when the facts
leaked out, as they were bound to do.

(It was babu Sita Ram who "caught it" first,
though. Within two days Samson discovered that
Sita Ram had been sending official telegrams in code
on his own account, very cleverly designed to cause the
high commissioner to give those last minute instructions. It was obvious that a keener wit than the babu's
had inspired him; but, though he was brow-beaten for
an hour he did not implicate Yasmini. And after he
had been dismissed from the service with ignominy
she engaged him as a sort of secretary, at the same
pay.)

But that was not all, either. The murderer of Mukhum Dass was refusing stolidly to plead guilty to
another charge, and Blaine's butler had come out with
the whole story of the burglary. Parliament would
get to hear about it next, and then there would be the
very deuce to pay. The police were offering the murderer what they called "inducements and persuasion";
but he held out for "money down," and did not seem
to find too unendurable whatever it was that happened
to him at intervals in the dark cell. There are limits
even to what an Indian policeman can do, without
making marks on a man or compelling the attention of
European officers.

On top of all that, Samson had to hand Dick Blaine

a check amounting to a month's pay, look pleasant while he did it, and—above all—look pleasant at the coming durbar.

On the other hand, there were people who enjoyed themselves. Sialpore, across the river, was a dinning riot of excitement—flags, triumphal arches, gala clothes and laughter everywhere. Dick Blaine, driving Tess toward Yasmini's palace in the very early dawn, had to drive slowly to avoid accident, for the streets were already crowded. His own place in the procession was to be on horseback pretty nearly anywhere he chose to insert himself behind the royal cortège, and, not being troubled on the score of precedence, he had Tom Tripe in mind as a good man to ride with. Tom could tell him things.

But he waited there for more than an hour until the royal elephants arrived, magnificent in silver howdahs and bright paint, and watched Tess emerge with Yasmini and the other women. Tess wore borrowed jewels, and a veil that you could see her face through; but Yasmini was draped from head to foot as if the eyes of masculinity had never rested on her, and never might. Things were not going quite so smoothly as they ought, although Tom Tripe was galloping everywhere red-necked with energy, and it was nearly half an hour more before the escort of maharajah's troops came in brand-new scarlet uniforms, to march in front, and behind, and on each side of the elephants. So Dick got quite a chance to "josh" Tess, and made the most of it.

But things got under way at last. Dick's *sais* found him with the horse he was to ride, and the procession gathered first on the great *maidan* (open ground) between the city and the river, with bands in full blast, drums thundering to split the ears, masters of ceremony shouting, and the elephants enjoying themselves most of all, as they always do when they have a stately part to play in company.

Utirupa led the way in a golden howdah on Akbar, the biggest elephant in captivity and the very arch-type of sobriety ever since his escapade with Tom Tripe's rum. Akbar was painted all over with vermilion and blue decorations, and looked as if butter would not melt in his mouth.

Next after Utirupa the princes rode in proper order of rank and precedence, each with two attendants up behind him waving fans of ostrich plumes. Then came a band. Then Samson, and a score of British officers in carriages whose teams were nearly frantic from the din and the smell of elephants and had to have runners to hold their heads—all of which added exquisite amusement. Then another band, and a column of the maharajah's troops. Then more elephants, loaded with the lesser notables; and after them, a column nearly a mile long of Rajput gentry on the most magnificent horses they could discover and go in debt for.

After the Rajput gentry came a third band, followed by more maharajah's troops, and then Yasmini on her elephant, followed by twenty princesses and Tess, each with a great beast to herself and at least two maids to wave the jeweled fans. Then more troops, followed by Dick and Tom Tripe together on horseback leading the rank and file. Trotters jogged along between Tom and Dick, pausing at intervals to struggle with both forefeet to remove a collar bossed with solid gold that he regarded as an outrage to his dogly dignity.

And the rank and file were well worth looking at, for whoever could find a decent suit of clothes was marching, shouting, laughing, sweating, kicking up the dust, and having a good time generally. The water-sellers were garnering a harvest; fruit- and sweetmeat-pedlers were dreaming of open-fronted shops and how to defeat the tax-collector. The police swaggered and yelled and ordered everybody this and that way; and nobody took the slightest notice; and the policemen did not dare do anything about it because the crowd was too unanimously bent on having its own way, and therefore dangerous to bully but harmless if not hit.

Half-way down the thronging stream of men on foot came another elephant—a little one, alone, carrying three gentlemen in fine white raiment—Bimbu and Pinga and Umra to wit, who, it is regrettable to chronicle, were very drunk indeed and laughed exceedingly at most unseemly jokes, exchanging jests with the crowd that would have made Tess's hair stand on end, if she could have heard and understood them. From windows, and roofs that overhung the street, people threw flowers at Bimbu, Pinga and Umra, because all Hindustan knows there is merit in treating beggars as if they were noblemen; and Bimbu wove himself a garland out of the buds to wear on his turban, which made him look more bacchanalian than ever.

In and out and around and through the ancient
city the procession filed, passing now and then
through streets so narrow that people could have
struck Utirupa through the upper story windows; but
all they threw at him was flowers, calling him
"Bahadur," and king of elephants, and great prince,
and dozens of other names that never hurt anybody
with a sense of pageantry and humor. He acted the
part for them just as they wanted him to, sitting bolt
upright in the howdah like a prince in a fairy story,
with jeweled aigrette in his turban and more enormous
diamonds flashing on his silken clothes than a courte-
san would wear at Monte Carlo. And all the other
princes were likewise in degree, only that they rode
rather smaller elephants, Akbar having no peer when
he was sober and behaved himself.

And when Yasmini passed, and Tess and all the
other princesses, there was such excitement as surely
had never been before; for if you looked carefully,
with a hand held to keep the sun from your eyes, you
could actually see the outlines of their faces through
the veils! And such loveliness! Such splendor!
Such pride! Such jewels! Above all, such fathomless
mystery and suggestion of intrigue! Pageantry is
expensive, but—believe Sialpore—it is worth the price!

And then in front of the durbar hall in the dinning,
throbbing heat, all the animals and carriages and men
got mixed in a milling vortex, while the notables went
into the hall to be jealous of one another's better
places and left the crowd outside to sort itself. And
everything was made much more interesting by the
fact that Akbar was showing signs of ill-temper,

throwing up his great trunk once or twice to trumpet
dissatisfaction. His mahout was calling him endearing names and using the ankus alternately, promising
him rum with one breath and a thrashing with the
next. But Akbar wanted alcohol, not promises, and
none dared give him any before evening, when he
might get as drunk as he wished in a stone-walled
compound all to himself.

Then Samson's horses took fright at Akbar's
trumpeting, he getting out of the carriage at the durbar door only in the nick to time. The horses bolted
into the crowd, and an indignant elephant smashed the
carriage; but nobody was hurt beyond a bruise or two,
although they passed word down the thunderous line
that a hundred and six and thirty had been crushed to
death and one child injured, which made it much more
thrilling, and the sensation was just as actual as if
the deaths had really happened.

And inside the durbar hall there was surely never
such a splendid scene in history—such a sea of tur-
bans—such glittering of jewels—such a peacocking
and swaggering and proud bearing of ancient names!
Utirupa sat on the throne in front of a peacock-feather
decoration; and—marvel of marvels!——Yasmini sat
on another throne beside him, unveiled!—with a genuine unveiled and very beautiful princess beside her,
whom nobody except Samson suspected might be Tess.
She wore almost as many jewels as the queen herself,
and looked almost as ravishing.

But the Princess Yasmini's eyes—they were the
glory of that occasion! Her spun-gold hair was mar-
veled at, but her eyes—surely they were lent by a god

for the event! They were bluer than the water of
Himalayan lakes; bluer than turquoise, sapphire, the
sky, or any other blue thing you can think of—laughing blue,—loving, understanding, likable, amusing
blue—two jewels that outshone all the other jewels in
the durbar hall that day.

And as each prince filed past Utirupa in proper
order of precedence, to make a polite set speech, and
bow, and be bowed to in return, he had to pass Yasmini first, and bow to her first, although he made his
speech to Utirupa, who acknowledged it. So, when
Samson's turn came, he, too, had to bow first to Yasmini, because as a gentleman he could hardly do less;
and her wonderful eyes laughed into his angry ones
as she bowed to him in return, with such good humor
and elation that he could not help but smile back; he
could forgive a lovely woman almost anything, could
Samson. He could almost forgive her that no less
than nineteen British officers of various ranks, as well
as one-hundred-and-three-and-twenty native noblemen
had seen him with their own eyes to make an official
bow to the consort of a reigning maharajah. He had
recognized her officially! Well; he supposed he could
eat his aftermath as well as any man; and he drove
home with a smile and a high chin, to unbosom himself to Colonel Willoughby de Wing over a whisky and
soda at the club, as Ferdinand de Sousa Braganza
reported in some detail at the Goanese Club afterward.

Late that night, when the fireworks were all over
and the lights were beginning to be extinguished on
the roofs and windows, it was a question which was
most drunk—Akbar, the three beggars, or Tom.

Tripe. Akbar's outrageous trumpeting could be heard all over the city, as he raced around his dark compound after shadows, and rats, and mice and anything else that he imagined or could see. What Tom Tripe saw kept him to his quarters, where Trotters watched him in dire misery. The three beggars, Bimbu, Pinga and Umra, saw three amber moons in a purple sky, for they said so. They also said that all the world was lovely, and Yasmini was a queen of queens, out of whose jeweled hand the very gods ate. And when people scolded them for blasphemy, they made such outrageously funny and improper jokes that everybody laughed again.

Drunk or sober (and more than ninety-nine per cent. of Sialpore was absolutely sober then as always) every one had something to amuse and entertain, except Samson, whose mental vision was of a great empty hole in the ground in which he might just as well bury all his hopes of ever being high commissioner; and poor Tom Tripe, who had worked harder than anybody, and was now enjoying the aftermath perhaps least.

Sialpore put itself to bed in great good temper, sure that princes and elephants and ceremony were the cream of life, and that whoever did not think so did not deserve to have any pageantry and pomp, and that was all about it.

Next morning early, Dick Blaine drove down to look for Tom Tripe, found him—bound him in a blanket—shoved him, feet first, on to the floor of the dogcart, and drove him, followed by Trotters in doubt whether to show approval or fight, to his own house on the hill, where Tess and he nursed the old soldier back to soberness and old remorse.

By that time Bimbu and Pinga and Umra were back again at the garden gate, sitting in the dust in ancient rags and whining, *"Bhig mangi, saheebi!"* "Alms! heavenborn, alms!"

"You are a fool," said the crow. "Am I?" the hen answered. "Certainly you are a fool. You sit in a dark corner hatching eggs, when there are live chickens for the asking over yonder." So the hen left her nest in search of ready-made chickens, and the crow made a square meal.—EASTERN PROVERB.

CHAPTER TWENTY-FOUR

A hundred guarded it.

IT began to be rumored presently that Utirupa had declined to recognize Blaine's contract with his predecessor. Samson's guarded hints, and the fact that the mouth of the mine remained blocked with concrete masonry were more or less corroborative. But the Blaines did not go, although Dick put in no appearance at the club.

Then Patali, who was sedulously cultivating Yasmini's patronage, with ulterior designs on Utirupa that were not misunderstood, told Norwood's wife's ayah's sister's husband that the American had secured another contract; and the news, of course, reached Samson's ears at once.

So Samson called on Utirupa and requested explanations. He was told that the mining contract had not received a moment's consideration and, with equal truth, that the American, being an expert in such matters and on the spot, had been asked to undertake examination of the fort's foundations. The new maharanee, it seemed, had a fancy to build a palace where the fort stood, and the matter was receiving shrewd investigation and estimate in advance.

Samson could not object to that. Those founda-

344

tions had not been examined carefully for eight hundred years. A perfectly good palace had been wrested away by diplomatic means, on Samson's own initiative, and there was no logical reason why the maharajah should not build another one to replace it. The fort had no modern military value.

"I hope you're not going to try to pay for your new palace out of taxes?" Samson asked bluntly.

But Utirupa smiled. He hoped nothing of that kind would be necessary.

Samson could not go and investigate what Blaine was doing, because he was given plainly to understand that the new palace was the maharanee's business; and one does not intrude uninvited into the affairs of ladies in the East. The efforts of quite a number of spies, too, were unavailing. So Dick had his days pretty much to himself, except when Tess brought his lunch to him, or Yasmini herself in boots and turban rode up for a few minutes to look on. The guards on the bastions, and in the great keep in the center, knew nothing whatever of what was happening, because all Dick's activity was underground and Tom Tripe, with that ferocious dog of his, kept guard over the ancient door that led to the lower passages. Dick used to return home every evening tired out, but Tom Tripe, keeping strictly sober, slept in the fort and said nothing of importance to any one. He looked drawn and nervous, as if something had terrified him, but public opinion ascribed that to the "snakes" on the night of the coronation.

Then about sundown one evening Tom Tripe galloped in a great hurry to Utirupa's palace. That was nothing to excite comment, because in his official capacity he was always supposed to be galloping all over the place on some errand or another. But after dark Utirupa and Yasmini rode out of the palace unattended, which did cause comment, Yasmini in man's clothes, as usual when she went on some adventure. It was not seen which road they took, which was fortunate in the circumstances.

Tess was up at the fort before them, waiting with Dick outside the locked door leading to the ancient passages below. They said nothing beyond the most perfunctory greetings, but, each taking a kerosene lantern, passed through the door in single file, Tom leading, and locked the door after them. That was all that the fort guards ever knew about what happened.

"I've not been in," said Dick's voice from behind them. "All I've done is force an entrance."

From in front Tom Tripe took up the burden.

"And I wouldn't have liked your job, sir! It was bad enough to sit and guard the door. After you'd gone o' nights I'd sit for hours with my hair on end, listening; and the dog 'ud growl beside me as if he saw ghosts!"

"Maybe it was snakes," Yasmini answered. "They will flee from the lantern-light."

"No, Your Ladyship. I'm not afraid of snakes— except them Scotch plaid ones that come o' brandy on top o' royal durbars! This was the sound o' some one digging—digging all night long down in the bowels of the earth! Look out!"

They all jumped, but it proved to be only Tom's own shadow that had frightened him. His nerves were all to pieces, and Dick Blaine took the lead. The dog was growling intermittently and keeping close to Tom's heels.

They passed down a long spiral flight of stone steps into a sort of cavern that had been used for ammunition room. The departing British troops had left a dozen ancient cannon balls, not all of which were in one place. The smooth flags of the floor were broken, and at the far end one very heavy stone was lifted and laid back, disclosing a dark hole.

"I used the cannon balls," said Dick, "to drop on the stones and listen for a hollow noise. Once I found that, the game was simple."

Leading down into the dark hole were twelve more steps, descending straight, but turning sharply at the bottom. Dick led the way.

"The next sight's gruesome!" he announced, his voice booming hollow among the shadows.

The passage turned into a lofty chamber in the rock, whose walls once had all been lined with dressed stone, but some of the lining had fallen. In the shadows at one end an image of Jinendra smiled complacently, and there were some ancient brass lamps hanging on chains from arches cut into the rock on every side.

"This is the grue," said Dick, holding his lantern high.

Its light fell on a circle of skeletons, all perfect, each with its head toward a brass bowl in the center.

"Ugh!" growled Tom Tripe. "Those are the ghosts that dig o' nights! Go smell 'em, Trotters! Are they the enemy?"

The dog sniffed the bones, but slunk away again uninterested.

"Nothing doing!" laughed Dick. "You haven't laid the ghost yet, Tom!"

"Have you got your pistols with you?" Tom retorted, patting his own jacket to show the bulge of one beneath it.

"Those," said Yasmini, standing between the skeletons and holding up her own light, "are the bones of priests, who died when the secret of the place was taken from them! My father told me they were left to starve to death. This was Jinendra's temple."

"D'you suppose they pulled that cut stone from the walls, trying to force a way out?" Dick hazarded. "The lid of the hole we came down through is a foot thick, and was set solid in cement; they couldn't have lifted that if they tried for a week. Everything's solid in this place. I sounded every inch of the floor with a cannon ball, but it's all hard underneath."

"I would have gone straight to the image of Jinendra," said Yasmini. "Jinendra smiles and keeps his secrets so well that I should have suspected him at once!"

"I went to that last," Dick answered. "It looks so like a piece of high relief carved out of the rock wall. As a matter of fact, though, it's about six tons of quartz with a vein of gold in it—see the gold running straight up the line of the nose and over the middle of the head?—I pried it away from the wall at last with steel wedges, and there's just room to squeeze in behind it. Beyond that is another wall that I had to cut through with a chisel. Who goes in first?"

"Who looks for gold finds gold!" Yasmini quoted. "The vein of gold you have been mining was the clue to the secret all along."

She would have led the way, but Utirupa stopped her.

"If there is danger," he said, "it is my place to lead."

But nobody would permit that, Yasmini least of all.

"Shall Samson choose a new maharajah so soon as all that?" she laughed.

"Let the dog go first!" Tom proposed. Trotters was sniffing at the dark gap behind Jinendra's image, with eyes glaring and a low rumbling growl issuing from between bared teeth. But Trotters would not go.

Finally, in the teeth of remonstrances from Tess, Dick cocked a pistol and, with his lantern in the other hand, strode in boldly. Trotters followed him, and Tom Tripe next. Then Utirupa. Then the women.

Nothing happened. The passage was about ten feet long and a yard wide. They squeezed one at a time through the narrow break Dick had made in the end of it, into a high, pitch-dark cave that smelt unexplainably of wood-smoke, Dick standing just inside the gap to hold the lantern for them and help them through—continuing to stand there after Tess had entered last.

"Jee-rusalem!" he exclaimed. "This is where I lose out!"

The first glance was enough to show that they stood in the secret treasure-vault of Sialpore. There were ancient gold coins in heaps on the floor where they had burst by their own weight out of long-demolished bags—countless coins; and drums and bags and boxes more of them behind. But what made Dick exclaim were the bars of silver stacked at the rear and along one side in rows as high as a man.

"My contract reads gold!" he said. "A percentage of all gold. There's not a word in it of silver. Who'd ever have thought of finding silver, anyhow, in this old mountain?"

"Your percentage of the gold will make you rich," said Utirupa. "But you shall take silver too. Without you we might have found nothing for years to come."

"A contract's a contract," Dick answered. "I drew it myself, and it stands."

"Look out!" yelled Tom Tripe suddenly. But the warning came too late.

Out of the shadow behind a stack of silver bars rushed a man with a long dagger, stabbing frantically at Dick. Tom's great barking army revolver missed, filling the chamber with noise and smoke, for he used black powder.

Down went Dick under his assailant, and the dagger rose and fell in spasmodic jerks. Dick had hold of the man's wrist, but the dagger-point dripped blood and the fury of the attack increased as Dick appeared to weaken. Utirupa ran in to drag the assailant off, but Trotters got there first—chose his neck-hold like a wolf in battle—and in another second Dick was free with Tess kneeling beside him while a life-and-death fight between animal and man raged between the bars of silver.

"Gungadhura!" Yasmini shouted, waving her lantern for a sight of the struggling man's face. He was

lashing out savagely with the long knife, but the dog
had him by the neck from behind, and he only inflicted
surface wounds.

"Hell's bells! He'll kill my dog!" roared Tom.
"Hi, Trotters. Here, you—Trotters!"

But the dog took that for a call to do his thinking,
and let go for a better hold. His long fangs closed
again on the victim's jugular, and tore it out. The
long knife clattered on the stone floor, and then Tom
got his dog by the jaws and hauled him off.

"You can't blame the dog," he grumbled. "He
knew the smell of him. He'd been told to kill him if
he got the chance."

"Gungadhura!" said Yasmini again, holding her
lantern over the dying man. "So Gungadhura was
Tom Tripe's ghost! What a pity that the dog should
kill him, when all he wanted was a battle to the death
with me! I would have given him his fight!"

Dick was in no bad way. He had three flesh
wounds on his right side, and none of them serious.
Tess staunched them with torn linen, and she and Tom
Tripe propped him against some bags of bullion, while
Utirupa threw his cloak over Gungadhura's dead body.

"How did Gungadhura get in here?" wondered
Tess.

"Through the hole at the end of the mine-shaft, I
suppose," said Dick. "I built up the lower one—he
came one day and saw me doing it—but left a space at
the top that looked too small for a man to crawl
through. Then I blocked the mouth of the tunnel
afterward, and shut him in, I suppose. He's had the
men's rice and water-bottles, and they left a lot of fag-

gots in the tunnel, too, I remember. That accounts for the smell of smoke."

"But what was the digging I've heard o' nights?" demanded Tom. "I'm not the only one. The British garrison was scared out of its wits."

Utirupa was hunting about with a lantern in his hand, watching the dog go sniffing in the shadows.

"Come and see what he has done!" he called suddenly, and Yasmini ran to his side.

In a corner of the vault one of the great facing stones had been removed, disclosing a deep fissure in the rock. One of Dick Blaine's crow-bars that he had left in the tunnel lay beside it.

"He must have found that by tapping," said Tom Tripe.

"Yes, but look why he wanted it!" Yasmini answered. "Tom, could you be as malicious as that?"

"As what, Your Ladyship?"

"See, he has poured gold into the fissure, hoping to close it up again so that nobody could find it!"

"But why didn't he work his way out with the crow-bar?" Dick objected from his perch between the bags of bullion.

"What was his life worth to him outside?" Yasmini asked. "Samson knew who murdered Mukhum Dass. He would have been a prisoner for the rest of his life to all intents and purposes. No! He preferred to hide the treasure again, and then wait here for me, suspecting that I knew where it is and would come for it! Only we came too soon, before he had it hidden!"

But it was Patali afterward, between boasting and confession, who explained that Dick was Gungadhura's

real objective after all. He preferred vengeance on
the American even to a settled account with Yasmini.
He must have found the treasure by accident after
crawling into the unsealed crack in the wall to wait
there against Dick's coming.

"The money must stay here, and be removed little
by little," said Utirupa.

"First of all Blaine sahib's share of it!" Yasmini
added. "Who shall count it? Who!"

"Never mind the money now," Tess answered.
"Dick's alive! When did you first know you'd found
the treasure, Dick?"

"Not until the day that Gungadhura found me closing up the fault, and asked me to dig at the other place.
The princess told me I was on the trail of it that night
that you went with her by camel; but I didn't know,
I'd found it till the day that Gungadhura came."

"How did *you* know where it was?" Tess asked,
and Yasmini laughed.

"A hundred guarded it. I looked for a hundred
pipal trees, and found them—near the River Palace.
But they were not changed once a month. I looked
from there, and saw another hundred pipal trees—
here, below this fort—exactly a hundred. But neither
were they changed once a month. Then I counted the
garrison of the fort—exactly a hundred, all told.
Then I knew. Then I remembered that 'who looks for
gold finds gold,' and saw your husband digging for it.
It seemed to me that the vein of gold he was following
should lead to the treasure, so I pulled strings until
Samson blundered, trying to trick us. And now we
have the treasure, and the English do not know. And

I am maharanee, as they do know, and shall know still better before I have finished! But what are we to do with Gungadhura's body? It shall not lie here to rot; it must have a decent burial."

Very late that night, Tom Tripe moved the guards about on the bastions, contriving that the road below should not be overlooked by any one. The moon had gone down, so that it was difficult to see ten paces. He produced an *ekka* from somewhere—one of those two-wheeled carts drawn by one insignificant pony that do most of the unpretentious work of India; and he and Ismail, the Afridi gateman, drove off into the darkness with a covered load.

Early next morning Gungadhura's body was found in the great hole that Samson's men had blasted in the River Palace grounds, and it was supposed that a jackal had mangled his body after death.

(That was what gave rise to the story that the English got the treasure after all, and that Gungadhura, enraged and mortified at finding it gone, had committed suicide in the great hole it was taken from. They call the great dead pipal tree that is the only one left now of the hundred, Gungadhura's gibbet; and there is quite a number, even of English people, who believe that the Indian Government got the money. But I say no, because Yasmini told me otherwise. And if it were true that the English really got the money, what did they do with it and why was Samson removed shortly afterward to a much less desirable post? Any one could see how Utirupa prospered, and he never raised the taxes half a mill.

Samson had his very shrewd suspicions, one of

which was that that damned American with his smart
little wife had scored off him in some way. But he
went to his new post, at about the same time that the
Blaines left for other parts, with some of the sting
removed from his hurt feelings. For he took Blaine's
rifle with him—a good one; and the horse and dog-
cart, and a riding pony—more than a liberal return for
payment of a three-thousand rupee bet. Pretty decent
of Blaine on the whole, he thought. No fuss. No
argument. Simply a short note of farewell, and a request that he would "find the horses a home and a use
for the other things." Not bad. Not a bad fellow
after all.

L'ENVOI

Down rings the curtain on a tale of love and mystery,
Clash of guile and anger and the consequence it bore;
The adventurers and kings
Disappear into the wings.
The puppet play is over and the pieces go in store.

Back, get ye back again to shop and ship and factory,
Mine and mill and foundry where the iron yokes are
    made;
Ye have trod a distant track
With a queen on camel-back,
Now hie and hew a broadway for your emperors of
    trade!

Go, get ye gone again to streets of strife reechoing—
Clangor of the crossings where the tides of trouble
    meet;
For a while on fancy's wing
Ye have heard the nautch-girls sing,
But a Great White Way awaits you where the Klax-
    on-horns repeat.

Back, bend the back again to commonplace and
    drudgery,
Beat the shares of vision into swords of dull routine,
Take the trolley and the train
To suburban hives again,
For ye wake in little runnels where the floods of
    thought have been.

Speed, noise, efficiency!   Have flights of fancy rested
     you?
A while we set time's finger back, and was the labor
     vain?
If so we whiled your leisure
And the puppets gave you pleasure,
Then say the word, good people, and we'll set the stage
     again.

CHAPTER TWENTY-FIVE

And that is the whole story

SMOKING a cigarette lazily on Utirupa's palace roof, Yasmini reached for Tess's hand.

"Come nearer. See—take this. It is the value, and more, of the percentage of the silver that your husband would not take."

She clasped a diamond necklace around Tess's neck, and watched it gleam and sparkle in the refracted sunlight.

"Don't you love it? Aren't they perfect? And now—you've a great big draft of money, so I suppose you're both off to America, and good-by to me forever?"

"For a long time."

"But why such a long time? You must come again soon. Come next year. You and I love each other. You teach me things I did not know, and you never irritate me. I love you. You must come back next year!"

Tess shook her head.

"But why?"

"They say the climate isn't good for them until they're eighteen at least—some say twenty."

"Oh! Oh, I envy you! What will you call him? It will be a boy—it is sure to be a boy!"

"Richard will be one name, after my husband."

"And the other? You must name him after me in some way. You can not call a boy Yasmini. Would Utirupa sound too strange in America?"

"Rupert would sound better."

"Good! He shall be Rupert, and I will send a gift to him!"

(That accounts for the initials R. R. B. on a certain young man's trunk at Yale, and for the imported pedigree horse he rides during vacation—the third one, by the way, of a succession he has received from India.)

And that is the whole story, as Yasmini told it to me in the wonderful old palace at Buhl, years afterward, when Utirupa was dead, and the English Government had sent her into forced seclusion for a while —to repent of her manifold political sins, as they thought—and to start new enterprises as it happened. She had not seen Theresa Blaine again, she told me, although they always corresponded; and she assured me over and over again, calling the painted figures of the old gods on the walls to witness, that but for Theresa Blaine's companionship and affection at the right moment, she would never have had the courage to do what she did, even though the guns of the gods were there to help her.

THE END